JESSIE

A NOVEL

JESSIE
A NOVEL

John Killinger

McCracken Press
New York

McCracken Press™

An imprint of Multi Media Communicators, Inc.

575 Madison Avenue, Suite 1006
New York, NY 10022

Editorial Director, William Griffin
Cover Art, Karen M. Pollpeter

Library of Congress Catalog Card Number: 93-078998

ISBN 1-56977-575-3

10 9 8 7 6 5 4 3 2 1
First Edition

Printed in the United States of America

5/95   PasTime   13.45

For my dear mother,
whose name was also
JESSIE,
and who might have been,
in certain places,
the Jessie of
this story.

JESSIE

A NOVEL

1

A little before ten o'clock on Christmas Eve, without a flicker of warning, the lights in New Haven's Pink Whale Saloon suddenly went out. One minute the jukebox was blaring, the syncopated tree lights were flashing, the purplish neon GENTS and LADIES signs were glaring, and faint aureoles of illumination were defining the two dozen booths where patrons congregated. The next minute, nothing.

Cries of disappointment arose in several areas of the darkness, followed by a few voices of protest and two minor bursts of profanity.

Then there was a momentary *zitsch* as of a lighter flint's being struck, and a small flame began to move over the face of the deep, producing a birthday cake adorned by a fiery crown of candles.

The cake, in turn, apparently propelled by three or four radiant faces behind it, began moving across the room, dividing the darkness as it came.

> Happy birthday to you,
> Happy birthday to you.

The entire room rang with voices as the cake arrived at its destination, some of them by this time having searched out and found an angelic-sounding descant.

> Happy birthday, dear Jessie,
> Happy birthday to you-u-u-u!

The full light of the cake illuminated the face of a young woman. Thirtyish, fair-skinned, with no makeup, but with dark, dancing eyes, she emitted a glow that inspired feelings of joy, hope, and peace.

"O-o-h-h-h," she moaned softly and happily.

"You're always doing things for other people," said the tall, freckled woman with cropped hair who appeared to preside over the cake. "It's time we did something to say how much we love you. Besides, you as much as admitted that people are usually too busy at Christmas to observe your birthday. Well, not this year, dearie."

"Enough speechifying," interjected a young, pretty girl sitting beside her. "Make a wish, Jess. Blow out the candles."

Looking at the expectant faces around the bar, Jessie's cheeks flushed. Slipping her hands under her thighs, she closed her eyes, rocked back and forth a moment, opened her eyes, and expelled a gentle stream of air until the last candle was extinguished. Whoever was stationed at the power switch when the lights went out now restored it to its original position. The jukebox, the blinking tree, the GENTS and LADIES signs, the bar lights, the soft globes in the booths resumed what they had been doing before the blackout. Bartenders and customers, like characters in a suddenly reactivated film, also returned to life.

"Roxie," asked Jessie, accepting a large knife from one of the bartenders, "I bet this was your idea, wasn't it?"

"I had a little help from Joan here," she replied, indicating the shorter, pretty girl beside her. "We thought it was time somebody paid some attention to you."

"Maybe they pay too much attention," Jessie said, dissecting the cake.

"Let's forget that for tonight," said Phyllis, an older, blonde-headed woman who had followed the cake to the table. "This is strictly a love night."

"Love night it is," said Jessie.

"Then you must accept my love."

The deep, rich voice belonged to someone edging through the group. A pair of large hands the color of coal surrounded Jessie's free hand and held it as she screamed "Thomas!" and half rose to accept the kiss he was carrying toward her cheek.

"Thomas, what are you doing here? You should be home with your family!"

"We are all here," he said, gesturing toward a smiling woman with a sleeping child in her arms and two young boys standing shyly by her skirt.

"But the children...."

"We promised the manager it is only for a few minutes. Besides, it is Christmas Eve."

"Here," said Jessie, gently guiding the woman and child into the booth where she had been sitting. "You must sit by me, Matilda. And little Leah. She is so beautiful."

"Now, Matthew," she said, hoisting the first boy onto the table so that his legs hung down beside his sleeping sister, "we must have you here where you won't miss anything."

"And, Mark," she said, easing herself onto the slight ledge of seat left by Matilda, "you will have to sit on Aunt Jessie's knee. Is that all right?"

The boys said nothing, but watched her with large, shining eyes as she turned her attention once more to Thomas and Matilda.

"We had to come," said Matilda. "No one has ever been so kind to us as you."

"But how did you know?"

"Roxie telephoned us," said Thomas. "We are very grateful to her."

"Here," said Jessie, sliding two small pieces of cake onto napkins and gently offering them to Matthew and Mark. "I bet you'll like this."

The boys' dark eyes looked inquiringly to their mother. When she smiled, the little dark hands reached out to accept the cake.

"We brought you something," said Thomas, laying a small sack on the table.

"So did we," said Joan, as both Roxie and Phyllis produced gift-wrapped packages.

Jessie reached into the sack. Removing the tissue paper, she laid a small brass turtle on the table, its back hollowed out to receive pieces of incense. The tissue also yielded a box of incense pellets.

"Oh, Thomas and Matilda, thank you."

"It is from our country," said Thomas.

"I will treasure it," she said, clasping the turtle to her cheek.

Then she opened the package from Phyllis. It was a tiny cut-glass bottle of perfume. The beveled edges reflected the light as Jessie turned it in her hand.

"Oh, Phyllis, it is so lovely. Um-m-m, and it smells heavenly. Thank you."

Finally she opened the package from Joan and Roxie, producing a pair of small, heart-shaped, gold-colored earrings, which she held excitedly to her chest.

"Oh, you know how I love little earrings! Thank you both so much."

"Happy birthday from all of us," said Phyllis.

"Oh, it's the happiest birthday!"

"We will never forget how you took us in when we arrived from Haiti," said Matilda. "Our money had been stolen, and the children were weeping from hunger, and we had nowhere to go. If you had not stopped in the street and asked how it was with us, I do not know what we would have done."

"Nor will we forget the trouble it caused you with your landlord and the other tenants," said Thomas. "We should have left, but you would not permit it."

"Of course you shouldn't," said Jessie. "It was just that they didn't realize. In *Baba*'s greater world, there are more people your color than theirs. If they had only seen the whole picture, they would have been kinder and more accommodating."

A camera flash suddenly arced behind Jessie. Joan gave a sharp tug on a tab of Polaroid film, separating it from the camera, and laid the film on the table. The dull rectangle began to brighten with colors and shapes, and within a few seconds appeared images of Matthew and Mark with light green icing highlighting their lips and cheeks.

Phyllis, sitting across from Matilda and Leah, stroked Matthew's back and smiled, remembering the first time she had heard Jessie refer to *Baba*. She had just met her at a bar in another part of town when she blurted out her sadness; her husband had left her and her mother had died, both within the space of six months. "I will ask *Baba* to help you," Jessie had said.

Phyllis had not known who *Baba* was. At first she thought it must be a friend of Jessie's. Then, seeing the puzzlement in her eyes, Jessie had laughed and explained that *Baba* was her name for God.

"Ever since I was a little girl," she had said. "It sort of solves the sex problem for God. Neither male nor female, but very intimate."

Phyllis had smiled. "Our *Baba*, who art in *Baba*-land," she had thought. "How nice!"

Jessie was so unself-conscious about her *Baba*. She spoke of *Baba* as matter-of-factly as if she were talking about her mother or father or a favorite aunt. No one who knew her very long failed to realize that *Baba* was as real and as present to her as her own hands or the face she saw when she looked in a mirror.

One of the bartenders reached around Thomas to set a full pitcher of beer on the table.

"Time to freshen up," he said, snatching away the empty pitcher and disappearing almost as quickly as he had come.

"What a wonderful Christmas gift this is!" said Jessie. "Your love, this cake, Matilda, Thomas, the children. I think I'm going to die of happiness tonight."

She brushed Mark's cheek with her hand, disturbing some of the crumbs and icing that had stuck there.

"It makes it harder to tell you," she said.

"Tell us what?" asked Roxie.

Jessie reached over and laid a cupped hand on the sleeping infant's cheek. Then she softly touched Matilda's shining braids.

"I think it's time to leave."

"You mean leave New Haven?"

"Yes. I've been feeling it for some time now. Tonight I began to know for certain."

"But why? Where will you go?"

"I don't know," said Jessie. "It's just something I feel. I've been talking with *Baba* about it. Perhaps somewhere in the South. Maybe Virginia, Tennessee, Georgia, Alabama."

"But you can't just leave us for no reason," said Joan. Her face was creased with pain. "We won't let you."

Jessie smiled and laid a hand on hers.

Phyllis leaned over from behind Jessie and clasped both arms around her neck. "Joan's right," she said. "We won't let you leave us."

"Oh, but, Miss Phyllis," said Thomas, "Jessie must go wherever *Baba* sends her. What if she had not come to New Haven when she was sent here? Then we would never have met with her." His face was an ebony mask of earnestness.

"Thomas is right," agreed Roxie. "But surely it won't be for a little while yet, will it, Jess? It's Christmas Eve, and this is a birthday party. We're still celebrating. More cake, anybody? Matthew? Mark?"

Matthew's eyelids had grown heavy. Mark was fighting to sit up.

"We must go," said Matilda. "We did not mean to stay this long."

Jessie gave each child a kiss as she helped to bundle the boys into their coats and scarves.

"Thank you for coming to my party," she said to each of them. "You've made it very special." She hugged Matilda and Leah together and gave Thomas a hug and a kiss.

"Blessed Christmas!"

"And to you," they said.

Afterward, Roxie, Joan, Phyllis, and Jessie sat in the booth, taking sips of beer and running their fingers in the icing and licking them.

"What will you do with your things if you go?" asked Joan.

"Ohhh, I don't have much."

"Your paintings?"

"There are only two or three. I'll give them away."

"Oh, not the two old men playing checkers in the park," protested Phyllis. "I love that one. Can I have it? I'll pay you for it."

"It's yours, dear. But not for pay. I'll be happy to think of it hanging in your apartment."

Everyone who had seen Jessie's paintings knew that she had enormous talent. There was a depth of humanity, of caring, in her works that made them special. Whatever the subject—children, old people, animals, flowers, a tumbledown house—each picture seemed to guide the eyes of the beholder to some new insight, some connection between the particular and the infinite, that compelled reverence as well as admiration, awe as well as joy.

Jessie had never had a showing. She was so generous with her works that she hadn't accumulated enough of them to mount an exhibit. If someone admired a canvas she was working on, she was likely to take it off the easel the moment she finished it and give it away.

Roxie and Joan had three of her paintings, one over the mantel in their living room, one above the tub in the bathroom, and one over the small table in the kitchen where they saw it each time they ate. This last one showed an enormous field of poppies, lupine, and daisies, with only a fifth of the canvas devoted to the sky, which was partially filled with fluffy cumulus clouds. In the center of the field, tiny but carefully defined, a mother and two children sat having a picnic on a gaily colored quilt. A small kitten stood on its hind legs, peering into the picnic basket. The aura of happiness shared by the mother and children was nothing short of blissful.

Joan, who was prone to occasional moods of depression, sometimes made a pot of tea and sat at the table for an hour or more, gazing at the scene. By the time she had emptied the pot, she always felt centered and hopeful again.

"How will you support yourself if you leave your job?" asked Roxie.

"I'll find something. I don't need much."

"You live on less than anybody I know," said Phyllis. "Sometimes I'd swear you're like one of those plants that live on air."

"*Baba*'s world is unbelievably rich," said Jessie. "Sometimes, the less we have, the more we see."

"The more some people see," corrected Roxie. "There are a lot of people who aren't exactly ennobled by poverty."

"Well, I admire you," said Joan. "I wish I could live as simply and happily as you do."

Jessie reached out to touch Joan's cheek. She loved the open, trusting face, younger than Roxie's and Phyllis's. Younger than her own.

"You will see," she said. "Listen to your heart."

She would miss the three women. She knew

she would. They had been close friends for a couple of years now. First, Roxie, whom she had met at the copy machine while working as a temp in the same office; Roxie was coming down with the flu; that evening Jessie showed up at her door with a thermos of soup and a single rose in a vase. Joan was not in that night; she had gone to a movie with a date, but they met a week later. And Phyllis had been last, that time at the bar.

But Jessie had a strange view about such things. She believed that it was possible, on the one hand, to be absent from friends and yet feel their presence strongly, and, on the other hand, to be present with them in the flesh and yet feel their absence in the heart. She would keep her friends by giving them up, by following *Baba*'s lead wherever it took her.

"One thing bothers me," said Roxie, giving her head a quick tilt to the right and running a hand through her short hair. It was a gesture Jessie had seen many times. "Who will be there to sort things out for you when you get into trouble?"

Jessie smiled and ducked her head in a little movement toward the side.

"You know what I'm talking about. Like that time you talked the Puerto Rican girl, what's her name, out of going through with her abortion, and her social worker got so mad he came to your apartment with blood in his eyes. Jess, I think he would have harmed you in some way if

I hadn't been there."

"And the time you took that old man's side in the grocery store," added Joan. "The one the clerk was shoving around because he didn't have the money for the things he had brought to the counter. Jeez, Jess, Rox really flattened him!"

Joan was proud of Roxie for her size and strength. At six-feet-two in her stockinged feet, she easily towered over most men. And, unlike many tall women, she had never seemed to find her height or her raw-boned physicality embarrassing. She ran five miles a day and worked out regularly at an exercise spa.

"I'll try to behave," said Jessie.

"I know you," said Roxie. "You can't help what you do. But I'll worry about you. Maybe you shouldn't go."

"I'll be fine. Really, I will."

By this time the four women were holding hands in the middle of the table, largely unconscious of what they were doing. They clearly felt strongly about their relationship.

From a radio at the bar, the soft, crisp tones of "Silent Night" drifted across the room. It was midnight and the bar was closing.

"Merry Christmas," said Jessie.

"Happy birthday," said Phyllis.

"Yes," said Joan, joined by Roxie, "happy birthday."

2

On New Year's Day Jessie boarded a bus bound for New York City, where she would transfer to another bus going to Knoxville, Tennessee. Her body felt a little stiff and her eyes were slightly sore; she had been up with her friends until almost three o'clock. They had wanted to see her off at the station, but she had asked them not to. She knew it would be harder that way. She knew also that Joan would probably load her down with more food than she could eat. As it was, she had gotten off with a small sack of muffins, some apples, and a six-pack of Cokes.

There hadn't been many people waiting at the bus station, probably in deference to the holiday. Jessie noticed one family, whom she took to be Middle-Easterners, waiting for a bus to Boston, for she heard the mother mention Boston to the children. The four children were well dressed, but apparently the family was relatively poor. Two of the children complained that they were hungry. The father told them they would have something to eat when they arrived at their destination.

Jessie gave them her muffins, apples, and Cokes. The parents at first expressed reluctance, but, seeing her willingness, thanked her and allowed the children to accept. The children were wide-eyed with wonder as they reached into the sack and produced its contents.

On the bus to New York there were only seven or eight people. One older couple sat together, and the others scattered throughout the coach.

Jessie looked out at the barren land along the interstate and thought of the adventures that lay before her. She had never been to the South before. She wondered what it would be like, and what *Baba* had in store for her.

Occasional snowflakes fell into the bus's windpath and were swept rapidly alongside. The sky was leaden and oppressive, like a great prison that cast a spell of individuation and loneliness on the people in the bus.

Jessie felt a thrill at seeing the tall buildings of New York. The driver sped along the Major Deegan Expressway and then down the streets of Manhattan, turning expertly onto a ramp, and drove through the nearly empty corridors to the Port Authority Bus Terminal. Opening the door with a whoosh, he announced that this was the termination of the journey, directing those going farther to consult the board in the terminal for more information.

Jessie removed her tote bag from the overhead rack and followed the other passengers. The air in the garage was cold and refreshing. She passed through the station, where dispatchers' voices were echoing hollowly in the cavernous room, mixing absurdly with the strong odor of disinfectant, and continued out onto the sooty-smelling sidewalks beyond. She arched her neck, looking up at the various buildings, then strolled around to the nearby New York Public Library. The library was closed, of course, but she felt invigorated by merely standing in front of it, staring at the great lion statues and imagining what a wealth of art and information the enormous building contained.

Back in the station, after having consulted the dispatch board, Jessie bought a glass of fruit juice and sat on a bench to drink it. A young girl, perhaps fifteen or sixteen, walked resignedly to the same bench, dumped her knapsack onto the floor, loosened her pea coat, and sat down with a collapsing motion.

Jessie eyed her appraisingly. She was quite a nice looking girl, with smooth, white skin; dark, straight hair almost to the shoulder; and good, solid features, all in pleasant proportion. With one hand, she pulled the navy-colored knit hat off her head and struck it absentmindedly but forcefully against the other hand. Jessie read it as a gesture of despair. When she caught the girl's eye, she smiled encouragingly at her. The girl smiled back, weakly, as if wishing to acknowledge the overture but confessing at the same time that she was depressed and bereft of energy.

When the dispatcher called for passengers to board the bus for Knoxville, Jessie saw the girl reach for the straps of her knapsack, and hung back long enough to let her start for the bus. Then she followed her aboard and asked if she might sit by her. The girl's eyes darted quickly around the bus as if to say, "There are plenty of other seats," but she smiled weakly and pulled her coat into her lap, clearing the way for Jessie to slide in beside her.

"Thank you," said Jessie, who then maintained a discreet silence as the bus pulled away from the station, negotiated several rapid turns, eased into the fume-filled darkness of the Lincoln Tunnel, and finally stretched confidently onto the virtually empty lanes of the New Jersey Turnpike.

Once, as the bus turned south at the early stages of the turnpike, the girl looked back wistfully at the skyline of the city, muted by morning fog. Then she settled into her seat and looked straight ahead, oblivious of the vast oil tanks, the planes descending into Newark Airport, and other scenery flashing past the window.

At last, after she perceived that the girl was beginning to relax, Jessie spoke to her.

"Trouble at home?"

The girl responded instantly, as if she had been expecting the question.

"Yes."

"Parents?"

"My mother. We don't live with my dad anymore."

"You're going to your dad's?"

"I would if I knew where he is."

"So where are you going?"

She shook her head.

"Just away?"

The girl nodded.

"It's tough sometimes, isn't it?" said Jessie.

Another nod.

"Drugs?"

A pause, then another nod.

"You a social worker?" asked the girl.

"No," said Jessie, smiling.

"Teacher?"

"No. Nobody special."

"Where are you going?"

"South. I'm not sure exactly where."

"Are you running away too?"

"No."

She didn't tell the girl about *Baba*. She had found that strangers were often put off by references to mysteries like that.

They fell silent again, letting their relationship grow without hurry or pressure. When the bus pulled into the station in Trenton, New Jersey, and the girl showed no signs of disembarking, Jessie asked, "Can I bring you a cup of coffee?"

"No. But you can bring me a Coke if you want to. Here, I'll give you the money." She fished in her knapsack for a purse.

"My treat," said Jessie, swinging lightly into the aisle and off the bus.

When she came back with the Coke, the girl's composure was surer and brighter.

"My name's Carol."

"Jessie."

"So, Jessie," asked Carol as the bus lurched

backward, then forward, roaring out of the station, "what's it all about?"

"It?"

"Life. The mess we're in. Relationships, non-relationships, the whole nine yards."

Jessie smiled and took her free hand.

"Well, for starters, it's about finding out who you are and where you belong. When that happens, you begin to see that the world is a pretty okay place after all, sort of like a great flea market of the spirit where you can find just about anything you want or need to make you happy and comfortable."

Carol didn't smile, but she looked trusting, so Jessie proceeded.

"And it's about God, and how we fit into God's design for the world and everything in it."

"Heavy."

"Not really. That's when it gets light. But maybe that's too far ahead for you right now. You seem to really be hurting."

Carol smiled a faint, deprecatory smile.

"Wanna talk about it?"

Soon Carol was pouring out a painful tale of parental estrangement, sexual involvement, drugs, fights with her mother and her boyfriend, disinterest and failure at school, and attempts at suicide.

"You poor thing," said Jessie. "How old are you?"

"I'll be sixteen next week."

"And away from home for your birthday?"

Carol turned away and looked out the window. Flat fields stretched endlessly on both sides of the bus, with black and white cattle gathered around small mounds of hay.

"Are you still doing drugs?" asked Jessie.

Carol said nothing.

"I know it's none of my business, Carol, but you need some help. You've taken on an awful lot to deal with alone."

Still nothing.

"Where are you going?"

"Philadelphia."

"Do you know someone there?"

Negative nod.

"Listen, Carol. I have a friend in Washington— a rabbi and his wife. They have a daughter about your age. I know they'd be willing to help. What if I take you there?"

Carol looked doubtful. "They're Jews?"

"Yes. And wonderful people. You'd like them."

"Are you Jewish?"

"Part, I think."

"How do you know them?"

"The rabbi and I were in school together. We're good friends."

Carol was quiet for a minute. Then she said, "My ticket is only to Philadelphia."

"We can fix that easy enough."

"I don't have much money."

"No problem."

"You'd do that for me? But you just met me."

"It feels like we're old friends, don't you think?"

Carol smiled warmly for the first time since Jessie had seen her in the station.

"Okay."

At the station in Washington, Jessie telephoned her friends Ray and Rachel Steltemeier. Carol didn't hear all the conversation, but she heard such phrases as "darling girl," "trouble at home," "for a little while," "help for Rachel," "wonderful friend for Julia."

By the time Ray, a short, heavy, thick-bearded man wearing a lumberjack mackinaw over his white shirt and black trousers, pulled up in front of the bus station and half-invited, half-shoved them into his yellow Volkswagen beetle, Carol was feeling comfortable and even a little excited about the arrangements.

"So," said Ray as he piloted them away over streets slushy with snow that had fallen during the night, "how're tricks, Trixie?"

The question was addressed to Jessie, who sat in front with him.

"Great," she said. "And even better with the chance to see you and Rache."

"Julia will love it," he said. "We talk about you all the time."

"Liar."

"It's true. Ask Rache. We were talking about you just last night. Your name came up when we were discussing New Year's resolutions."

"Don't kid me. I'll pull your beard."

"It did, seriously. We said we had to see you in the new year. How's that for prophetic resolution-making?"

"Oh, Ray," she said, "you never change. And I'm glad. We deserve a few good things that stay the same."

"Carol, ever been to D.C. before?" he asked.

"Once, with my eighth-grade class."

"Then you remember the Lincoln Memorial over there." He gestured as he turned onto the bridge leading to Alexandria. "And if you look back as we cross this bridge, you can see the Washington Monument, our nation's first space needle."

Carol turned and looked through the small rear window of the VW. Already she could feel the warmth and love of the home to which she was going.

"This is Old Town," he said as they sped along streets lined with quaint shops and restaurants. In the early dusk, Christmas lights were shining in the greenery on the utility poles and across the streets; electric candles glowed warmly in the windows of houses and apartment buildings. "We live here, just a few blocks along."

Rachel was as thin as Ray was heavy, and her fine black hair was rolled up in braids on the back of her head. There was an air of old-country fun and gaiety about her that won Carol's heart immediately. And when Julia came in from a visit to a friend's house, bearing a gift of warm popovers and strudel, the two girls instantly hit it off together. Carol was happy she had encountered Jessie and that the encounter had led to this wonderful family.

"So, Carol," said Ray after a sumptuous meal accompanied by sweet white wine and followed by the popovers and strudel, "how about coming to live with us for a while? We could use another girl around here."

Carol was grateful for the way she was being invited, not coerced. Her eyes were dancing as she shook her head yes.

"And we'd like to keep your buddy here too if she will stay."

"Oh, yes," said Rachel, "please do, Jess."

"I'd really like to," said Jessie, "but I'm afraid I have to move along."

"Old *Baba* at you again, is it?" said Ray.

Jessie flushed.

"Baba?" asked Carol.

"You haven't told her about *Baba*?" said Ray.

Although she was obviously a little uncomfortable with how Ray had introduced the subject, Jessie explained to Carol about *Baba*.

"Baba is my old childhood name for God. It isn't masculine and it isn't feminine, so it avoids all the hassle about whether God is male or female, or, as some people insist today, even both. Maybe you remember in the Bible how Jesus taught his disciples to call God *Abba*, for Father? Well, *Baba*, I realized one day after I had used it for years, has the same letters in it,

and it carries the same connotations of personal intimacy for me that *Abba* did for Jesus."

Carol had a gentle, wistful look in her eyes.

"We never talked about God in our house," she said, "except maybe in a cursing sort of way."

Jessie reached over and put an arm around her shoulders. "Brace yourself, dear," she said. "You are going to hear a lot about God in this house. Rabbi Steltemeier is a bigger evangelist than Billy Graham."

Rachel and Julia both laughed at the joke.

"Don't worry," continued Jessie. "God is not like a medicine you have to take. God is the sum of everything good and clean and pure and wonderful about the world. You will like it!"

"Guaranteed," added Ray, "or my grandfather's name wasn't Moshe Aaron Rabinowitz."

Everyone laughed this time, Carol a little more uncertainly than the others, and the strudel was passed around again.

"*Baba* or no *Baba,*" said Ray to Jessie, "we are keeping you until after Sabbath. Then you can continue on your high and holy mission if you must. But until then you are in our charge. Right, gang?"

"Right!" shouted Julia.

"Please, Jessie?" Carol implored.

"All right," said Jessie, "I surrender. Till Sunday."

"Ta raaaaah," Ray said into his clenched hand, as if he were blowing a trumpet.

Carol felt her life getting better already.

3

The snow that began on New Year's Day, when Jessie and Carol arrived in Washington, continued through the night and all day Thursday, paralyzing traffic in the city and suburbs, lying deep and cold as the Sabbath approached.

By late Thursday, Carol was exhibiting signs of restlessness. She moved from window to window, peering out at the drifting snow and wondering aloud if it would ever stop. That evening she only picked at her food and asked to be excused to her room.

Jessie and Rachel looked inquiringly at Julia, but Julia shrugged her shoulders and said maybe she was missing her mother.

On Friday morning the snow had stopped, but the city lay in the grip of a cold wave. The slush in the streets turned crusty, and cars could be heard spinning their tires and crunching ice.

Shortly after breakfast Carol said she wanted to go for a walk. Julia said to wait until she had finished her cocoa. She would show her the school Carol would be attending with her, as well as her favorite record shop and pizza parlor.

"Julia, don't you have some extra boots Carol can use?" asked Rachel.

"Yeah, Mom, I think they're in the hall closet."

When the girls had gone, Rachel went into the kitchen and returned with a fresh pot of coffee. She and Ray and Jessie sat quietly a moment, sensing the fresh aroma from their cups and cradling the warmth in their hands.

"Drugs," said Ray.

"I'm afraid so," said Jessie.

"Is she a user?" asked Rachel.

Jessie shook her head. "I think so. I asked her, and she didn't deny it."

"I've seen a lot of them," said Ray. "She has all the symptoms. Dreamy look. Short attention span. Unexplained nervousness. Need to get out. She's got the problem, Jess."

Jessie's eyes focused on her cup, then on Rachel, and finally on Ray.

"Does this mean you don't want her? I mean, with Julia and all? I'd understand."

Ray looked at Rachel. No words were exchanged, but apparently Rachel communicated something.

"We'll help her," said Ray. "Or at least we'll try. Kids on drugs are sometimes completely unmanageable. You realize that. She may not want to be helped."

"Don't worry about Julia," said Rachel. "She has her head screwed on straight. Carol's being here won't pose a threat to her."

"*Baba* knew what *Baba* was doing," said Jessie. "Carol really needs you."

At mid-morning, Rachel and Jessie went to the grocery store to buy things for the Sabbath meal and the remainder of the weekend. When they returned, Julia was there without Carol. Ray was on the telephone.

"Where's Carol?" asked Rachel.

"Gone," said Julia. "She disappeared from the record store. We went in to listen to some new tapes. I took a Michael Jackson tape into one booth, and she went into another booth with a tape she had found. When I came out, I looked in the booth and everywhere for her, and she was gone. She had just vanished, like into thin air. I waited thirty or forty minutes, thinking she would show up, but she never did."

"Who is your father talking to?" asked Rachel.

"Somebody he knows at the police station. They haven't seen her either, but I guess Dad figures they can watch for her."

Ray hung up the phone about that time.

"I gave him a description of Carol," he said. "He said he'd put out an APB and let us know if anyone spots her. He's also checking with the NYPD to see if she has a record with them."

"Poor Carol," said Jessie. "She must be so frightened."

"Of what?" asked Julia. "Nobody's done anything to hurt her or scare her."

Jessie put a hand on Julia's arm and pulled her close. "Some people don't need anything outside themselves for that," she said. "They carry around their own ghosts and goblins."

"What'll we do?" asked Rachel. "We can't simply sit here and do nothing."

"Right," said Ray, heading for the coat tree where his mackinaw and a long scarf were hanging. "I'm going to go look for her."

"I'll go too, said Jessie.

"And so will I," added Julia.

"Julia," said Ray, "you go with Jessie. The two of you take the area near the riverfront—all the pizza joints and galleries and shops—anywhere she might have wandered. I'll cruise around the other parts of town. She can't have gone too far unless she took a bus, and I don't think she'd do that."

For two hours, Julia and Jessie trudged up and down the streets of Old Town, looking in restaurants, bakeries, shops, and museums, but there was no sign of Carol. They even searched the whole of the Torpedo Factory, a large, hangar-like structure near the river that once produced torpedoes but had since been converted into a warren of small art studios. Jessie's eyes scanned the better canvases as they hurried from cubicle to cubicle, and she thought how much fun it would be to have her own gallery there, where she could work and talk with all the browsers who stopped by.

On the way back to the Steltemeiers' house, they heard a sudden crunching noise at the curb and saw the familiar yellow Volkswagen pulling alongside them, its tiny wipers valiantly attempting to deal with the thick paste of salt water and snow slung constantly by passing cars.

They knew from Ray's face that he had had no luck, and he knew because Carol was not with them that it had been the same with them.

But the VW had barely crunched its way into a parking space before Rachel burst out the front door onto the porch to shout, "They've found her! Sergeant Goldstein called half an hour ago. She's down at the station."

Ray, who had put one foot out of the VW and half stood outside to hear what she was saying, darted back in, restarted the engine, rocked them forward out of the parking space, and shot off into the street again.

They found Carol slumped unhappily in a big wooden armchair at the side of Sergeant Goldstein's office. He was continuing to work at his desk, typing reports and answering phone calls, but he was clearly in charge of Carol's presence and blocking any attempt she might make to take herself elsewhere.

"Carol!" said Jessie, dropping to her knees in front of the sullen-looking girl. "We were so worried!"

"Patrol picked her up at the Arena Health Spa," the sergeant was saying to Ray. "Trying to make a hit, they figured. Kept asking around for somebody to i.d. a pusher for her. Girl at the desk called the precinct house, said it looked like they had a runaway hanging out in the gym."

"You didn't bust her?" asked Julia.

"No, miss. We didn't have nothing to charge her with. I just held her till the rabbi could get here and collect her."

"Thanks, Artie," said Ray. "I owe you one."

"Pleasure. Hope she don't make trouble

for you."

"You didn't say if you found a record on her in New York."

"Nope. Nothing under the name you gave me.

"Thank God for that. Come on, children, let's go home to Mama."

Even the somber events of the day did not totally manage to eclipse the joy of Shabbat as the evening fell. Strong smells of rosemaryed lamb, spiced cabbage, and freshly baked challa bread filled the house and greeted Jessie and Carol with special pungency as they descended from upstairs.

Julia had the honor of saying the first blessing as they all stood around the table. She draped a small, delicately woven white cloth over her head, one point hanging over her forehead, and looked quaint and demure as she folded her hands, closed her eyes, and intoned the familiar words of the Hebrew prayer.

Ray poured red wine into all their glasses and served their plates from the dishes arranged before him.

The conversation was lively and touched on many subjects—Ray and Jessie's days in school; Rachel and Ray's first date; the congregation they had served in Natick, Massachusetts; a crazy woman who was convinced that alien creatures had bugged the synagogue and were listening to the prayers and readings in order to infiltrate the congregation; Julia's distress with the chicken pox; her unhappiness at not having a Christmas tree like many of her non-Jewish friends; her parents' eventual consent to her having a very small one in her room, which turned out, when Ray brought it home, to stand nearly six feet tall, demanding three additional strands of lights.

Carol, who had responded only glumly to this point, asked, "But isn't that against your religion or something?"

Rachel laughed. "Something, I expect. This rabbi was never very orthodox. I have even heard him praying to *Baba*."

Ray raised his eyes ceilingward and then, without turning his head, shifted them toward Jessie, who winked at him.

"Speaking of which," he said, "it is time we read the Torah and said our prayers. Julia, will you please bring the scroll?"

"Yes, Papa."

Easing away from the table, Julia slipped to the side of the room and opened an ornate box atop the sideboard. Extracting a scroll by its wooden handles, she carried it reverently to her father.

"I think we should ask Jessie to read tonight, don't you?" he said.

"Oh, yes," said Rachel.

Jessie opened the scroll to the book of Numbers. Her eyes shone as she began to read about the spies Moses sent into the land of Canaan before the Jews entered the land. She ticked off the names of all the places they went—Zin, Rehob, Hebron, Ahiman, Sheshai, Eshcol. They cut down a single cluster of grapes in the valley of Eshcol that was so big, two men had to carry it on a pole between them. After forty days, they returned to Moses and Aaron and showed them the grapes. But when the people were eager to enter the land, the spies said no, the inhabitants were giants. "We seemed to ourselves like grasshoppers," they said, "and so we seemed to them."

"Now I'm going to skip over to the book of Joshua and read some more," said Jessie. And she read the part about the priests encircling the city of Jericho and blowing their trumpets, after which all the people raised a great shout, as Jehovah had instructed them, and the walls of the city fell down, so that the Israelites marched straight into the heart of the city without interference.

There was silence in the room when she stopped reading. It was as if something mystical were happening, as if there were an invisible connection between the scriptural events and the people around the Shabbat table. They could all feel it, even Carol.

"Carol?" asked Jessie.

"Yes."

"I think the passages were especially for you tonight. Did you sense that?"

"I felt something."

"Your life has been like the first story—giants

in the land, fear, the feeling that you were doomed to failure. But *Baba* is going to transform all that, as in the second passage. When *Baba* becomes involved in your life, there is nothing you cannot conquer—not fear, not sickness, not even death. Do you believe this?"

"I—I want to believe."

Then something very strange happened, something Ray and Rachel and Julia would talk about the rest of their lives. Jessie stood and walked around the table to Carol. Carol stood up as if on cue. Jessie reached out with both hands and took Carol's face between them. Afterward they would remember that a kind of light hovered over Carol's face, as if an electric current had passed through Jessie's hands into her body. One thing they knew for certain: Carol had slumped immediately to the floor, as if she had suddenly and inexplicably fainted.

Ray leapt up and helped her into her chair, and she began to regain her senses.

"What happened?" asked Rachel. "Are you all right?"

"It was so peaceful," said Carol. Her tongue seemed thick and her speech was slow. "So very...very...peaceful."

Together they held hands around the table as Ray recited some prayers. When he had finished them, he began singing a Yiddish hymn. Rachel and Julia joined in. So did Jessie.

Carol sat with an expression of great contentment on her face, beaming before some unseen source of blessing.

The next hymn was a rhythmical chant, very minor and syncopated. Without a word of suggestion, Jessie and Ray stood up, lifting Rachel and Julia and Carol as well, and they all danced back and forth around the table to the beat of the music. When it ended, they collapsed into their chairs with laughter.

"*Baba* has honored our household," said Ray.

"Praise *Baba*," said Julia.

Jessie smiled. She was more confident than ever about her journey.

4

On Sunday morning the three Steltemeiers, plus Jessie and Carol, piled into the diminutive VW for the trip to the bus station. There they all scrambled out and stood noisily waiting for Jessie's bus to be called.

"I feel as if I've gained five pounds," said Jessie.

"Me too," said Carol. "You'd better take me with you and not leave me with these people."

Rachel and Julia could not get over the change in Carol since the Shabbat incident. She was a totally different person—jolly, lighthearted, tender and caring all at the same time. She had told them all about her drug habit and how she had craved first marijuana and then cocaine, buying crack from other students at school. Friday, when she had disappeared from the record store, she had felt desperate for a fix. She was just waiting for another chance to lose her guardian family—for good, if necessary—and find a source of supply. She had even considered prostitution as a means of financing her habit. And then had come that unforgettable experience at the dinner table, when *Baba* had intervened in her life. It had changed her destiny forever, she was convinced.

That very evening she had begun insisting that she go with Jessie wherever it was that Jessie was going. She would be no trouble, she promised, and, besides, Jessie could use a companion.

But Jessie had said no. Carol needed to be in school. She could stay with the Steltemeiers for a few weeks, and then, if she felt like going home, they would help to arrange matters with her mother.

In the end, Carol had admitted that perhaps that would be best. She knew she owed a lot to her mother and would like a chance to make it up to her. Besides, she would miss Julia if she left the Steltemeiers now. The two of them had become amazingly close in the few days they had shared a room.

"Don't stay away, kiddo," said Ray as he enclosed Jessie in a bear hug.

Jessie and the women also had a great hug. She and Carol clung to each other for an inordinately long time, rocking back and forth, conveying deep meanings of friendship and alliance without uttering a syllable of speech. Even as they parted and Jessie mounted the steps to the bus, an almost visible bond seemed to extend between them. Ray and Rachel understood, and perhaps Julia too, that it would sustain Carol as almost nothing else in the months and years ahead.

Jessie sat on the side of the bus next to them, so that she could still see and wave to them until the bus pulled out of the station. She barely noticed the huge man who sat next to her, his bulk filling his own seat and part of hers as well. Only as the bus pulled away from the city streets and accelerated over the bridge leading to the interstate highway in Virginia did she turn to look at his face.

Like the rest of the man, the face was over-sized, with flesh lying in great folds at the base of his jaws. Yet it was a kindly face, with soft, warm eyes and a shock of brown hair falling boyishly across his forehead. The man's enormity obviously imposed added stress on his breathing, for it was quite audible and was frequently punctuated by heavy sighs.

"Hi, I'm Sam," he said when he saw that Jessie was looking at his face. He thrust a large, hamlike hand a few inches in her direction.

"Hello. I'm Jessie," she said, slipping her small hand into his, but giving him a firm grip nevertheless.

"I'm going to see my daughter in Charlottesville," he said. "She got married last

June and she's been sick since September."

"Not pregnancy?"

"Nope. Doctors don't know what it is. She's been at the university hospital there the last two months. First they thought it was chronic appendicitis. Then they decided it was Crohn's disease. But they did all those fancy X-rays and CAT scans and everything, and figured it wasn't that. You know what Crohn's disease is?"

Jessie said she didn't.

"It's an inflammation of the bowels that causes serious problems. Sometimes they can treat it by medication and sometimes they have to operate, take out a section of the intestines. Eventually, they keep doing that, you have to have a colostomy."

"But that isn't what she has?"

"Nope. They thought it was, 'cause she kept vomiting and having diarrhea, the way you do when you have it, and she lost a lot of weight. She wasn't ever as big as me, but she was a good size. She says she's down about fifty pounds now."

"What are they doing for her?"

"Nothing right now, except giving her some medicine to keep her stomach quiet and feeding her intravenously for a while until they can figure out what it is."

"I know she'll be glad to see you."

"She don't know I'm coming. I didn't know myself till yesterday. I moped around the house all weekend thinking about her, you know the way you think about your baby girl and all, and finally my wife upped and said, 'Well, why don't you go down to see her.' So I called up my boss—I work at a tire warehouse up in Silver Springs—and told him I needed a couple days off to go see my baby, and he said, 'Okay, things are kinda slow right now, why don't you do that?' So here I am, on my way to see her."

"What's her name?"

"Billie. Well, it's really Willena, for my wife's sister, but we always called her Billie, ever since she was a little girl."

"Have you been to Charlottesville before?"

"No, ma'am. Well, not really. I been through it the time I helped move Billie and Howard's furniture down to their house. It's in the country about twenty miles the other side of town. But I didn't stop. Just went through."

By now, the bus was sailing rapidly along the straight highway. The sun had broken through some early morning clouds and was making the snow on the hills sparkle like white satin. The road was mostly dry, but mounds of dirty snow stood at the edges.

Jessie found her eyes involuntarily registering the telephone poles as they whipped by, a hundred and one, a hundred and two, a hundred and three, a hundred and four...

Her mind went back to Carol at the station, and to Rachel and Ray and Julia. She said a little prayer to *Baba* for them, asking that Carol remain healed of her drug habit and that the four of them have a happy, wholesome relation-ship over the weeks—and possibly months—ahead.

Then she prayed for Sam and his wife, and for Billie and her husband Howard. She inter-ceded with *Baba* for the doctors at the hospital, asking that they might be caught up in God's great healing program, so that their vast medical knowledge and expertise would be used to their utmost, and that one of the doctors would sud-denly experience a breakthrough in Billie's case and begin an effective treatment for her.

"You a woman of faith?" Sam interrupted her train of thoughts.

"Oh, yes."

"Me too. I mean, I'm a man of faith. I pray every day for my baby. Sometimes six, seven times a day. Whenever I think about it. I know the doctors do their best, and I wouldn't want to do without them, but they don't know every-thing. Can't, in this complicated world. They need help from the Man Above."

Jessie smiled at the simple expression. She did not judge it, for she knew that God always makes allowances for human contrivances in the realm of faith. Even *Baba*, she thought, is a lim-iting term. All language is, when it comes to God.

"Sam," she said, "I have a feeling you are going to find Billie much improved when you get there today."

"I hope you're right. It would sure make me

feel good."

"There isn't anything the Man Above can't do."

"You're right about that."

Sam took Jessie's comparatively small hand in both of his as he was getting off the bus in Charlottesville. "Sure made me feel better talking with you, miss," he said. "I'm going to tell Billie all about our conversation."

Jessie's heart was warmed by his simple good-will.

"Give her a kiss from me, and my best wishes," she said.

"I will indeed."

Jessie felt the bus shift as the large man stood and moved his weight into the aisle. He turned again when he had gotten off the bus and waved a last farewell.

Dusk was beginning to fall as the bus roared down Interstate 81 toward the Tennessee border. Jessie was mesmerized by the beauty of the hills and the late afternoon shadows they cast. What a master artist *Baba* is, she thought, to have molded such incomparable grace into common fields and hills.

Once, she laid her head back in the corner formed by the seat and the window and dozed for a few minutes, enjoying a sort of dream as she did. It was a dream about God as a great shepherd, big as a cloud, coming across these lovely hills in search of her as a lost sheep somewhere among them. Then, inexplicably, she herself was the shepherd, and she was looking for lost sheep.

When she awoke, she breathed a prayer of thanksgiving for the dream, which produced a sense of joyful serenity in her heart, and then for the mission *Baba* was giving her. She didn't yet know what it was, but she knew she was already being obedient to it, that she was drawing nearer to it with each passing mile. Somewhere out there were the sheep she must find.

In Tennessee, there was only a dusting of snow on the hills and valleys, and where the sun had reached during the day the bare fields were showing in great dark patches. The light had faded now to an intense red glow along the western horizon, and Jessie's pulse raced at thoughts of the adventure that lay before her.

5

Jessie had been in Knoxville several days awaiting guidance about her mission. She wasn't sure if it lay in the city of Knoxville itself, where she saw plenty of need, or somewhere further west or south. She was staying at the YWCA, a large, well kept building in the central part of the city, as her funds were extremely limited. She was beginning to be open to the possibility of a job, if this was where she was to remain, and had already approached one firm specializing in the placement of temporary secretaries and office helpers.

When the young man interviewing her at the employment office asked if she had any special talents, she mentioned that she had done some paintings. He asked if she were familiar with Gatlinburg and Pigeon Forge, neighboring communities with numerous shops and galleries devoted to arts and crafts, especially those indigenous to the mountain areas.

When she said she was not, he suggested that she make a trip over there and see if she might make a connection. Next day she went to the station and caught a bus bound for Gatlinburg, and soon found herself walking the streets lined by shops of every kind and bordered by fast-running brooks with trout swimming in them. Beyond the brooks, the mountains stretched suddenly and mightily, giving the town the appearance of an Alpine village.

One small section of shops, in fact, bore the name Alpine Village. Its brick sidewalks led to a large fountain surrounded by winter flowers, and beyond these lay a donut shop with the most delicious pastries Jessie thought she had ever eaten. She sat on a bench finishing a cinnamon twist and a carton of milk while she looked up at the towering hills and forests.

"Europe couldn't be better than this," she thought.

After inquiring at several galleries, she discovered one filled with soft, gentle watercolors of Appalachian scenes so poignant she had to spend a few minutes in front of each, studying its rich composition and marvelous detail. A small, white-headed woman with sharp features and eyes like a bird's sat behind a desk reading a book. From time to time she looked up to observe Jessie's absorption in the paintings, and finally she spoke.

"My son does these. He works at a printing factory over in Knoxville and does these in his spare time."

"They're beautiful," said Jessie. "I love them."

"He hopes to make a living at it someday, but he's just getting started now. The market's sort of depressed, I'm afraid. People don't have much money to spare for anything they don't absolutely have to have."

"But his prices are so reasonable."

"Oh, they're that. But people still don't have the money. Most artists 'round here would starve to death if they didn't have jobs to support themselves."

"Have you had this shop long?"

"'Bout six months. No, seven, in a week and a half."

"Your son is fortunate to have you here to represent him."

"Yes. He couldn't have the gallery if I weren't free to keep it open. My husband died three years ago. There's just me and the boy, and I don't have anything else to do."

Jessie continued studying the pictures. She was especially taken by one of a farmyard with an old bucket sitting near a well. A doe was carefully advancing on the bucket to see if there was anything in it; her fawn was standing a few paces behind her. The hairs on the animals were so finely rendered that she almost reached out to feel them. In fact, she caught her hand in midair about to touch the canvas.

"You're the second person I've seen do that," said the woman. "You must have some artistic blood in you yourself."

Jessie blushed without thinking why, and acknowledged the woman's keenness of perception. She said she had come to Gatlinburg for the day to see whether there was anything she might do there to earn a living for a while.

"As an artist?" asked the woman. "Or clerking?"

"Either," said Jessie. "I'm not particular."

"Well, I don't know of any jobs open right now. This is slack season, as you can tell. Most shops close up at four or five in the afternoon. Not like spring and summer and fall, when all the tourists come to town, though we did have a sight of them during the Christmas vacation, with all these new decorations the city put up.

"As for being an artist, my son'd have to see some of your work before giving a judgment on that. He's talked of getting a couple of other artists' work in here besides his, thinking it would entice more customers by offering a wider range of choices."

"I'm afraid I don't have anything to show just

now. I arrived in Knoxville a few days ago from New England, and didn't bring any paintings with me."

"Knoxville, you say? That's where my son and I live. Why don't you go back there in the back room, if you like, and paint up something sort of fastlike right now? I mean, if you really want to."

"You mean now?"

"Sure, honey. My son won't mind. He's got all kinds a canvases and paints and brushes in there. He works here on weekends when he's managing the studio."

The woman was so friendly and inviting that Jessie couldn't resist. Perhaps *Baba* had planned it this way. Within a few minutes, she was alone in the back room, where a skylight provided plenty of natural light, sketching on a small canvas.

When she first wondered what to paint on such short notice, she thought of Ray and Rachel and Julia and Carol at the Sabbath meal, and what a warm picture they would make. She smiled as the sketching pencil flew over the canvas, roughing in the familiar faces and figures. Soon she was at work with some oils she found in a box; the warm features of the bearded rabbi and his family were rapidly coming to life on the easel.

An hour passed. The woman, who introduced herself as Mrs. Moorefield, looked in to ask if she'd like something to drink. When she returned with a Coke, she stopped to look at Jessie's progress.

"Say, you're *good*," she said, her face hanging a bit slack in appreciation.

She studied the emerging portraits a moment longer.

"Tell you one thing," she said. "That sort of thing won't sell around here. Only pictures of barns and woods and flowers and things like that. People like what's already familiar to them, and whatever they've already seen pictures of. Only thing that counts, my son says, is what they already know done better than anybody has done it before. But you're sure good, I'll say that for you."

Absorbed in her work, Jessie was unaware of the passing of time. She had completed the background of the painting and most of the details of the table setting. Positioning the Torah scroll in the foreground of the scene, she left the scroll box open on the sideboard by the wall and showed the scroll itself, with a decorative sash around it, lying on the table near the figure of Ray. Now she was adding details to the portrait of Julia, the demure young girl with head bowed and hands folded, standing behind the table. With minute touches of yellow, orange, and white, she imparted a sheen to the kerchief on Julia's head, suggesting a glow from the candles in the menorah. The whole room was beginning to shimmer in the radiance of the candlelight, with an interplay of highlights and shadows that suggested the special mystery and solemnity of the occasion. The wine goblets in particular stood out; their molded surfaces glinted softly and magically in the half light.

Jessie prayed for each of the members of Ray's family as she worked on their representations. She had given thanks for Ray's faith and scholarship, and for the irrepressible vivacity of his spirit that seemed to bubble up and burst effervescently on everyone around him. She asked *Baba* to preserve these special qualities and to empower him to impart the faith to his congregation in a full and satisfying way. For Rachel, she asked strength and wisdom for the maturing years, that she would continue to be a good wife and mother and to deal resourcefully with the unique challenges of being a rabbi's spouse. As she continued to add detail to the characterization of Julia, she prayed for Julia's safe and happy passage during the difficult years of adolescence, and asked that *Baba* would incline her always to understand the centrality of *Baba*'s place in her personal affairs as well as in the whole of human destiny.

The details of Carol's portrait were left till last, and Jessie lingered over them with loving care. The casual viewer would have taken her for a pretty sister, or perhaps a cousin visiting in the home, her face filled with wonder before the miracle of grace and fellowship commemorated by the meal and the prayers. A hint of titanium gave a special luster to her eyes, and her cheeks were flushed with color highlighted by the glow of the candles. Her chin was slightly dropped, to suggest an attitude of humility and reverence. But there was no denying that the major theme of her character was joy and peace. She virtually radiated these qualities, just as the Torah scroll and Julia's scarf bespoke the presence of tradition and the entire family projected a sense of trust and stability.

Jessie was dwelling lovingly on Carol in prayer as she made the final adjustments to her portrait, asking that *Baba* surround her with a special shield of love in the coming weeks, powerful enough to withstand all temptation and despair, when Mrs. Moorefield spoke to her from behind. "Lord, child, you really get into your painting, don't you? I bet you didn't even hear me come in or notice when I switched on the lights over an hour ago. It's plumb dark outside, and folks have all closed up around us."

"Oh!" said Jessie, startled. "I'm so sorry, Mrs. Moorefield. I completely forgot the time. I've probably made you late for dinner."

"Oh, no, child, don't worry about that. I enjoy seeing anyone as engrossed in their work as you have been. Let me get over here where I can see what you've done."

Moving closer to the painting, she stood with her hands on her hips, surveying the canvas. Then she lifted her glasses that hung on a chain around her neck and placed them on her nose and looked again, more intently than ever.

Then she removed the glasses and stepped back a few inches, maintaining her silence.

"I don't rightly know what to say. Honey, that's a masterpiece you've done. I wouldn't believe anyone had done it right here in this back room, and in a single afternoon, if I hadn't seen it with my own eyes. Why, it's better'n anything I ever saw in one of those museums, the time I visited my sister Hattie in Chicago. I'm completely flabbergasted. For once in my life, I'm speechless. And you'd have to know me better to realize what a miracle that is."

Jessie was happy with her sense of achievement. "They're friends of mine," she said. "In Washington." She almost said Alexandria but decided it was easier to say Washington than explain where Alexandria was.

"You mean they're real people? Well, don't that beat all. And here you've painted them right here in this store room. Brought them to life again—and I do mean life—here in Gatlinburg, Tennessee. What a world we live in!"

Mrs. Moorefield looked at her watch. "You did say you was going back to Knoxville tonight, didn't you, hon? Or did I just assume it?"

Jessie nodded yes.

"Do you have a car?"

"No, I came on the bus."

"Then I tell you what. Why don't you ride back with me? We can stop at the Cracker Barrel out in Pigeon Forge and get some supper on the way, and I'll drop you off wherever

you're going. You do have a place you're staying?"

"Oh, yes. I'm at the Y."

"Fine. And I tell you what we're gonna do
with this here masterpiece you've just created."

She picked it up gingerly in both hands, careful to touch only the edges of the canvas.

"It's okay to handle it this way, isn't it?"

"Sure," said Jessie.

"Let's just hang this in there in the studio like
it was one of Harold's paintings. We'll put a sign
under it like the others, with a title and a price,
and your name, of course, and let Harold discover it when he comes in to work tomorrow. He's
off tomorrow, as it's Saturday, and he always
handles the place by himself on Saturdays. I'd
love to see his face when he sees it. He won't
know where in the world it came from. My
phone'll ring two minutes after he sees it. It'll
take him that long to recover from the shock."

Jessie followed her into the gallery.

"Let's see," said Mrs. Moorefield, "where's the
best place for it? Some place where he won't see
it right at first, but, when he does, will have the
right kind of impact. Ah, how about over here,
where this picture of a split-rail fence is hanging? That'll be perfect, I think. Jessie, you take
down that picture—it's just on a nail—and I'll
set this right on the nail in its place."

The new painting fit perfectly in the space,
and showed to even greater advantage under the
intense track lighting from the ceiling.

51

"My, that's beautiful," said Mrs. Moorefield, standing back to admire it again. "That's the finest painting that's ever hung in a shop in this town, I'll guarantee it. Harold's going to be so surprised!"

She went to the desk and took out a slip of paper. "What do you want to call it, honey?" she asked.

"How about *Shabbat*?"

"'Sha-what'? What's that?"

"*Shabbat*. It's the Yiddish word for *Sabbath*."

"Oh, *Sabbath*. I see. All right. Here, why don't you print it yourself. I'm sure you can print better'n me, and besides, you probably know how to spell it."

Jessie accepted the pen and printed the word *Shabbat* in neat block letters.

"Now put your name under it," said Mrs. Moorefield.

She wrote *Jessie*.

"Jessie what?" asked Mrs. Moorefield.

"Just Jessie."

"Don't you have a last name?"

"I haven't used one for years."

"Well, okay. I guess that's acceptable. There's that girl Madonna, and some fellow named Prince. Nothing wrong with that, I suppose. But we need to put a price on it. What do you normally get for a painting like this?"

"I don't know," said Jessie. "I usually give them away."

"Well, you'll do no such thing as long as I'm

around. Would five hundred dollars sound fair to you? It's worth a lot more than that in some places, I know, but around here that's about as much as a painting will fetch."

"That's fine."

"If it sells quickly, we'll know to ask more for the next one. But I reckon that's not bad for an afternoon's work, looked at that way. Print five hundred dollars down in the corner there." She pointed to the right-hand lower corner of the slip.

When Jessie had printed the number, Mrs. Moorefield took the slip and dropped it in the plastic holder beside the painting.

Then she stepped back to survey the scene again. Once more she put the glasses on her nose and studied the details.

"That painting's a miracle," she said. "A beautiful miracle. Harold's going to fall all over himself."

6

Jessie picked up a phone message from Mrs. Moorefield about four o'clock Saturday afternoon, just as she was returning to the Y from a street fair in downtown Knoxville with a new friend, a Thai girl named Jasmine. Jasmine, a new exchange student at the University of Tennessee, was staying at the Y until the new semester began in late January. It was a cold, cloudy day, and the fair had not been very successful; gusts of wind flapped the awnings of the booths angrily, driving people away within minutes of their arrival.

Jessie dialed the number on a phone in the lobby. Mrs. Moorefield picked up the receiver on the third ring.

"Hello."

"Hello."

"Oh, Jessie, dear. This is Rowena Moorefield. I just had to call and tell you about Harold and your painting. It was the funniest thing. He didn't get to the studio till about ten this morning. There wasn't anybody around for a while, so he went back to the workroom, made some coffee, and started on a framing job he had left unfinished. Then he heard the bell ring when some customers came in, so he left what he was doing and went out to meet them.

"When he got there, they were all gathered in front of your painting, and he listened to their comments and compliments, thinking they were talking about his painting of that old fence, which was really sitting in the corner behind the desk. Then they moved on and were chatting about one of his paintings, but he still didn't pay any attention till after they left the shop.

"He had started to go back to the workroom when he spied the fence painting where we left it. He said his head whirled around so fast to see what those customers had been talking about that he nearly dislocated his neck. And then he saw your painting—what did you call it, *Shabbit*?"

Jessie didn't answer. She wouldn't have hurt Mrs. Moorefield's feelings for anything.

"Well, he said he nearly flipped. He couldn't believe his eyes. We had watched a TV program together last night, and I fixed his breakfast this morning, and I hadn't breathed a word about you or the picture. It didn't take him half a minute to get on that phone and give me the tenth degree.

"'Where'd that new painting come from?' he wanted to know.

"'What new painting?' I said, innocent as a peach with no fuzz on it.

"'You know darned well the one I mean, unless some leprechauns got in here in the night and painted one.'

"'What does it look like?'

"'C'mon, Mom, I can't stand this. Where'd it come from?'

"Well, I finally had to tell him all about you coming in and me inviting you to use the paints in the back room, and us having dinner together and everything."

"I hope he wasn't mad," said Jessie.

"Mad? Honey, I haven't heard or seen that man so excited about anything since the time he got a triple-slammer in a high school ballgame and brought home two winning runs. He says you've got more talent than any artist since one of the Wyeth fellows—I never can remember which one is which—and he's dying to meet you. He says, 'Can you get her over for dinner tonight or tomorrow?' So I'm asking. It's a command performance."

"Oh, Mrs. Moorefield, I'd love to come. But I can't tonight. I've promised a friend to go for pizza. But I'm free anytime tomorrow."

"That's great. Whyn't you come for dinner after church? Harold can pick you up at the Y about twelve-thirty. That all right? It's only fifteen minutes to our place."

"That's wonderful. I'll be down at the front door."

"And, honey, do you like fried chicken? Course you do. Everybody likes fried chicken. We always have fried chicken on Sundays, except sometimes when we have beef roast. But tomorrow I planned to have fried chicken."

"That's great, Mrs. Moorefield. I know it will be delicious.'

Pizza that night turned out to be more than either Jessie or Jasmine had bargained for. Their pies were delivered to the table by the gruff, middle-aged owner of the restaurant, who had been complaining to every set of customers that his regular waiter had called in with the flu and his good-for-nothing son was God knows where, probably sitting in some porno flick with his beer-drinking, deadbeat friends. When Jasmine took a bite of her pizza and remarked that it was not very hot, it was just the spark needed to ignite the owner's temper. Turning abruptly from the adjacent table, where he was in the midst of taking an order, he snatched up the remainder of Jasmine's pizza and shouted at her as he whirled away and started toward the kitchen. "Why don't you damned Japs go back home? I don't remember anybody asking you over here."

Jasmine sat with a stunned expression on her face and then put up her hands to conceal her weeping and discomposure. All the other customers lapsed into silence. The air was charged with tension. Jessie stood up like an indignant totem pole.

The owner slammed a couple of oven doors and crashed a large pizza down noisily on the counter top.

"I had enough of them slant-eyes in Vietnam to do me for two lifetimes," he said quite audibly, as if explaining his behavior to himself and whoever else wanted to listen. He returned, bearing a pizza and a pitcher of beer, which he set down briskly on the table behind Jasmine.

"Mister," said Jessie, "I don't know what's bothering you, but you owe this young woman an apology."

He looked around with indignation burning in his eyes.

"I don't owe nobody nothin'," he said. "Why don't you and your friend just get out of here while the gettin's good?"

"Look," she said, pointing to Jasmine, whose face was still buried in her hands.

The man looked, and for a moment his resolve seemed to weaken. Then, pursuing his way to the ovens, he said over his shoulder, "Go on, get outta here. And take your yellow friend with you."

At this point, Jasmine sprang up and rushed toward the door.

Jessie hesitated a moment, then followed her. She found Jasmine standing at the curb, her frail body wracked with tiny convulsions. Jessie put her arms around her and gently rocked her, soothing her with, "Dear Jasmine, don't cry. He doesn't know you. Whatever was bothering him had nothing to do with you. He will be sorry in the morning."

"I am so ashamed," said Jasmine. "Buddhists are not supposed to weep over such transitory matters, but I cannot help it. He treated me as an enemy."

"You needn't be ashamed. Your reaction is very natural."

"I know. But I should overcome the natural."

"Oh, sweetheart," said Jessie, "there are many wonderful things in your religion, and I would be the last to criticize it. It has brought many of your people to a high degree of saintliness and asceticism, and perhaps even very close to God. But it is an important part of my belief—maybe the most important part—that we do not have to do anything or be any certain way in order to draw near to the deity. The deity has already drawn near to us."

"How do you mean?" asked Jasmine, sniffling but showing interest in what to her was obviously a novel idea. "I was always taught that the religious life is a ladder by which we ascend to higher existence."

Jessie lifted the corner of her jacket and gently wiped the tears from Jasmine's cheeks.

"There are many of my faith who persist in believing that too," she said. "But the truth is that God has already come down the ladder to meet with us on the lowest rung. We don't have to be a certain way to please God. God is pleased with us as we are. God accepts our humanity. Much better than we do, I'm afraid."

"But shouldn't we strive to be as good as possible?"

"Oh yes, we should. But not as a requirement for being loved and accepted by God. Only because we are so happy that God does love and accept us. On any other basis, we tend to set up false distinctions among ourselves, and even to deceive ourselves about our own goodness or worthiness."

Jasmine's face was a picture of earnest thoughtfulness.

"But what of that man in there?" she asked. "Would not God regard him as being lower than a dog? He is certainly cruel and insensitive."

"Yes, he is insensitive. But I believe that God loves him all the same, and that we should do likewise, despite his unkind behavior."

"Oh, Jessie," said Jasmine. "I have very

much to learn. I hope you will be my teacher. Buddha would approve of you and your wisdom. I know it."

"I have much to learn from you, my dear. Do you feel like going someplace else to eat? There is a McDonald's only a couple of blocks in this direction. Would you like to get a hamburger?"

"Oh, yes. I am okay now. And I would like to have a hamburger under the famous golden arches."

"Good. Perhaps tomorrow we can come back to visit our friend in the pizza parlor and see if we can be friends with him. But for tonight he must unfortunately live with whatever demons are trying to destroy him."

"Jessie," said Jasmine as they went off down the street arm in arm, "tell me something truly. I am not really a slant-eyes, am I?"

Jessie stopped her under a street light and held the smaller girl's face in her hands a minute.

"No, my dear," she said, "you are not a slant-eyes, although there would be nothing wrong with that if you were. You are only one of the most beautiful people I have ever met."

"Thank you," said Jasmine shyly, lowering her eyes. Then she smiled. "And so are you," she said. "Also one of the most beautiful people in the world."

The next morning, Sunday, dawned cold and clear in the city of Knoxville. Jessie awakened soon after daylight. Not wishing to disturb the other women, and especially Jasmine, who had still not completely adjusted to having traversed numerous time zones, she quietly slipped into her clothes, ran a brush through her hair, pulled on her jacket, and went out for an early walk. She liked the deserted streets and felt invigorated by the fresh, cold air.

She talked to *Baba* as she walked, praying especially for the man in the pizza parlor. She hoped that *Baba* would help her to minister to the man, to build some bridge of understanding that would lead to friendship, so that he could share his inner pain and frustration and thus be open to healing.

Turning the corner of an unfamiliar street, she heard the sound of hymn-singing inside, and realized she was at the door of an old church building. Instinctively she turned, walked up the few steps, and pushed through one of the heavy doors separating the cold air outside from the only slightly warmer air inside. The hymn had ended and a priest was facing the altar, intoning a prayer. She genuflected, made the sign of the cross, and slipped into a pew about a third of the way down the aisle. She knelt on the kneeling bench, conscious of the near emptiness of the vast room, yet feeling the warmth and comfort of being with fellow worshipers, however few in number.

After the sacrament, the priest stood at the door to greet the congregation.

"Hello," he said as he took Jessie's hand. "You're new in this parish, aren't you? I'm

Father Donlevy."

"Yes," said Jessie, noticing that he was younger than he had sounded and looked, at least from a distance. She saw that his skin was rather pockmarked and scrofulous, and imagined this was the reason for the thick, tangled beard, which was even longer than her friend Ray's. "My name is Jessie. I'm staying at the Y."

"Great, Jessie," he said. "Why don't you come around next Friday for the fellowship dinner? Six o'clock, in the church hall next to the sanctuary."

"Thank you, Father. I might do that."

"Please do," he said, giving her hand an extra squeeze. "We need some younger folks."

Jasmine and the other women at the Y were up when Jessie returned to the Y. She sat at a long table with several of them as they enjoyed some juice and sweet rolls.

"You must be a Catholic," said Susan, a middle-aged woman with thin, reddish hair that was apparently unmanageable, for it projected erratically in every direction from her pale, freckled head.

"I enjoy worshiping in Catholic churches," said Jessie, reaching for a crumb that had eluded her and fallen on the table.

"I can't say that I enjoy worshiping anywhere anymore," said Dana Crouch, a small, wiry woman with lips as thin as a hairpin. "I think churches have all outlived their usefulness. All they want anymore is numbers and money, numbers and money."

"Oh, I don't agree with that," said Wanda Mae, a heavy blonde woman in her thirties with arms that continued to vibrate long after she had moved them. "I love my church."

"You a Baptist?" asked someone.

"No, Assemblies of God," she said.

"Thought you might be a Baptist," said the woman who asked. "You sound like one."

"And how is that?"

"I don't know. But you do."

Jasmine sat listening to the conversation without betraying half the confusion Jessie was sure she must be feeling.

"Speaking of church," continued Wanda Mae, "it's almost time for Sunday school. Would any of you gals like to go with me? There's a bus stopping at the front door at nine-thirty."

"What time do you get back?" asked Jessie, thinking she and Jasmine might accompany her.

"Oh, 'bout one o'clock, I expect. It's hard to tell. Depends on how long Donny Jim's sermon is. He can get real wound up some Sundays and don't quit till nearly twelve-thirty."

"Sorry," said Jessie. "I have to be here at twelve-thirty to meet someone. But maybe Jasmine'd like to go."

"Her?" said Wanda Mae. "She ain't a Christian, is she?"

Jessie waited for Jasmine to respond in her own behalf. When she didn't, Jessie said,

"Jasmine is a Buddhist. I thought she might be interested in observing worship in a Christian church."

"Well, I dunno," said Wanda Mae. "Our church don't take much to spectators, especially foreign ones."

"I guess that lets me out then," said Dana, "'cause I'm not ever going to be more than a spectator again, long as I live."

Jessie smiled appreciatively at her.

"That's all right," she said. "Jasmine and I will find something else to do, won't we? Maybe we'll walk down by the river and watch the boats."

She reached out and laid her hand lightly on Jasmine's. Jasmine's liquid brown eyes glowed with gratitude.

"I'll go with you," said Dana, "if you promise not to stop in any churches you happen on along the way."

Later, the three women did take a walk down to a park along the river.

"Did you have a bad experience in church?" Jessie asked Dana as they sat in a restaurant having a cup of coffee.

Dana was silent for a moment, as if deciding whether to trust her companions with the information. "I was married to a minister. Fifteen years. Put up with more sh...more trouble...from good Christians than I ever knew was in the world. Then my husband decided to take up with a choir director half his age. Silly fool! The church put both of us out faster'n you can say Jack Robertson, or whatever his name is."

"Was this recent?" asked Jessie.

"Four years ago. I stayed in that town till last summer, when my youngest graduated from high school. Then I got out as fast as I could."

"And you came here," said Jasmine.

"Not directly. This is the third place I tried to find work. Finally landed a job last week as a packing clerk at a wholesale drug company. There aren't many jobs for older women with no special education and no experience, I can tell you."

"I know," said Jessie. "I've been looking for work too."

"But Dana," said Jasmine, "didn't the members of your church support you when you had your trouble? I have read that Christians are instructed to love one another."

Dana regarded Jasmine, and a sly smile pursed her thin lips.

"I've heard that all my life too," she said, "but don't you believe it. In all my years in the church, I never had more than misery from most folks. It was as if they existed solely to pick on the minister and his family. They half-starved us to death and complained if I bought as much as a piece of costume jewelry or a new pair of shoes. As soon as I did, someone would say they were paying my husband too much. I put up with that garbage most of my adult life, and then my husband up and ran off with that damned little choir director."

She laughed and lit a cigarette.

"Well, at least he set me free from all that. I reckon I owe him for that."

"Poor Dana," said Jessie. "You have suffered so much."

Jasmine looked at Jessie. "I do not understand," she said. "When you spoke of God's coming down the ladder to dwell with people, I thought Christianity sounded very beautiful. This does not sound so nice."

"God's part is always beautiful," said Jessie. "Unfortunately, our part isn't. Perhaps this is why true Christianity always promotes the coming rule of God and not the church itself."

"But is not the church a part of God's rule?"

"Not as we know it here on earth. That church is always contaminated by selfish, unspiritual people. But in the world to come everything will be as God wants it."

"It is all very mysterious to me," said Jasmine. "But you help me to believe in it."

Dana blew a long stream of smoke, sat meditatively for a moment, flicked the ash from her cigarette, and said, "Damn if you don't almost help me to believe in it too."

7

Not wishing to make Harold wait, Jessie was inside the front door of the Y at twelve-twenty-five. She was wearing a denim skirt, a black pullover sweater and stockings, and her only jacket. She wore no makeup, her face shining with good health and a joyous heart.

No more than two minutes had passed when a powder-blue van appeared at the curb. A tall, broad-shouldered, curly-haired man stepped out and approached the door.

"Are you Jessie?"

"Yes," she said, extending her hand. She had to look up rather sharply, as he stood several inches taller than she.

"I'm Harold."

He smiled as he said his name, and large dimples appeared beside the corners of his mouth.

They both knew that something special existed between them from the moment they met. It was almost as if they had known each other before their meeting, and the meeting itself merely confirmed the fact.

"I guess Mom told you about how surprised I was at finding your painting in the studio," he said as they drove through the back streets.

"Yes."

"I mean, I was totally flabbergasted. I couldn't have been more surprised if I had looked up and seen the *Mona Lisa* hanging there. It's a wonderful painting. Incredible, really. I can't believe you did it in half a day. It would have taken me a month, even if I could do something like that."

"Oh, but your paintings are so tender and sensitive," she said. "I hope your mother told you how much I liked them."

He smiled broadly, and she saw the dimples again.

"Oh, yes. Mom talks a lot, as you probably gathered. She told me everything."

Harold stopped the van in the driveway of a large old brick house in a pre-World War Two neighborhood of moderately sized yards, large oaks and sugar maples, and generally neglected homes. The Moorefield residence, by contrast, was neat and gave every appearance of having received consistent care and attention.

Jessie heard the leaves of two large magnolia trees rattle in the wind as they passed between them on the way to a porch that extended three quarters of the way across the front of the house and halfway around the other side.

The aroma of fried chicken greeted them as they stepped through the doorway by a heavy wooden door with a large panel of thick, beveled glass.

"Hey, Mom, we're here!"

They found her in the big, old-fashioned kitchen, removing a pan of biscuits from the oven.

"Just in time," she said, setting the biscuits on an old table in the middle of the room, laying the oven mitts beside them, and wiping her hands on her apron. Then she gave Jessie a hug.

"I thought Harold would go crazy waiting for noon to come," she said. "If he'd had his way, he'd probably have been at the Y by eleven-thirty."

Harold grinned. The dimples were there again.

"Hope everybody saved room for apple pie and ice cream," said Mrs. Moorefield after they had all eaten enormous helpings of fried chicken, potatoes and gravy, broccoli-and-cheese casserole, three-layer salad, and biscuits and jam.

"Harold, you fill Jessie's coffee cup again while I get it."

"Where did you get your art training?" Harold asked after Jessie had pushed away the half piece of pie she couldn't finish.

"Nowhere, I'm afraid."

"I don't believe it," he said. "You mean it's all natural?"

She shook her head gently in self-deprecation. "I've just always liked to draw and paint since I can remember. And I've tried to learn little things from all the artists I've liked."

He talked about what he saw in her painting of the Sabbath meal, and how it seemed to breathe an air of deep and meaningful reverence.

"There's something—well, transcendent—about it, if you know what I mean. It seems to say that all life, and especially life around a table where people know God and love each other, is sacramental."

He smiled again. "I know I'm putting it awkwardly, but your picture makes me feel spiritual, as if I've just entered a great cathedral or heard a wonderful piece played on the organ."

"Thank you," she said, returning his smile.

"That's the nicest compliment I've ever heard."

The afternoon sped by with talk of many things — Harold's education, his training at the Cincinnati Art School, Mr. Moorefield's career as a shop teacher at a local high school, his illness and death from a brain tumor three years ago, Mrs. Moorefield's faith and courage at the time, Harold's decision to move back to Knoxville and open the gallery in Gatlinburg, his work at the printing plant, Jessie's friends in New Haven, her vagabond habits, Ray and Rachel and Julia, and, of course, Carol and Jessie's fond hopes for her as part of the Steltemeier household. Before they realized it, dark had fallen and the logs in the fireplace had burned to ashes, leaving a diminishing red glow under the grate.

"Harold," said his mother, "get some more wood for the fire while I make us a pot of tea."

Then they talked about Jessie's future relationship to the gallery and where she intended to live.

"I may be wrong," said Harold, "but I figure we'll be able to sell at least one of your paintings a week, Jessie. Maybe more during dogwood time in the spring and in the summer and during foliage time in the fall, when the town is packed with tourists, maybe less at times like now, when business is slow.

"We need to talk about percentages, I guess. I'm not much of a businessman, but we probably ought to draw up a contract of some kind.

Would sixty-forty seem fair to you? Sixty per-cent for you, forty for the gallery. If you don't think so, we could make it seventy-thirty."

"Sixty-forty is fine. And I don't need a contract unless you want one. However you want to do it is fine with me."

"Where do you plan to live? You can't stay at the Y forever, can you?"

"I hadn't really thought about it. I suppose not."

"Why don't you stay here awhile?" asked Mrs. Moorefield. "You can have Mr. Moorefield's room. It has a nice big bed. Till you get a little more settled, at least. And you could ride over with me and paint at the studio."

Jessie looked over at Harold, whose eyes were filled with pleasure at the idea.

"Thank you," she said. "I'll think about it. But I'll probably find a little place of my own somewhere. It would be enough having my paintings in your studio without having me around underfoot all the time."

It was almost seven when Harold let Jessie out at the Y. Inside she found Jasmine waiting alone for her on the worn chrome-and-plastic sofa in the lobby.

"Hi, Jasmine," she said. "Are you up to trying for pizza again tonight?"

Jasmine's big brown eyes dilated slightly at the thought, but she said, "Whatever you wish, Jessie."

They stopped first at a large supermarket

whose sign boasted WE NEVER CLOSE. Jessie bought a small, colorful bouquet of carnations, daisies, mums, and baby's breath. The choice was somewhat limited after the weekend, but most of the flowers still looked fresh and pretty.

Things at the pizza restaurant appeared to be much more under control than on the previous evening. Apparently the waiter with the 'flu had recovered sufficiently to return to work, and another young man, whose obvious resemblance marked him as the owner's son, was assembling pizzas near the bank of ovens.

The owner, who was behind the counter when Jessie and Jasmine entered, looked at them with momentary astonishment, and was rendered nearly speechless by the sweetness of Jessie's smile as she laid the flowers on the counter and said, "These are for you. May we come in and eat here tonight?"

Flushed and embarrassed, the man gestured awkwardly with his head, his hands being presently occupied with a large pizza he was holding.

"Uh, sure, sure," he said. "Sit anywhere."

In a few seconds, the man appeared at their table with two glasses of water and menus. "I'm sorry about last night," he said, looking at some indeterminate location across the room, not at either of them. "Order anything you want. It's on the house."

Later, when the number of customers had

dwindled, the man returned to their table with refill pitchers of beer and Coke.

"I'm really sorry about last night," he said sheepishly. "I didn't mean those things. It had been a helluva day and I was shorthanded and working my butt off, and I was just out of line."

"Won't you sit down?" asked Jessie, gesturing toward an empty chair.

"You girls live around here?" he asked, turning the chair around and sitting astraddle it.

Jessie didn't miss the symbolism of his placing the chair back between them. Obviously he had reasons to place barriers between himself and others.

"We're at the Y," said Jasmine softly.

"Yeah? Going to the university?"

"I am," said Jasmine. "Next week."

"You speak pretty good English," he said.

"Thank you. In my country we study English from childhood."

"Could you use a job? I need a waitress four, five nights a week. It pays minimum, but you keep all your tips. That can run thirty or forty dollars a night if we're busy."

Jasmine looked at Jessie as if asking her permission.

Jessie smiled approvingly.

"Yes, thank you. I would like to work."

"Great! My name's Mike. Mike Pieratti. Everybody just calls me Mike."

"I am Jasmine. And this is my friend Jessie."

"Pleased to meet you."

He looked directly into Jasmine's face now, no longer ashamed. "I'm real sorry about last night," he said. "And thanks for coming back. That took some guts."

Jessie smiled at him. "What you are doing takes guts too, Mike. Thank you for being nice to us after such an awkward beginning."

"I'm usually a pretty decent guy," he said. "Only lately things don't seem to have gone so well. My wife run off with a guy 'bout six months ago. Then my daughter and her husband moved to St. Louis, and that robbed me of my little granddaughter Michelle, who I used to see every day. And hell, I just ain't been doin' so hot for a while."

He reached in his hip pocket and pulled out a large billfold attached to his belt by a chain.

"Look. Here's a picture of that little angel. Three years old. Ain't she cute?"

Jasmine and Jessie both looked at the photograph of the dark-haired little sorceress standing on one of the booth tables in the restaurant. There was a big slice of pizza in her hand, and she was holding it near her mouth as if about to bite the tip off.

"She is lovely," said Jasmine.

"She's a doll," said Jessie.

"He is really a very nice man," said Jasmine as she and Jessie walked through the chilly, somewhat foggy evening back to the Y.

"He is, isn't he?" said Jessie.

A moment later Jasmine said, "What if we

had not gone back? We would never have known, would we? Except you knew, Jessie. I think you knew. You are very wise."

"I am not sure if it is wisdom," said Jessie. "I think maybe it is more a matter of hope and trust. If you cannot believe in people, then the world has come to a sad pass."

"As with Dana."

"As with poor Dana."

8

On Tuesday after he got off from work, Harold picked up Jessie and took her to look at some apartments she had circled in the classified ads. The search was successful only in revealing the variety of locations and scale of prices; she didn't see anything that really appealed to her nor had she fully acceded to Harold's insistence that she remain in the area, at least until she had had time to assess the marketability of her art.

She had not yet told him about *Baba* and the divine claim on her life. And he was as intent as a young man could be on getting better acquainted with an eligible young woman who had captured his fancy.

On Wednesday morning she received a message at the Y to telephone Mrs. Moorefield, or Rowena, as she insisted on being called.

"Hello, Rowena."

"Jessie, hon, can you hold the phone a minute?"

When she came back on the phone, she explained that she had been concluding a small transaction and was just seeing the customer out of the gallery.

"Guess what, Jessie," she said, a note of excitement in her voice. "A nice Jewish couple studied your painting yesterday. They would think about it before leaving town today, and they were waiting when I arrived this morning. 'We want that painting!' they said. Not only that, they said that if you do any more scenes like that one, for me to send them pictures and the price, and they would consider buying more. What do you think of that?"

"Oh, Rowena, that's wonderful!"

"I thought so too. I tried to phone Harold, but he's out on a delivery and hasn't come back yet. Why don't you come over and have supper with us tonight, and Harold'll have your money for you?"

"Well, I suppose I could, if you don't think it would be an imposition."

"Imposition? Lord, child, you're no trouble at all. Besides, Harold would shoot me if I didn't use the opportunity to have you over to the house. He hasn't talked about anything else since he met you on Sunday."

Harold was all business when she came for dinner that evening—at least, as far as a love-struck young artist could be all business. He handed her an envelope with his studio name printed on it, containing a check for three hun-

dred dollars and signed "Harold J. Moorefield."
He was brimming with enthusiasm for her
future as an artist and what it would mean to the
Moorefield Galleries.

"That Jewish thing is probably a gold mine,"
he said. "I don't know anybody else who does
that sort of thing. Oh, they probably do in New
York or Los Angeles. But not around here. And
I bet nobody ever thought how many Jewish
people come through Gatlinburg in a year.
We've just sort of assumed that everybody was
Christian, and we've got all those Christian
bookstores and places filled with Precious
Moments dolls and the like. But you've made
me realize that there are bound to be a lot of
Jews too, maybe even some Buddhists and
Muslims and who knows what else. We'll have
the only gallery in town that caters to them!"

Jessie had not seen the marketing side of
Harold before, and it amused her. He was like a
young boy laying plans for an exciting future.

She didn't mind painting an occasional
Jewish scene, she said, but she wasn't always
sure what she would paint until she actually
stood before a canvas.

It was time, she decided, to tell him about
Baba, and *Baba*'s extremely strong role in her
life. She didn't dwell on the explanation, but she
told him enough to give him a good idea of how
unpredictable it made her life.

"Oh golly, Jess," he said when she had
explained it to him, "I knew you were special the

minute I laid eyes on you. Before that, even, when I saw your painting. You had to be different from anybody else I've ever known to make a picture like that."

"I was afraid it might put you off."

"Oh no, Jess, no, not at all. I respect you for it. It's a very spiritual thing, and I honor that. We've never been heavy church-goers ourselves, but we do belong to a little Methodist church a few blocks from here, and I understand what you've said."

Although Harold was pressing her to ready some more paintings, Jessie decided to withdraw from active life for a few days to consult with *Baba* about what she should do. Accordingly, she rode the bus to Gatlinburg, used some of her money from the painting to rent a room in a small, inconspicuous motel fronting on a rocky, mountain stream, and devoted herself to praying.

One day she walked several miles to the national park and hiked over steep, snow-packed trails, through tall trees and past icy creeks, stopping occasionally to bask in the wonders of *Baba*'s world and seek *Baba*'s guidance about the future.

Originally it had been her impression that she would go deeper into the South than Tennessee, that Knoxville was merely an intermediate or staging point where she would be given further direction about where to go. Now, with her friends at the Y, in whose lives she had already become enmeshed, and with the relationship to Harold and Rowena, and the naturalness of an income from her art, she was beginning to feel that perhaps her mission was here, at least for the foreseeable future.

She was especially guarded against a too-easy acceptance of this possibility because of her feelings for Harold. It was true that she found him very likeable and attractive, and that something inside her responded naturally and warmly to something deep and true inside him. But this only tended to make her wary; she had no wish to betray her allegiance to *Baba* through a selfish infatuation or commitment to another human being.

"Oh *Baba, Baba*," she said one day as she sat on a log, the sun on her back and her shoes resting on the icy crust of snow in the log's shadow, "help me to know what to do. I don't want to betray you, ever."

Finally, on the third day of her journeys into the woods, Jessie was certain about the immediate future. She felt centered and good about remaining in the area for an indefinite period, and seeking *Baba*'s will and purpose for her being there.

She had eaten very little during the three-day period, for she had always prayed best and thought most clearly when taking little nourishment. Now, relaxed in heart and mind, and feeling the need of reentering the everyday world, she was ravenously hungry. She smiled as she tramped down the steep trail and saw three squirrels playing tag in the snow, their bushy tails wigwagging as if they were speaking to one another in semaphore code. *Baba* had indeed created a spectacular world, and she was grateful to be alive in it.

She thought she might reach the town early enough to catch Rowena and invite her to dinner at one of the many restaurants in Gatlinburg, but by the time she reached the gallery it was dark. So she walked along the streets until she found an eatery that appealed to her, went in, and enjoyed her first meal as one who intended to reside in the region. She felt once more like a citizen with roots.

That night she wrote a long letter to Roxie, Joan, and Phyllis, telling them about her journey on the bus, her meeting with Carol, the events in Alexandria, the sale of her first painting, her friends at the Y, the beauty of the Gatlinburg area in winter, her decision to stay there a while, and, discreetly but openly, her friendship with Rowena and Harold. She then wrote an only slightly less lengthy letter to Carol and the Steltemeiers, which she concluded with a very encouraging postscript to Carol alone.

She slept that night with the window open toward the creek, so that the cold mountain air carried in with it the uneven melody of the water gurgling over the rocks and along the torn boundaries of ice and snow.

Next morning wondrously refreshed, Jessie

went off under a bright winter sun in search of a realtor's office—she had seen many along the three or four main thoroughfares of the town—that might offer listings of apartments and condominiums. Although it was after nine o'clock, most of them were still closed. When she did find one open, she entered and for a few moments studied a list of available places in a booklet she found in a rack by the door. A pleasant-faced man in his late thirties greeted her.

"I'm Chip Delaney. Can I help you?"

Jessie looked up, returned his smile, and said, "I hope so. I'm looking for a little place to rent. Do you handle rental properties?"

"Oh yes, ma'am," he said, "lots of them. This is a good time to be looking. Bad time to be renting, if you're the owner, good time to be looking if you want to rent. Plenty to choose from."

They went inside. A fireplace at the side of the room was in the first, energetic stage of burning. Dry wood crackled and sent sparks flying onto the dark stones of the wide hearth. Blackened spots on the pine floor beyond indicated that sometimes the sparks made it farther than the hearth. Original watercolor scenes of the mountains hung on three walls, lending patches of color to the otherwise plain, naturally finished knotty pine. The fourth wall was mostly window and opened onto a creek and the woods behind the office.

Jessie defined for the realtor the sort of place she wanted, telling him about her arrangement to sell paintings through Harold Moorefield's gallery and specifying that she would like at least one room with sufficient light to serve as an artist's studio. Chip Delaney checked his memory but could not recall the Moorefield Galleries.

"But that doesn't mean a thing," he said. "Galleries in this town are thicker'n fleas on a hound dog."

Presently Chip suggested that they drive around and see a few of the places his agency represented. After he had made a few phone calls to check on keys and availability for showing, they went out, got into a large Rover parked alongside the office, crunched out into the street, and drove off, the all-weather tires singing merrily on the pavement.

They had looked at four apartments in three locations before Jessie apologized for taking up so much of Chip's time. None of the places had remotely appealed to her. They all had an air of hasty, improvised construction that was totally out of keeping with the natural beauty and primitive dignity of the mountains around them. One had the appeal of being beside a small creek, but it was partially underground, the lighting was too poor, and it gave off an odor of dampness and mildew.

Chip, however, was indomitably cheerful.

"You're not taking my time," he said. "This is what I live for. But I tell you what. It's my coffee and sweet roll time. I don't usually eat breakfast before coming to work. What say we stop at a roadside place out this way and have something before going to the next places on my list?"

Jessie was only too glad to agree. They stopped at a small establishment with an old-fashioned counter and stools. Chip picked out a straight wooden booth and ordered coffee and sticky buns for both of them.

They chatted about many things — Chip's growing up in nearby Maryville, his wife and children, Jessie's life in several places, her happiness with the mountains around Gatlinburg, her deep faith that God was still in charge of the world despite all the unrest and disorder in it. It was after talking about this that Chip smiled and said he was really a minister by calling, but worked in real estate to earn a living.

"Really?" asked Jessie. "What church?"

"Baptist." The waitress had just refilled his cup and he took a cautious sip. "That's why I have to work at something else to make a living. There're more Baptist preachers in these parts than there are — "

"Fleas on a hound dog," she finished the sentence for him, grinning as she did.

"Right. That's what I tell people. The truth is, I got run off from my church over in middle Tennessee for being too liberal on the Bible."

"What do you mean?"

"I mean, I couldn't agree with them fellers who insisted that God dictated every word in the

Good Book verbatim, just the way it appears in the King James version or the RSV or whatever the heck kind of translation you're using."

"You mean you're not allowed to hold personal views about the Bible?"

"Not if you want to be a minister in the Southern Baptist Convention."

"But I thought Baptists had always insisted on freedom of belief."

"Not these Baptists."

"Did they really run you off?"

"Darn right. We had a self-appointed group of laymen come to our home one night, vigilante-style, who wanted to know where I stood on the inspiration of the scriptures.

"I said I believed they were divinely inspired. They asked, 'Every word?' I said, 'That's a moot question, because we don't have the original manuscripts.' They said it wasn't moot with them, did I believe it or not? I said if that was the way they insisted on putting it, not. They said, 'We thought so. We just wanted to hear you admit it.'"

And that was that? Could they dismiss you for that?"

"No, not really. But they went to the board of deacons and got them so riled up about having a pastor who 'didn't believe the Bible' that I went ahead and resigned without waiting for a business meeting. Even if I had survived a vote by the congregation, there was no way I could continue to minister in that church."

"Do most Baptists believe the way those men do?"

"You mean, about the Bible? I'm not sure. I suppose so. At least, they've managed to win most of the votes at the annual convention meetings the last few years. Most of my minister friends from seminary days have either left the church or are wishing they could."

"But isn't it wrong for Christians to get so bent out of shape over an issue like that? Shouldn't we all be focusing on love and fellowship instead of divisive ideas?"

"That was my position exactly. But now I'm selling real estate instead of ministering in a church."

"I'm sorry. I bet you were a good minister."

Chip grinned. "Probably better than I am a realtor. But we do what we have to do."

"I'm sorry about those places we looked at," said Jessie. "They just weren't what I had in mind."

"I don't blame you. I couldn't stand them either. Say!" He paused as if he had just had a sudden idea. "You said you like walking in the mountains, which means you'd like to be close to the park. Do you think you'd be interested in a small house?"

Jessie said she hadn't hoped for a house, but was not opposed to the suggestion.

"I know a fellow who has an unusual place over in a small community near here named Cartersville. Do you know where that is?"

She shook her head no.

"I could run you over and let you see it. It's three or four miles from here. This little place is an old schoolhouse that's been converted into a residence. It only has two rooms, I think, and a small kitchen and a bath. The man who owns it lived there until he got married recently, and his wife made him move to Knoxville. He said he doesn't want to sell it in case the marriage doesn't work out and he has to move back."

"Do you know how much he's asking for it?"

"No, but it couldn't be much. Probably less than an apartment."

After making a call to learn that the key was under a stone by the front steps, they soon drove back through an open space and a clump of maple and gum trees to reach the little house. It had a three-foot foundation wall of creek stones and mortar. Above that, the frame building had obviously been repaired and given several coats of red paint, emphasizing its original character as a schoolhouse. There was even a small bell tower at the peak of the gable in front. When they passed through the alcove to reach the front door, they saw a bell rope of recent vintage. Originally a single room, the building had been divided approximately in the middle by a cedar wall. In the front room, a large fireplace had been built of creek stones on one wall, and opposite that sat a large overstuffed sofa in a flowered design. As Chip and Jessie entered, they passed under a low ceiling that upon examination turned out to be a loft holding a double bed, a chest of drawers, and a chair. A ladder constructed of two-by-fours ran straight up the right-hand wall, giving access to the loft area. The back half of the building was subdivided into a large kitchen area with rough-hewn cabinets on two walls, bright yellow appliances, Scotch-plaid indoor-outdoor carpeting, a round table and four wooden chairs, and a small bathroom. The kitchen carpet extended right into the bathroom.

Jessie was ecstatic, especially when she learned that the three acres the house was on abutted directly on the National Park, and that there was a creek and a waterfall less than five hundred feet from the forest's edge.

"And look," she fairly squealed, "there's even a skylight in the kitchen. It will be a perfect place to paint. And I can see the birds and squirrels right outside the window."

"And probably 'coons and deer and an occasional bear," added Chip.

"Oh, I do hope I can afford it. I will be so disappointed if I can't."

She could. Chip had asked the price when he called about finding the key. It was only two hundred and twenty-five dollars a month, seventy-five dollars less than the cheapest apartment they had viewed.

"Oh," she said, her enthusiasm momentarily dampened.

"What is it?" asked Chip.

"Will I need a car?"

"Depends on where you want to go," said Chip. "The little town of Cartersville is only half a mile on down the road. They have a couple of grocery stores, post office, two or three churches, garage, maybe a drug store, grade school. Most anything you'd need. Gatlinburg is about three miles back the other way. What do you think?"

"No problem at all," she said, relieved. "I'm an avid walker, and those distances are nothing."

So it was settled. *Baba* had not only led her to Knoxville and Gatlinburg, but had provided the perfect place for her to live. Chip said she could move in immediately. They signed the papers at his office and had a sandwich together. Then he drove her to the motel to settle her bill and get her tote bag, and then took her out to the house and turned the keys over to her.

The owner had left the electricity on to keep the heat pump going and prevent the pipes from freezing, and the water was provided from a deep-well pump in the backyard. She could go by the utilities office in a day or two and sign up for the electricity, or she could, if she liked, merely check with the owner and pay him the amount he was billed each month.

That evening she had a simple meal of soup, salad, and bread that she had obtained in the nearby village. She built a roaring fire in the fireplace and sat before it drinking a cup of hot chocolate.

"Baba," she said, "you really know how to do things up right!"

Then she prayed for all her friends, including Dana Crouse and Mike Pieratti and Chip Delaney. It had given Chip such pleasure to find her this agreeable little house. She hoped he wasn't too unhappy about not being able to pursue his ministry in a church.

9

Harold and Rowena were delighted with Jessie's arrangements. Within two days of hearing, they descended upon her with a dozen canvases, an easel, a box of paints and brushes, two gallons of fixative, a gallon of turpentine, several sacks of groceries, and a large potted schefflera.

Harold had also brought a cold bottle of Veuve Clicquot champagne and three glasses. After they had carried everything into the house and placed the schefflera by the sofa in the living room, he opened the bottle, and they all toasted *Baba*, the house, Jessie, Rowena, Harold, and their working relationship, in that order.

While they were sipping champagne and talking, Jessie suddenly shushed them and pointed to the kitchen window. There, creeping stealthily toward a piece of salt block she had erected atop a stake, was a large deer.

"To the deer," said Rowena, lifting her glass.

"To the deer," they happily rejoined.

Jessie was in no hurry to begin a new painting. She knew Harold was anxious to have a steady flow of her works, and she did not want to disappoint him, but she knew it was important not to try to outrun *Baba*. She needed time to go into the woods and pray, to center herself, to feel an absolute congruency between *Baba*'s will and whatever she attempted to do.

For several days she took long walks into the forest, discovering neglected trails, rollicking streams, waterfalls, outcroppings of huge boulders, and soft mountain dells where wild flowers grew beneath the winter snows. She sat on rocks or logs and listened to the breeze whispering in the trees or made clucking noises to the little animals that came up to her. She saw deer regularly, and they cautiously approached and nuzzled her. Once she came upon a great black bear near its cave in a hollow between the hills. It had come out to forage and drink from a nearby stream, and regarded her curiously when it saw her perched on a rock near the water. She guessed that the bear was pregnant and nearing her delivery time, and she spoke gently to her of the cub she carried in her womb. The bear listened, arched her neck calmly in the late morning sun, and went on about her business.

Like a child growing inside her, Jessie felt the direction of her work maturing in her heart, and one day it was time to begin the birthing process. Her first project was an ambitious one involving a large crowd of people in biblical dress listening to a woman addressing them.

The scenery suggested a wilderness setting; the woman was sitting atop a large rock like many she had herself studied in the nearby forest. Her face would be the focus for the entire painting — soft, mystical, visionary, full of *Baba*'s love and grace — and all the other faces would be turned to her, basking in the shared warmth and radiance.

Although she worked with incredible speed, Jessie did not want to rush the painting. Some days she walked into Cartersville and sat at the cafe or the local lounge making sketches of people she saw. A waitress named Alma was very friendly to her at the cafe, and kept her coffee cup full while stealing glances at her sketch pad.

"Gee, that's great," she would say. Or, "Honey, you're terrific."

Two or three days after the picture was finally completed, Jessie walked into Gatlinburg, carrying it under her arm.

"Jessie!" exclaimed Rowena. "Come here, girl, let me see what you've done."

Jessie leaned the large canvas against a wall and began removing her coat and scarf. Not satisfied with the lighting where it was, Rowena moved it nearer the front window and continued to study it.

"Oh, Jessie, it's — it's magnificent! I don't know how to talk about it, it's so — so different. I mean, it's not just a great painting, it sort of takes your breath away. Know what I mean? I don't know how else to put it."

"Do you like it?"

"*Like* is too weak a word for this, honey. And you don't *love* it either. It's powerful. It grips you here"—she placed a doubled-up fist against her chest—"and doesn't let go of you."

She walked back a couple of paces, stared at it some more, then advanced toward it, lifting her glasses, and studied the details.

"We can't let this go for what the other one sold for," she said. "With your permission, I'm going to put a thousand dollars on this one."

Jessie didn't say anything. She was glad Rowena was affected by the painting, and hoped Harold would like it as well.

"Harold will be thrilled," said Rowena. "I can't wait for him to see it. I'm going to call him this minute and tell him to come right over."

"Can he do that?"

"Honey, for something like this he can. And for you he can. He's been moping around lately, complaining that he hasn't seen you for days."

Harold was away from the printing plant, however, and she was unable to reach him.

"Well, it'll have to wait till tomorrow," said Rowena. "But I tell you what, girl, it's almost lunch time. Why don't I close up, and let's go up the street to this new place I've found and have lunch together?"

At lunch they talked about how Jessie liked her new home, about the slow times in the town, and about Harold's work. Rowena asked Jessie what she called her new painting. "I'd like to call it *Hearing the Word*."

Rowena fished in her purse for a pen and piece of paper. "I forget so much these days," she said, "I have to write everything down."

The next day, during a routine visit, Trish McCann, a woman reporter for the *This Month in Gatlinburg* magazine, who was visiting several galleries and specialty shops for a feature on trends and happenings, saw the painting. "Jessie," she read the artist's name beside it. "Who is that, Mrs. Moorefield? I've never heard of her. Does she exhibit in any other galleries around here?"

Trish brought in a photographer to shoot some photos of Rowena standing beside the picture. She wanted to have Jessie in them too, but Jessie didn't have a phone.

Apparently both Trish and the photographer, a man with the local paper, told almost everybody they saw about the remarkable painting at the Moorefield Galleries. Soon there was a steady stream of visitors to the studio, most of whom had never heard of it before.

Before the week was out, a retired university professor and novelist, D. M. Birkenstall, purchased the painting. Rowena asked to delay delivery of the painting; she wanted to keep it on display until the first of the month.

Most viewers spoke of the extraordinary power of the composition and of the beautiful face of the woman proclaiming the Word. Some said they found a mystical quality in the painting that gave them an unusual sense of both peace and excitement. Many of the women who saw it remarked on the added confidence it imparted to them as females. "Do you suppose," several of them asked, "there were a lot of women preachers in the early church?"

A carload of women from Cartersville thought they spotted resemblances in the portrait to three or four people they knew. From that moment on, recognizing the real-life originals in the painting became a nearly full-time fad among the citizens of Cartersville. Visitors trouped into the studio twenty or thirty a day, always asking to see "the painting." Sometimes they were great hulking men with beards and lumberjack coats who Rowena was sure had never been in an art gallery before.

Even though Jessie's picture had not appeared in a brochure or paper, people soon spotted her when she came into the village to buy supplies or to do more sketches. She was pointed out as eagerly as if she had been a well-known celebrity. People began coming up to her in the cafe or the post office and offering to serve as models for future paintings. Mothers volunteered their children, and people frequently suggested particular friends. Several went out of their way to speak kindly to Jessie, and two sought her out to invite her to speak to the local art and poetry guild.

Only in the second week did a few people begin to profess outrage at the subject matter of the painting, declaring it a violation of New Testament principles and therefore a sacrilege. The minister of the local Baptist church, Dr. Jack Garbie, announced that he was going to preach a sermon on women keeping silence in the church and had a packed sanctuary that Sunday. Many members of his congregation, especially female members, thought he was over-reacting and frankly disagreed with the substance of his sermon. But they admitted that they enjoyed the hubbub occasioned by the emergence of Jessie as a person of note in their community.

At first, Jessie was dismayed by all the attention, and particularly by the negative reactions. For two or three days she took long walks across the mountains, sitting on rocks near the peaks and watching the hawks cutting graceful circles in the sky while she talked with *Baba* and tried to feel the divine confirmation upon what she had done.

Eventually she realized that she had never done anything to solicit the attention of others or to inflame them by what she did or said. If people chose to react strongly to her work, she could not be responsible for them. She must continue to follow *Baba*'s guidance as closely as possible and not be overly concerned about the consequences.

But she did find herself spending more and more time alone, either painting or walking in the forest. And she felt extremely conspicuous about making any sketches in the lounge or cafe. Sometimes she sat on a bench outside one of the grocery stores making quick studies of people coming and going, but she was very careful not to let anyone see her sketching.

She was already at work on a new painting, which depicted two women who appeared to be disciples of Jesus, for a small cross burned like a flame on their foreheads. They were passing through a crowd of people, healing ill and crippled persons when they touched them. At one side there was a man throwing away a pair of crude crutches he would no longer need. In the foreground there was a formerly blind woman excitedly pointing to her eyes because she could now see. The scene was one of a near pandemonium of joy as the two women, strong and healthy and confident, worked their way down the street.

When Harold came to see her on a Sunday afternoon, she yielded to his entreaties to let him see it, even though it needed several days more work.

"What do you call it?"

"*Martha and Mary in the Marketplace.*"

"It's already breathtaking."

"Do you recognize anyone in it?"

"That man there. The crazy one. Is that old Lucius, the wild man who walks the highways around here?"

She nodded.

"And those Down's syndrome children there.

I think I've seen them around Gatlinburg."

"Who are the two women? Are they people around here?"

"No. They're friends of mine up north. Their names are Roxie and Joan."

"I think I've heard you speak of them."

"Yes."

He went to the refrigerator, took out a beer, opened it, and took a drink as he walked back to the painting.

"I wonder what kind of reaction this one will cause," he said.

"Does it worry you?"

"No. Just curious."

While they were eating dinner that night, there was a noise. Jessie went to the back door and switched on an outside light. There stood two raccoons, unfazed by the brightly burning bulb.

"Wait a minute," Jessie said, "I'll get you some bread." She returned to the table, carried some bread to the door, and held it as each took a piece and waddled off into the woods.

Harold was astonished at their friendliness.

Jessie shyly ducked her head. "I'm afraid I've been too generous with them," she said. "I may be teaching them to depend on me."

Afterward, sitting before the fire and drinking some Belgian coffee Harold had brought, they talked about *Baba* and how Jessie's new direction in painting had grown out of her extended conversations with *Baba*.

"I know you really wanted me to do some more Jewish paintings," she said, "and maybe even some from other viewpoints as well. But the more I prayed and meditated, the more I knew this was where *Baba* was leading me."

"Have you got this thing about women and ministry?"

"I don't know," she said. "Not really. It isn't something I've thought a lot about. But I do feel strongly that women have been much more central in the Jewish-Christian experience than has generally been acknowledged. I'm not exactly a feminist, at least not for feminism's sake. But I think the world would be a lot closer to *Baba* today if people had emphasized the nurturing side of life more and the competitive, acquisitive side less. The old 'make love, not war' thing."

"I couldn't agree more," he said, suddenly leaning over and giving her a kiss on the cheek.

"Don't try to distract me," she laughed, "when I'm trying to deliver a serious speech."

"Sorry," he said. The firelight danced in his eyes and made deep shadows in his dimples. "I don't think you realize how much you affect people. There's something so special about you that nobody can be around you without having either their best or their worst brought out. And I think it's the same with your paintings. Some people are going to be wonderfully changed by them—have their very best thoughts and manners drawn out from somewhere deep inside them. And others—well, I hate to think about

them. They just can't stand to be around anything good."

10

If *Hearing the Word* had stirred up a lot of people, both for and against it *Martha and Mary in the
Marketplace* did even more. The same woman
who bought the first instantly bought the second
as well, saying they were companion pieces and
shouldn't ever be separated. She also gave her
permission for the Moorefield Galleries to keep
both of them on display for an indefinite time, as
she said she did not wish to deprive the public of
an opportunity of viewing them. Besides,
Rowena confided to Harold, she was cagey
enough to realize that the publicity would treble
and quadruple their value.

Dr. Birkenstall, who Rowena had learned had
a Ph.D. degree and used to teach in a
Midwestern university, gave out publicly, for
anyone who might be interested, that she personally considered Jessie's talent to lie among
the front ranks of all of those in contemporary
American art. As for her subject matter, well, it
just might be the most important statement ever
made on the contribution of women to the religious sensibilities of the Western world, and
possibly the Eastern as well.

A reporter at a television station in Knoxville,
a fan of Dr. Birkenstall's, picked up this interest-

ing tidbit of information and had little difficulty persuading her boss that the paintings of this unknown artist whom everybody was raving about just might make an excellent trailer for the six o'clock news. Carolyn Cushman, the reporter, telephoned Moorefield Galleries to make arrangements for filming a segment around the two paintings. Rowena took the call and gave Ms. Cushman Harold's work number. Harold was delighted at the prospect of publicity for his gallery, but was not altogether encouraging about Jessie's availability or willingness to permit the taping of her paintings.

Ms. Cushman could not believe anyone would refuse a lot of free PR.

"You haven't met Jessie," said Harold.

"Well, tell me how to reach her and I'll give her a call and persuade her."

"Afraid I can't. She doesn't have a phone. She lives in a little place next to the national park out in Cartersville."

"Where's that?"

"A few miles from Gatlinburg."

The conversation concluded with Harold's agreeing to drive out to Jessie's that evening to see if she would be willing to participate in an interview.

A little after six Harold drove into Jessie's yard, hoping to take her to dinner as well as see her about the interview. The house was totally dark. Supposing she might be at the cafe, he drove into the village. But she was not there, so he drove back to the house. Still dark. He sat for a few minutes wondering what to do.

Then, on a hunch, he took a flashlight from the dashboard, went around to the back of the house, and started up the nearest trail. Ten minutes later, he found Jessie sitting on a rock in a clearing where she could watch the rising moon.

"Harold," she said when she recognized the face half-masked in darkness.

"Jess," he said, turning the light in her direction. "Thought I might find you up here."

They sat on the rock together, discussing the pros and cons of Jessie's appearing in Carolyn Cushman's news segment. In the end, it was Harold's reasoning that helped her to decide. "If this is some kind of mission you're on," he said, "then surely the more publicity it gets, the better."

The program was taped three days later at the gallery. Jessie appeared at the gallery that morning with her hair and skirt wet, for she had walked to Gatlinburg through a heavy mist and occasional showers. Harold had offered to pick her up, but she had declined, saying she would need the time to compose herself for such a public occasion. Carolyn Cushman came with an entourage of cameramen, technicians, makeup people, and a cue-card manager. As she sat on a stool being prepped for the camera and tested for lighting, Jessie was rubbing her head with a towel, trying to get her hair dry.

When the cameras began to roll, Ms.

Cushman put herself into a kind of psychic over-drive and breathily introduced herself and the segment. The staid little community of Gatlin-burg, Tennessee, she announced, was presently being shaken by the big, big art of a little lady named Jessie—no last name—who lived in a former schoolhouse (still shot of Jessie's house) on the edge of the national forest. Although she denied being a feminist, Jessie was racking up more points for feminism than anyone since Bella Abzug and Gloria Steinem. Her most recent paintings, now owned by well-known local novelist and university professor D. M. Birkenstall but still on exhibit in the gallery of Mr. Harold Moorefield (shot of Harold and his mother), were vivid reinterpretations of the role of women in the early Christian movement.

"What exactly are you trying to say in your paintings, Jessie?"

Jessie smiled slightly and said she would let the paintings speak for themselves.

"But you seem to be saying that women played a much bigger part in the growth of early Christianity than history has recorded. Is that a fair interpretation?"

"You could read that into them," admitted Jessie.

"I have a statement here," said Ms. Cushman, looking at a half-sheet of paper she reshuffled from under her stack of notes, "from prominent clergyman Dr. Reginald P. Waterson, pastor of the University Avenue Church of Christ in

Knoxville. Dr. Waterson says, and I quote, 'It would be most unfortunate if this newly discovered talent were put in the service of confusion, destabilization, and even evil by supporting the arguments of certain godless forces today seeking to promote the cause of rebellious women at the expense of society and the church.' What do you say to that, Jessie?"

Jessie looked straight at her questioner and not into the camera. "That's preposterous," she said. "I am not trying to promote any cause at the expense of society and the church. Did someone really say that? I can't believe that any reputable minister would make a statement so filled with polemic and—and hogwash."

At this point one of the cameramen trained his camera on first *Martha and Mary in the Marketplace* and then *Hearing the Word* for fully five seconds each, while Ms. Cushman read a brief statement from Dr. Birkenstall about the enormity of the paintings' significance. Then Ms. Cushman concluded the take with a query about whom to believe in the "great controversy" racking the ordinarily quite traditional little mountain town; and there was a final reminder that the public could see the paintings at the Harold J. Moorefield Galleries between the present date and the end of February. As the cameras faded out, they showed the glamorously costumed and cosmeticized Ms. Cushman, the interviewer, a false smile plastered on her face, side-by-side with the plainly dressed Jessie, the artist, her hair still hanging limp from the dampness and her face bereft of makeup. Viewers would have had to be blind to miss the aura of simple integrity and inner beauty of the artist.

When the segment aired on the evening news and again on the ten o'clock edition, it was seen by thousands of people in East Tennessee, North Georgia, southern Kentucky and Virginia, and western North and South Carolina. The Rev. Dr. Reginald P. Waterson wasted no time in telephoning several conservative ministers, the chairman of the local Republican Party, and the president of the Women for Civic Decency League to alert them to the dangerous presence of "that subversive woman in Gatlinburg." A number of women, including several female ministers and a few seminarians, made notes of the name of the Moorefield Gallery, intending either to visit the gallery to see Jessie's paintings or to write a supportive note to the courageous artist. Several persons, some male, some female, telephoned the TV station to protest the airing of the segment. One of these, which the confused receptionist was later unable to identify as either male or female, threatened to blow up the station if anything like the segment was ever shown again.

Jessie, meanwhile, walked home in the rain, feeling that she had made a very foolish showing, but determined to continue work on her third painting, *Miriam in Triumph,* in what she was now beginning to call her "Women in

Religion" series. It showed the prophet, the sister of Moses and Aaron, leading a dance of the Hebrew women, timbrels and castanets ringing and clashing, after God had closed the Red Sea upon the pursuing armies of the Egyptian pharaoh.

The following Saturday night, an exhausted and frustrated network editor, who was working on the final edition of a nationwide news and variety program to be aired on Sunday morning, needed a two-minute segment to replace a section of the show that had been cancelled at the last minute because of a legal problem. His assistant dropped in his hand a videotape that she had made for her personal use from a news broadcast of their affiliate station in Knoxville. He was tired and wanted to get back to his apartment for a few hours' sleep before returning to the studio at five A.M.

On Sunday morning the entire nation heard about Jessie's paintings and the controversy they were stirring up in the sleepy little resort town of Gatlinburg, at the edge of the Great Smoky Mountains.

There was one oddity about the report. The editor, noting that there was no last name given for Jessie, marked an X on the script, intending to have research check for it. Due to his weariness and the lateness of the hour, the matter went unresearched, and the Sunday morning announcer read the report as applying to one "Jessie X."

"Roxie!" shouted Joan as she removed a bagel from the toaster in their kitchen in New Haven. "It's our Jessie."

"Did you see her?" asked Phyllis excitedly when she phoned Joan and Roxie three minutes later.

"That interviewer was an airhead!" Carol said at the Steltemeier breakfast table in Alexandria.

"Honey, I need to talk to you," said Dana out loud in the lounge at the Knoxville Y. "You and I have a lot to discuss."

"Right on, Jessie," said Jasmine and her two roommates at the University of Tennessee. "We're on your side!"

At the hour when the program was being aired from New York and fifty percent of the population of Cartersville and Gatlinburg were in the Sunday school and church of their choice, Jessie was hiking to the top of the tallest mountain in the vicinity; she was praying for all her friends, asking *Baba*'s help with the painting about Miriam, and stopping to share her bag of popcorn with the birds, squirrels, and chipmunks she saw along the way.

"Oh, *Baba*," she said when she stood at the top and looked across the undulating hills and forests below, "I want so badly to do your will. Forgive me if I make a mess of things. I love your world and your plans for it. Please help me to fulfill your intentions for my ministry here, whatever happens to me."

11

One morning not long thereafter, Jessie was working in her kitchen studio when she heard tires crunching on the gravel in the driveway. She looked out to see Chip Delaney's Rover parked there. She was delighted to see him and put on a pot of coffee. She offered to take it in the living room, but he insisted that she go on working on her painting.

"You've really become a celebrity," he said.

"I'm afraid so."

"I told my wife I was coming out. She said to tell you how much she appreciates what you are doing, and that she understands part of what you must be going through."

"Thank her for me."

"Jessie, we know how mean some of these people can be. We're worried about your being out here by yourself."

"I'm not alone," she said. "*Baba* is here."

"But *Baba* doesn't always keep us from harm," he said, "contrary to the promises of TV evangelists. Sometimes our faithfulness to *Baba* is what puts us in harm's way."

Jessie continued painting.

"We'd like you to consider moving in with us for a few weeks. Or at least till this thing blows over."

"What thing, Chip?"

"You don't really know, do you? I mean, you don't understand the size of the brouhaha you're stirring up, or the viciousness of some of the powers you've offended."

Jessie laid down her brush, took a sip of coffee, and looked at him.

"There's a monstrous evil loose in this country, Jessie. It coils like a snake through the underbrush of the whole nation, and strikes at people like you whenever it wants to. It's filled with hate and poison, and it can't stand goodness. It especially can't stand goodness! Don't you know that?"

His voice had been rising and the words were coming more rapidly. It was clear that he was upset about what might happen to her.

"I know about evil, Chip. But I also know about good. Good doesn't thrive by hiding or being afraid of evil. In fact, when it begins to hide and fear, it becomes a little part of the evil itself, and the evil wins.

"I respect your feelings for me, and I appreciate them. You are wary for me because you yourself have been hurt. I know that. But don't you see, Chip, I'm doing *Baba's* will, not my own. And in the end *Baba* will win, even if I get hurt in the process. My life is nothing. *Baba's* glory is everything."

Chip didn't know how to argue any further against such logic because deep down it was what he also believed. He got up to pour himself another cup of coffee and look at the painting of Miriam.

"It really is powerful," he said. "I'm a man,

but it still excites something primitive and elemental in me."

"That's because this is part of your history too. It isn't just for women. People are mistaken if they think I'm doing this for women. I'm doing it for all of us, men as well as women. It's a part of all our heritage. You have as much female ancestry as you do male. Part of the sickness of our time, the evil you spoke of, stems from the one-sidedness of our contemplation of the past. Women are trying to redress that now, to remind us that love and nurture and compassion have as much place in human history as war and hunting and making money. *Baba* is a God of love and nurture and compassion, and only those people who don't know *Baba* are always going around preaching hate and ugliness and divisiveness."

"I know that," he said, looking out the window at a deer standing at the edge of the woods and watching the house. "God, don't I know it."

A few days later, Jessie carried the completed *Miriam* painting into town and presented it to Rowena, who said it spoke to her even more than the previous paintings, if that was possible. On her way home, she heard a truck slowing down as it approached from behind her. It passed, then stopped and backed up.

"Hey, Jessie, is that you?" called the driver as he rolled down the window.

It was Mike Pieratti. Jessie was surprised to see him, and crossed the highway to get in the truck. She was further surprised, when she reached the passenger side, to discover who was sitting in the passenger seat. It was Dana Crouch, her friend from the Y.

"Dana!" she exclaimed. "What are you doing here? I didn't know you and Mike knew each other. Nothing has happened to Jasmine, has it?"

"Oh no," laughed Dana. "She's fine, I guess. No, Jasmine introduced me to Mike when I quit my job at the drug company. That's another story. Boss thought his position entitled him to perks I wasn't willing to grant, and all that. Mike hired me, and I've been working for him the last couple of weeks."

She looked over at Mike, and they beamed at each other. Jessie could see there was more than a business relationship between them.

"I'm glad we spotted you," said Mike. "We went to the gallery and saw your paintings. Mrs. Moorefield told us you'd just been there and we might find you on your way home."

Jessie got in and directed them to her house, where she made a pot of coffee and sliced some fruit on a plate.

"Say, this is some place," said Mike.

"It's wonderful," said Dana. "So peaceful and quiet. Must be great for a painter."

"Hey," said Mike, "it's a hard place to find for a pizza delivery."

Jessie laughed.

"Your paintings are fabulous," said Dana.

"We saw the TV program about them—or I did. I think Mike was still at the restaurant. That interviewer was the pits, but at least it was good publicity. And then the national coverage! We didn't know we were living at the Y with a prospective celebrity."

Jessie was happy to see Mike and Dana together and to realize what a difference their finding each another had made in their attitudes. They both seemed more content and fulfilled.

"I wanted to talk to you, honey," said Dana, "about something that's rather important to me."

"I'll wander outside," said Mike.

"No, you can stay," she said. "We've talked about this ourselves."

"I know. But I think I'll go out anyway. I'd like to look around, maybe have a smoke."

Jessie smiled at Dana after Mike left and inquiringly glanced in his direction.

"It's crazy, isn't it?" said Dana. "Our backgrounds are so different. But he's really a great guy. What do you think?"

"I think he's a good man."

Dana nodded. "But that isn't really what I wanted to talk about. I need some advice, or at least someone to bounce some ideas off of. Jessie, what would you say if I said I'm thinking of going to seminary to become a minister?"

Jessie looked at her thoughtfully and took a drink of coffee.

"I know. I didn't like being in the church when my husband was a minister, and now I'm talking about becoming one myself. But it's the strangest thing. It's like something was happening to me inside, some great change, and it was just beginning when I met you. And then when I heard about your paintings and the direction they were taking, I knew it was happening. And when I stood there and looked at them an hour ago, all three of them—that nice lady showed us the one that hadn't been hung yet—I knew, Jessie, I knew. I felt it deep down inside. God wants my life in some special way, Jessie. It's absolutely crazy, I admit, but I feel happier than I think I've ever been in my whole life."

"And Mike?"

"Mike is totally supportive. That's crazy too. He's Catholic, if he's anything. Hasn't been to church for years. But he listens to me so sympathetically. He even says he'll help me to go to school if I'll let him."

"Where would you go?"

"I don't know. Louisville, Nashville, Atlanta. I haven't got that far yet. But what do you think? Am I being completely insane?"

Jessie smiled. She set down her cup, got up, and went over to Dana. Taking her by the hand and lifting her to her feet, she simply put her arms around her and held her for a minute. Then she said, "I think it's all beautiful. You, Mike, ministry. Everything."

Dana cried. "I told Mike you'd understand," she said. "I knew you would."

Jessie waved to them as Mike backed up his

truck and turned around to leave. "Be very good to them," she said to *Baba*. "They've both been hurt so much. Don't let them be hurt anymore."

A little before dark, Harold appeared with an invitation to join him and Rowena for dinner in Gatlinburg. Jessie washed out her paintbrush — she had been applying gel to another canvas — splashed some water on her face, threw out some bread for the raccoons, and went with him.

"Jess," he said while they were waiting for their dinners, "Mom and I think it's time to raise the price again on your paintings. *Miriam* is outstanding. And with all the publicity you've been getting, we think your work is worth more. A lot more, in fact."

"That's right, honey," said Rowena. "You ought to be getting what they're really worth in the marketplace. You're not just an unknown any more, you're a nationally known artist." She put a lot of emphasis on the word "nationally."

"What price are you thinking?" asked Jessie.

"We were talking about four thousand," said Harold.

"Four thousand dollars per painting?"

Harold nodded.

"We've already had a dozen calls from all over the country," said Rowena, "people wanting a chance at your next one. Four thousand is cheap in that kind of market."

Jessie picked up a pack of sugar from the bowl on the table and played with it for a moment. Rowena and Harold watched her face, which was shadowed by concern.

"No," she said. "I don't need the money. I'm getting more now than I can spend. I've already paid next month's rent, and I have two or three hundred dollars. That's more money than I've ever had, I think. My paintings are for people. I don't want to make them inaccessible to people who don't have a lot of money. In fact, I've worried before that they are already beyond the reach of the poor."

Harold looked at Rowena. "I told you," Rowena said.

"I know," he said.

"I realize that's not exactly fair to you," said Jessie. "After all, it penalizes the gallery when I won't let you raise the prices. I tell you what. Why don't we make a new agreement? You give me enough for rent and food every month, and then let the gallery take whatever is left over."

"Oh, honey, we couldn't do that," said Rowena.

Jessie stared at the crumpled sugar sack in her hand. "I had even been wondering," she confessed, "how I could work it out with you to give away a painting occasionally. There's a beautiful little church off the road between here and Gatlinburg, a little Catholic chapel"— "Rymer's Chapel," said Harold, nodding—"that doesn't have a very nice altar painting. I'd like to do one for them, if I had your permission."

Harold and Rowena assured her they didn't want her to feel obligated to them, that she was always free to paint what she wished for whomever she wished. And they seemed to understand her reluctance to charge more for her art. The world would be a better place, they said, if there were more folks like her. In the business world, said Rowena, people seemed to just naturally think in terms of profit and more profit, whatever the traffic would bear.

Later that week, after a day in the woods, Jessie began another painting, this one of Mary, the mother of Jesus. After making several sketches, she decided on one depicting Mary as a pregnant maid sitting in a field and playing with a group of children. One of the children, a small girl, was standing in her lap and reaching up, trying to put a flower in Mary's hair.

Jessie had the feeling, once she had settled on the sketch, that this was the painting she would like to give to the little chapel.

It was perhaps more than a coincidence that Jessie decided to give her Mary the face of her friend Carol and that that very afternoon, when she walked into the post office, she had a letter waiting from Carol. It was a warm, happy letter exuding enthusiasm for Jessie's newfound notoriety, which Carol knew was assured after she had seen the segment of the national TV program.

She was having a wonderful time with Julia and her parents, she said, and was doing extremely well in her schoolwork. She had recently talked on the phone with her mother, and hoped to visit her during a brief recess from school in early March. Ray and Rachel had given permission for Julia to accompany her, and the two girls were excited about their joint excursion.

Ray and Rachel were both fine, and Ray sent word to Jessie that she might be able to out-Michelangelo Michelangelo, but he bet her six strawberry blintzes she couldn't out-Chagall Chagall. Carol said she wasn't sure what that enigmatic message meant, but Ray said he was sure Jessie would understand.

Carol concluded her letter by saying how awfully much she missed Jessie and how hungry her heart was for her. She had not mentioned it yet to Ray and Rachel, but she wondered how Jessie would feel about it if she were to come to visit her during the week-long Easter vacation in April.

Jessie, moved and overjoyed at the prospect, went back inside the post office—she had read the letter standing just outside in the afternoon sunlight—and telephoned the Steltemeier residence immediately. Yes, she told Carol after speaking briefly with Rachel, by all means, come. They would have a wonderful time together. She would introduce her to all her new friends in Tennessee. And by then she would have something special she wanted to show her—something she hoped Carol would like very, very much.

12

In early February there was an unusually heavy snowstorm over the mountains around Gatlinburg. A low-pressure cell had located itself between Memphis and Nashville, and a Bermuda high was standing off the coast of South Carolina. The resulting air flow was pumping vast quantities of moisture up from the Gulf of Mexico; the cold front that had dropped temperatures in the Smokies into the low twenties was turning it all into frozen precipitation. Knoxville had six or seven inches; at the higher elevations some reporters had measured more than twenty inches. The mountain roads had been closed for the last twelve hours; there were drifts in the passes estimated at ten to fourteen feet deep.

In her bright kitchen studio with the plaid carpet, Jessie was painting red and yellow poppies in the sunlit field around Mary and the children. She was also thinking about her animal friends, asking *Baba* to take good care of them so they wouldn't freeze or starve before the snow melted. While the snow was still ankle-deep, she had waded out to fill the birdfeeders with sunflower seeds, even though she knew that the squirrels would probably get more of the seeds than the birds. She also had put extra corn under the heavy fir trees, where the deer and opossums and raccoons would find it; that is to say, if the snow did not drift under the low-hanging branches. The bears, she realized, would merely curl up in their caves and sleep tightly until the storm was over.

About three in the afternoon, the power went out. Jessie had been warned by an old man at the hardware store that winter storms often put the electric company out of business for three or four days; the repair trucks could not get up into the distressed areas until the snowplows had done their work; a deep snow could keep them operating day and night for a week at a time. The grinding noise of the plows had already passed her house several times that day, and she imagined what a gargantuan effort was necessary to keep civilization operating even at a minimum.

Laying her paintbrushes aside for a few minutes, she stepped out on the back porch, where she had thought to store nearly a cord of wood; she brought in several split logs to keep the fire going warmly. Back at the painting, she was deciding whether there was enough natural illumination from the windows and skylight to continue, when she heard a knock at the front door.

She opened it to find a bulky snow creature standing there.

"Oh Jessie, I didn't know what else to do." It was Alma, the waitress from the cafe in the village. "He's dying, I know he's dying."

Her face was a mask of fear and distress, and she was completely oblivious to the bits of snow falling from her coat and scarf onto the floor.

"Who's dying, Alma?"

"Billy Gerald," she said, "my boy. I know he's got appendicitis, and we can't get him down to the doctor in Gatlinburg. The sheriff tried to call the state patrol and the road crew, but the lines are all down. There's no way to get him into town. Two or three have tried, and they got stuck in the drifts. The wind blows the snow back as fast as the plows clear it off. He's got a high fever and is out of his head, and he's gonna die 'cause there's nothing we can do about it."

The words had poured out in a torrent, and the tears had begun running down Alma's rosy cheeks before she had finished two sentences. "He's gonna die. I know he's gonna die."

"Hush, Alma. We don't know that. *Baba* may have other plans," said Jessie. "Come on, put your scarf back on while I'm getting into my boots and coat. We must get back to him as fast as we can."

The snow was up to the women's knees as they struggled back toward Cartersville. Fortunately, Alma's extra adrenaline gave her added strength to keep forcing her way along; Jessie had no trouble in the snow. It took them fully forty-five minutes to cover the half-mile into town, and another ten minutes to reach Alma and Billy Gerald's little apartment in an old house on the far side of the village. Billy Gerald's father, Alma had once confided to Jessie, had never married her and had in fact deserted her before Billy Gerald was born. She had worked as a waitress then, and had gone back to work six weeks after the baby was born.

Alma increased her speed almost twofold the last hundred yards or so, screaming into the hush of the wintering world, "We're coming, Billy Gerald! We're coming, honey! Hold on! Hold on just one more minute."

Alma pulled back the storm door and shoved the inside door open; she hadn't bothered to lock it. There was total stillness in the apartment except for the noise of the two women stamping their feet and racing toward the bedroom.

"Oh, Billy Gerald! Billy Gerald!" Alma called, sinking over the quiet form on the bed, taking his cheeks in her hands. He was cold, or was it her hands that were cold? "Oh, speak to me, honey! Open your eyes. Mommy's back, dear. Mommy's back."

There was no sound, and the boy's eyes did not open.

"Oh God, Jessie," said Alma. "We're too late, we're too late!"

"No, we're not," said Jessie, calmly and firmly pulling the distraught woman back by the shoulders. "Here, dear, you go in the kitchen and heat him some soup or something. Leave us alone for a minute. I'll call you."

Her eyes frantic, her heart believing the worst, Alma pulled back and slowly went through the door and into the hallway leading to the kitchen.

When she returned three or four minutes later

with a cup of soup she had heated on the gas stove, Billy Gerald was sitting calmly in bed, two pillows propped behind his back. Jessie was gently rubbing his temples.

"Hi, Mom," he said when he saw his mother with the soup.

"Oh, Billy Gerald," she cried, "you're okay, you're okay! Oh, baby, you're okay, you're all right! Jessie has made you all right!"

Alma tried to get Jessie to spend the night with them, as it was already dark outside, and the snow was still coming down. But Jessie said she needed to keep the fire going in her house so the water pipes wouldn't freeze. There was enough reflective illumination from the thick blanket of snow to make travel possible even without a flashlight. Along the roadway Jessie found herself praising *Baba* for the quiet wonder of the world around her. Snowbanks made the usual contours of the bushes and fence rows indistinguishable; most of the trees looked like enormous ghosts under their white robes. The wet flakes felt cool and refreshing to Jessie's cheeks; she was so exhilarated that she lifted her face and let them fall ticklingly against it.

The logs she had left in the fireplace had burned down to embers, but it took only a couple of minutes to restore roaring flames. The snow that had blown in upon the logs on the porch sizzled as it melted and fell among the ashes. Jessie warmed her hands and feet before the fire, then sat on the hearth with her back to it for a few minutes, watching the shadows dance around the room.

She was at the point of going to the cupboard for a kerosene lantern she had seen there a few days earlier when she heard a scratching noise at the back door. Hastily fetching the lantern, she opened the door and saw a German shepherd lying meekly at the threshold, large and bloody, its head on its paws, trying to look up at her with its one clear eye. The other was covered with blood and snow, and she could see a gash above it. The dog lifted one paw slightly, as if motioning to the doorway, and whimpered softly.

"Oh, you poor dear," said Jessie, "you look as if you've just had the fight of your life. Can you move? Come on in if you can."

The big dog lay there, as if the pain of having come that far was all it could endure.

Jessie got some towels and spread them on the floor in front of the fireplace. Then she stooped down beside the dog, managed to get her arms under its body, and carried it inside, where she laid it on the towels. In the light from the fire, she took a pan of lukewarm water and began gently bathing the dog's wounds.

"I believe you've been in a fight with a bear," she said softly. "You have too many cuts to have been hit by a car. Besides, there aren't any cars moving around anywhere tonight."

The great dog lay quietly as she sponged off the blood, first from its body and then from its head. The eye that had been encrusted with blood and snow appeared to be all right, but the area around it was badly swollen from the cut sustained above it.

When Jessie had completed the task of bathing the dog's wounds, invoking *Baba*'s healing on each one, she opened a can of beef and vegetable soup and put it on the propane stove to heat. When it was barely warm, she poured it into a shallow bowl and held it low for the dog to eat.

"What's your name, big fellow?" she clucked to him as he lapped up the soup. "You don't have a collar anymore, if you ever did. Is it Prince? Devil? Tiger? Bob? None of the above, I see. Well, what would you like me to call you? I tell you what, you look a little like that TV detective with the bad eye and the disheveled raincoat. What's his name, Columbo?"

The dog finished the soup and looked up at her more brightly.

"Is that it? Columbo? You like that name? Okay, Mr. Columbo, that's what it will be. Jessie and Columbo. Columbo and Jessie. Does that suit you?"

She rubbed the fur under his neck, which was one place not affected by whatever conflict he had been engaged in, and he seemed to regard her gratefully.

She set a large pan of water beside him, which he thirstily devoured. Then she opened some more soup for her own supper, and unwrapped a partial loaf of bread she had covered with plastic wrap.

"Here," she said, offering part of the bread to Columbo. "I forgot to give you your bread with the soup."

Jessie slept that night on a sleeping bag she rolled out beside Columbo in front of the fire. She wanted to be there if the dog needed her. And it was the warmest place in the house. Twice in the night she got up to add logs to the fire. Once it had nearly gone out, and it took her a minute or two to get it started up again. She lay there on her pallet thinking about the events of her life the past few weeks, and how wondrous were the ways of *Baba*.

Perhaps Columbo was part of *Baba*'s plan too. She felt happy and comfortable with the big dog lying there beside her. Sometimes she needed another creature of flesh and blood to talk to and to touch. She thanked *Baba* for sending him, and for the healing she could already sense occurring in his cleaned wounds.

Before she went back to sleep, she saw the great head of the dog raise and pivot in her direction. Then it went back down, and she heard a contented sigh as he adjusted his body to a more comfortable position.

13

The snow stopped late in the night. When Jessie stirred and looked outside a little after daybreak, there were no tracks anywhere. Even her trail through the snow the evening before had been covered over. The fir trees were bent low under their heavy burdens of white. Snow stood three feet deep against the front door and was halfway up the windows around the house, imparting a strange, bluish light to the lower areas of glass. Even on the sheltered back porch, the snow was a couple of feet deep at the edges, and in the doorway where she had discovered Columbo, there were several inches of newly drifted snow.

The only activity was the darting about of birds in the feeder and in the nearby trees. Three cardinals, several sparrows, a starling, two crows, and some finches were all chattering and playing gaily in the brightness of the new day.

Columbo raised his head and watched her as she moved around, but did not himself offer to rise.

"Still stiff, old boy?" Jessie asked.

She put on her boots, coat, and gloves and went out onto the back porch, where she took a shovel and began clearing a path through the yard to the edge of the woods. Then she opened the door and asked Columbo if he wanted to go out.

Slowly he gathered his resolve, made a couple of tries, and managed to shift his weight and get his feet under him. He stood unsteadily a moment, then moved toward the opening, looked questioningly at the strange white world, and ambled down the path. In a couple of minutes he was back again.

"Good boy," said Jessie. "Now I'll bet you're hungry. Let's see what we can find for a big dog with a voracious appetite."

She worked most of the morning on her painting. Even without electricity, her studio was much brighter than usual, for the snow reflected the sunlight. As she worked on the portraits of the children, she found herself giving one of them Billy Gerald's freckled face and short, reddish hair. She also pondered painting Columbo into the scene, but decided to postpone that for another picture.

Shortly after noon, she put on her boots and coat, called to Columbo, and went out for a walk in the sparkling wonderland. Anxious to see if her woodland friends were faring well, she struck into the forest and followed her usual path for a mile or so. Although there was plenty of snow in the woods, much of it lay in the trees above, leaving the trails themselves fairly passable. She had to be careful, though, because the sun was warming the overhead snow enough to send great masses of it dropping down through the branches.

Columbo showed surprising agility, considering the shape he had been in the night before, and was soon bounding through the snow like a young pup. Two or three times he left the trail to chase a squirrel up a tree. Once, at a higher elevation, he prowled and sniffed cautiously around some large rocks, leading Jessie to suspect that he was in the vicinity of the animal he had encountered the previous day.

"Be careful, my friend," she said, "or you may provoke your nemesis again."

The little village of Cartersville remained essentially snowbound for forty-eight hours, which was how long it took for the snowplows and salting trucks to clean the main highway leading in from both directions. Electrical capacity was restored at approximately the same time. Jessie hardly noticed when the lights came on, so intent was she on finishing her painting of Mary.

It had not taken that long, however, for word to spread through Cartersville of the seemingly miraculous recovery of Billy Gerald. Alma had unhesitatingly assigned his cure to Jessie's special powers, declaring to one and all that her son had really lost the battle to live when that remarkable woman effected a complete reversal of his condition. Some folks considered the report to be the fabrication of an hysterical woman, while others vowed that they had known Alma all her life and had never perceived her to be the least bit excitable or gullible. "If Alma says it happened," these latter said, "then it really happened."

Jessie thus became the topic of daily conversation in and around the small community. More than a few citizens resolved to approach her the first chance they got about various ailments and personal problems.

The day she spoke to the Women's Art and Poetry Guild, the crowd was almost too large. The committee in charge of the event had to make hasty calls to their husbands at the fire department and the local shrine to bring more chairs immediately to the arts and crafts center. They also dispatched three ladies to the bakery for more refreshments.

"Ladies and gentlemen," said Eleanor Benton, the guild's president, "I am glad to be able to say 'gentlemen' today, for we normally do not have any men in attendance. I know it is a tribute to today's speaker that they have been attracted here, together with many of you who have also seldom attended."

She thanked the various persons responsible for the arrangements, including those who had brought in additional chairs and those who had prepared such lovely and abundant refreshments, which she knew they would all enjoy after hearing the speaker of the day. In introducing Jessie, Ms. Benton mentioned her recent notoriety "both at home and in the nation at large," her residence in the old Jumbletown schoolhouse — Jessie had never heard it called that before — and her obvious way of setting people around her at ease. All eyes focused on the simply clad, little dark-headed woman sitting quietly at the side of the small speaker's platform, her hands softly folded in the lap of her denim skirt. By her side lay a large, handsome German shepherd. Someone had suggested that perhaps the dog would be more comfortable waiting at the firehouse next door, as dogs did not usually accompany their owners into the arts and crafts center. Because the woman did not insist, Jessie merely smiled and entered the room, Columbo padding closely beside her.

On the opposite side of the speaker's lectern stood an easel bearing a painting covered by a decorously arranged light-blue cloth. In introducing Jessie, Ms. Benton alluded to the mystery painting beneath the cloth, which she said was Jessie's most recent "accomplishment" and would be "appropriately recognized" later in the program.

Jessie walked to the speaker's stand and began to speak, in a pleasant voice and manner that everyone could easily understand and relate to. She told them how much she had enjoyed her few weeks in the former schoolhouse at the edge of their town and spoke of the beauty and majesty of their mountain area. She had been few places, she said, where the bounty of God was so obvious in the glory of the daily scenery that surrounded the inhabitants wherever they looked.

As for her paintings, she said that they were merely windows focusing their viewers on certain moments in life and history when God had chosen to bless the world through the lives of faithful women servants. They were in no way a denial or denigration of the gifts of God given through male figures. They were simply reminders that the God of biblical understanding was impartial with regard to the sex, color, or even religion of the persons through whom God elected to bestow blessings.

The primary duty of an artist, she averred, is to see the world with excitement and bracket parts of that world in such a way that others take notice of them too. "The artist doesn't make beauty," she said. "The artist recognizes it and frames it for others to see."

After the applause, Ms. Benton introduced Father Milton McKeown, pastor of Rymer's Chapel Roman Catholic Church, who was present to receive the mystery painting as a donation from the artist herself. Jessie had already met with Father McKeown, a middle-aged Carmelite priest, and therefore didn't take long with the formalities of presentation. As she shook Father McKeown's hand, Ms. Benton unveiled the portrait of Mary, which she announced was entitled *Mary's Secret*.

More applause. Alma, who was sitting only a few feet from the painting, emitted a small shriek and exclaimed, "There's Billy Gerald!"

"And there's my Emma," said another.

"And the Hinson boy!"

There was general delight among the townspeople at recognizing their offspring in the painting. Everyone admitted that the portrait of Mary was extraordinarily transcendent and beautiful, but it was really the sight of the familiar that charmed them most.

Father McKeown was overwhelmed at his little chapel's good fortune. He knew that not only would the painting prove a blessing to all who looked upon it, but over the years it would bring many, many visitors whose sole object in coming would be to view it at firsthand. It would mean a steady stream of contributors in a parish that had always been small and enjoyed only meager revenues.

The only disgruntled guests at the presentation appeared to be the Baptist pastor, Dr. Jack Garbie, who had preached the now-famous sermon on women's keeping silence in the church, and three of his male parishioners. They hung back for a few minutes while a number of enthusiasic fans, mostly women, greeted Jessie. Then they drifted toward her in a group. Garbie began speaking to her before they had arrived fully in front of her.

"Are you a Catholic?" he asked, as if that might explain everything he found objectionable in her work.

Jessie looked up at the four men. Garbie was a tall, thin man in his mid-fifties. Bald on top, he carefully combed his graying hair across his head and lacquered it to keep it firmly in place. The square, rimless glasses he wore for far-sightedness made sections of his face look thicker than the rest. He gestured with long, thin hands extending from wrists that seemed to extend eight, perhaps even ten, inches beyond the cuffs of his jacket. Of the four, he was the only one wearing a white shirt and tie. The others were attired in colored shirts. One, a middle-aged man who looked as if he might be a store owner or an insurance agent, wore a hounds-tooth sports coat. The others wore ordinary jackets, one blue and one green.

When Jessie said no, she was not a member of the Catholic church but had many Catholic friends, the man in the green jacket asked, almost too quickly, "Are you a New Ager?"

"Pardon?" said Jessie.

"I ast if you're one of them godless New Agers that says people can be saved by repeating Satan's name or looking into a crystal ball."

"No, that doesn't sound like me," she said, smiling patiently.

"The point is, miss," said Garbie in a smooth, patronizing voice, "we are concerned about the doctrinal errors in your position, and the confusion they help to spread among ignorant people who don't know any better."

"Where'd you go to seminary?" asked the store owner or insurance agent.

"I didn't," said Jessie. "Why do you ask?"

"Because," said the man, "it is obvious that you have come under false teaching somewhere, and the seminaries today are full of false teaching."

"What false teaching?"

Garbie interposed himself. "He is referring to

your heretical position on women. All these paintings you've been doing. Representing women as the agents of God. The Bible is perfectly clear about the role of women in the world, that they are to be helpmates and servants of men, not speakers and leaders the way you represent them."

Jessie's eyes remained calm and pleasant.

"You mean," she said, "that's the way you read the Bible. I read the Bible too, and I see women there in a different way. Theirs was admittedly a patriarchal society, with men determining most of their affairs. But even between the lines it is obvious that Judaism and Christianity could not have existed as they did without the spirit and cooperation of women."

"What do you know about the Bible?" shot back Blue Jacket. "You done said you ain't been to seminary. Dr. Garbie here's got two degrees from a seminary besides his college degree, and that was before our seminaries got so many things wrong with them. He knows the Bible. Quotes it all the time in his sermons. An' if he says the women are supposed to keep silent in the churches, then women are supposed to keep silent."

"Let me be sure I understand," said Jessie. "You are all upset with me because I choose to represent women in the more creative, central roles of faith and not as mere helpers and maidservants. Is that right?"

"You are twisting the purposes of God," said

Garbie. "You and your kind. You are disturbing the household of God in our time, and He will not hold you guiltless for that."

"I know why you are upset," she said. "This is an age of profound changes in the world, not just in religion but in technology and government and many other things as well. People are naturally uneasy in such an era, and the first thing they wish to do is to try to hold everything in place just where it was. That's the way I see your position on women. You are fighting to keep women in what you think of as their place, the way people a few years ago opposed the desecration of the Sabbath by stores remaining open on Sunday. But you are putting your emphasis in the wrong place. If you really have faith in God, then you will trust God to bring in God's commonwealth despite anything that happens in society."

"You're just as ignorant as all the others," said the man in the sports coat. "You talk about having faith but you want to throw out the Good Book and not pay any attention to what it says."

Garbie was aware that a number of people around the room were watching the encounter between him and his deacons and the woman artist.

"Look, miss," he said, pointing his long finger about two inches from Jessie's nose, "we're just trying to give you a friendly warning. These are fast days we're living in, and there's plenty of us that love the Lord and are trying to keep His ways in spite of the godless secularism of people like yourself. We are going to do everything in our power to help Him triumph over you. Of course, we don't personally wish you any harm. In fact, I will pray every day for your soul's salvation. With God, all things are possible. But if you don't repent and change your ways, there's nothing we can do for you. The devil will just go on having his way with you."

Columbo, sensing the threatening tone of Garbie's voice and the finger thrust into Jessie's face, sat up in an alert position, his ears standing like two sentinels. Garbie noticed the dog out of the corner of his eye and lowered his hand, but his tone continued compulsive and threatening to the end.

He was just completing his sentence about the devil when a tall, well-groomed elderly woman stepped up, accompanied by a shorter, plumper woman perhaps ten years younger than herself.

"I heard that remark about the devil," she said. "Someone said you're Garbie, the Baptist preacher over here, and these are your deacons. I'm D. M. Birkenstall, Dr. Garbie, and this is my friend Delma Hirshfield-Jones. I own two of Jessie's paintings, and I am proud to be able to say that I do. I consider her not only the finest artist painting in America today but one of the finest who ever lived, and that includes Rembrandt and Michelangelo and Pablo Picasso.

"I admit to your face," she continued, "that I

don't have much use for your cheap, theatrical brand of Christianity. It does more harm to the Christian community than good. I find your kind of minister pompous, arrogant, ignorant, and offensive. You would have to make a lot of progress in your thinking to become medieval. I'm an Episcopalian myself, and I say thank God for the Prayerbook. At least it keeps stupid, self-serving oafs like yourself in the background and lets opinionated old ladies like myself worship in relative peace and protection.

"Now, if you are through badgering this wonderful woman, whom I am frank to say I regard as something of a saint, I will thank you to take your scruffy entourage elsewhere and let some people with the sense to know the hand of God when they see it admire and converse with this woman."

Garbie and the three men were so taken by surprise that they looked at each other and retreated with only one further utterance. It was spoken by Garbie when they were several feet away. "You haven't heard the last of this," he promised.

"Pifflesnort," said Dr. Birkenstall. "I'm afraid, my dear, there are more horses' asses in the world than there are horses."

Jessie laughed. Columbo lowered himself to a prone position again, relaxed but wary.

"You really are quite wonderful," said Dr. Birkenstall. "Isn't she, Delma? I can't tell you how profoundly your paintings move me. I have been a Christian all my life, and a university professor almost as long, and I have never been so deeply affected by anything, except maybe the Book of Common Prayer and Dante's *Divine Comedy*. The older I get, the less I enjoy Dante. You're a godsend, my dear."

"I second the motion," smiled Delma Hirshfield-Jones. "And that's one reason I'm here today, Jessie. May I call you Jessie? I'm spiritual-life chair for my diocese, and we've been planning a wonderful new service for Easter called *Women of the Tomb*. We're thinking of a huge rally to be held at sunrise in the convention center in Gatlinburg, with churches bringing busloads of people from all over the area. There'll be special music. We're commissioning a brand new anthem from John and Anne Prather, who write such wonderful things. There'll be a gigantic choir with hundreds of ladies from all over. And we'd like for you to be our speaker. D. M. here has agreed to loan us your paintings—the ones she has—and we want to have them flanking the pulpit. You would give the program just the added dimension it needs. You proved that this morning. People enjoy hearing you talk. Well, most of them, anyway." She tossed a glance in the direction taken by Garbie and his men. "What do you say, Jessie? Will you do it?"

"It would mean a great deal to all of us," said Dr. Birkenstall.

Jessie looked down at Columbo. She thought

what unexpected turns her life had taken in recent weeks.

"All right," she said. "I'll be glad to help."

14

For several days, Jessie spent a great deal of time praying in the mountains. While she in no way shrank from the pressure of her newfound notoriety, she found that it drove her more often and insistently into the presence of *Baba*, who alone could provide the strength and courage for confrontations like the one she had experienced with Dr. Garbie and his associates.

Sometimes, when she sat on a rock or a log to talk with *Baba*, Columbo lay quietly a few feet away, like a great bodyguard waiting patiently for his mistress to conclude her visit. Other times he would pad off quietly into the woods, following some mysterious scent or exploring the curiosities of the forest. But on these occasions he was obviously alert for the least sound of her motion; she would not take twenty steps before he quietly appeared and rejoined her.

The increasing fame of her paintings and the stories about her led to a sudden increase in her volume of mail, which Mary Patton, the woman who took care of the small post office in Cartersville, now insisted on sending to her house, as it was often more than Jessie could comfortably carry home, especially if she did not call for it more than once or twice a week. If

Jessie was not at home, old Bill, the mailman on her route, would leave it in a U.S. Mail sack by her front door and then pick up the sack the next time he came.

Many of the letters that arrived were pleas for help from desperately ill or poor people who said they had nowhere else to turn. Jessie would pray for them on her walks in the forest; she often sent a little money to persons whose needs she considered legitimate. Some people sent little gifts, mostly books, and asked her to remember them in prayer, which she was only too pleased to do.

She occasionally heard from Roxie and Joan and Phyllis, all of whom missed her dreadfully. Once she had a letter from Rachel, saying how beautifully Carol was doing and how inseparable she and Julia had become. They were counting the days, she said, until they could both come for Easter vacation.

There had also been a letter from Jasmine describing her new life at the university. Following Jessie's inspiration, she had assumed responsibilities in a Christian women's group at the school. She intended to remain a Buddhist, but was eager to learn more about Christianity, and most of the other girls had been very tolerant. When they learned that she was a personal friend of Jessie's, who had become one of their heroines, they insisted that she accept a minor office, something to do with interfaith programing; Jasmine acquiesced. Moreover, she had seen the fliers advertising the Women of the Tomb service on Easter, and had promptly organized a group of university women to come by bus for the occasion.

Jasmine was working fewer hours at Mike's restaurant, now that Dana was assisting full-time. Dana and Mike's romance, she reported, was progressing at surprising speed. They were talking about a late spring wedding.

Jessie had soon completed another painting, this one of the famous martyr Joan of Arc. It showed Joan in full battle armor, the sun glinting on its smooth contours and hinges, sitting astride a majestic horse on a hill overlooking the bedraggled army she commanded. She held her helmet in her arm, and tears of love and compassion streaked her face. A graceful white cross, edged in gold, was emblazoned on her horse's battle skirts. And there, standing poised and alert beside the horse, was a fabulous German shepherd dog. His coat was lustrous and his head looked proud and regal—indeed a true representation of Columbo since his wounds had healed.

She had also begun work on a painting of Rosa Parks, the dedicated black woman in Alabama who had defied the order and tradition that relegated her people to seats at the back of public vehicles. It would depict a defiant Rosa sitting cross-armed near the front of a bus while the frustrated driver looked on and a sheriff's deputy, truncheon in hand, stood over her, arguing for her self-removal. Outside the windows, there would be a number of faces looking in, witnesses to one of the great moments in history.

The model for Rosa was a warm, friendly woman named Sarah who worked as a dishwasher in the cafe where Alma was a waitress. Only one other face had begun to take shape at this point, and that was the visage of the bus driver, who wore square, rimless glasses and stood with his hat in his hand, revealing long strands of grayish hair combed across his balding head.

Harold and Rowena were delighted to have the *Joan* painting, which Jessie and Columbo delivered as soon as the paint was reasonably dry. Rowena was thrilled at seeing Columbo in the picture, for she was an animal lover and had taken an instant liking to him. It was late in the afternoon, so they closed up the gallery a little after five, and the four of them went to a restaurant for dinner. The hostess was about to object to Columbo's coming in, but then she recognized Jessie and was only too happy to admit him. There was scarcely anyone else in the restaurant that evening anyway, and the great dog lay quietly beside Jessie's chair.

Rowena described what the extensive publicity had done for their business. Attendance in the gallery had at least quadrupled since the television coverage, and people often lingered much longer than formerly, chatting about Jessie's works or sometimes just standing there reverently. They also tended to spend more time viewing

Harold's paintings as well. Sales of his canvases had increased so steadily that he had given up his job at the printing plant and was working full time on them.

Not everything they had to report was pleasant, however. Lately they had been receiving mysterious threats by mail about what would happen to their gallery if they continued to exhibit the "lewd and lascivious" paintings of that "secularist heathen" woman named Jessie, as one of the notes had put it. Also, said Rowena, there was the morning when she went to open the studio and found a spray-painted message on the door saying DEATH TO NEW AGE WHORES, with little crosses painted all around it.

"That's terrible," said Jessie. "I don't want to cause you any trouble. Maybe you shouldn't hang any more of my things for a while."

"Bosh," said Rowena. "They don't scare me."

Harold had been to the police with the letters and had photographed the message on the door before painting over it. The Gatlinburg police came by and looked at the gallery, studying Jessie's paintings when they did, but they said it was probably just some crank. They didn't get a lot of cases like that in the little town. When they did they were soon cleared up; everybody knew everybody else in those parts, and it was hard to keep that sort of thing secret for very long. But they said to report any more messages and promised to alert their patrols to keep an eye on the studio, especially at night.

"You're awfully quiet, Harold," said Jessie. "What are you thinking?"

"I don't know, Jess. It worries me, I admit. Not for us or the gallery. I don't think anyone would try anything here in town. But your place is another matter. I wouldn't want anything to happen to you."

"I've got *Baba* with me—and Columbo."

"I know. That relieves me some. But I'm still not exactly easy."

She put a hand on his wrist and stroked it softly. "I'll be all right. I really will."

Meanwhile, word was getting around about phenomenal happenings at Rymer's Chapel. *Mary's Secret* had been hung in an ornate, hand-crafted gilt frame over the altar in the little chancel. Father McKeown had set a large candlestick on either side of it, so that even in the evenings there was sufficient lighting to see the soft, radiant face of the expectant mother and the cheerful countenances of the young children gathered around her in the poppy field. A steady stream of visitors came to view the portrait, and there were almost always a few worshipers kneeling on the cushions at the altar rail to pray in the presence of this powerful reminder of divine love and grace.

The day after the painting was hung, a young woman with acute bursitis in one shoulder and the elbow on the opposite arm was staring at the face of Mary when she noticed that she no longer felt any pain. She rotated her shoulder, gently at first, expecting the pain to return, but it didn't. Then she flexed her arm to see if the elbow would hurt. It too was free of pain.

She was weeping tears of pure joy when she excitedly narrated her story to Father McKeown. "It's the first time in years that I have been without pain," she said. She asked if she could say confession and receive Communion. She had not been an active Christian since her graduation from high school.

The evening of the same day, the elderly gentleman who once cared for the church property was standing before the painting. He did not kneel because he had a degenerated hip joint and walked with a crutch. But something about his mood as he stood before the portrait led him to defy his circumstances and kneel anyway. When he arose, he did so with an ease and comfort he could scarcely believe.

"I feel like a young man again, Father," he told the astonished priest. "I can go up and down steps like a spring chicken!"

Other miracles were reported on succeeding days. A woman with cervical cancer felt better, went to her doctor, and got a clean report. A teenage girl with severe curvature of the spine had her back suddenly straightened. A man with inoperable melanoma was found to be totally cured. A woman with Alzheimer's disease suddenly recovered her memory and went home to lead a normal life.

Word spread instantly to the relatives of affected families. News reporters began calling from all over the country, tying up Father McKeown's phone line for hours at a time. LOURDES IN THE SMOKIES said a headline in a Chicago newspaper. MIRACLES IN THE MOUNTAINS read one in San Francisco. MYSTERY PAINTING PRODUCES HEALINGS said another in Montreal. There were even calls from news agencies in Paris and Rome, where attendance at Catholic churches soon increased in hopes that God was sending a new surge of spiritual power into the world.

Father McKeown did his best to be discreet in his replies to questions. Yes, Jessie was a relative newcomer to the mountains. No, he didn't know much about her background. Yes, she was an apparently very normal young woman, nothing unusual about her that he could see, except that she was obviously a person of deep spiritual commitment. Yes, she had painted other works too, and no, he had not heard of any miracles associated with the others. Yes, the painting was a gift to the chapel. Yes, she had discussed it with him before making the presentation. No, it was not a traditional portrait of Mary; it showed her pregnant in a field with a group of children. No, he didn't have any photographs of the painting; to tell the truth, he would prefer that none be taken just now, lest it disturb the chain of events that appeared to be related to the portrait.

Only once, in a conversation with a television reporter from a network agency in New York, did he mention the name *Baba*, which he had heard Jessie speak twice in their initial meeting. It was a sort of personal name for God, as he understood it, something she had used since childhood.

Once was enough.

Within a week, almost every television news program, major newspaper, and magazine in the Western hemisphere had divulged the private name the "miracle painter" Jessie, as she was called by several stories, used when addressing her God. Foreigners smiled about the eccentric inventiveness of Americans in almost every field, including their religion. Conservatives and fundamentalists clucked that she was obviously a kook and probably a tool of Satan to divert people from the true faith and the narrow way that leads to righteousness. Several New Age groups in Arizona and California began producing *Baba* literature and *Baba* wheels, the latter designed to bring about personal centering and increased Alpha waves.

Dr. Garbie, at the Baptist church in Cartersville, preached a much-talked-about sermon entitled *"Baba* and Babel,"* in which he declared that the invention of non-biblical names for God was heretical and blasphemous, and that Jessie would burn in the eternal flames of a bottomless hell for her unforgivable perfidy. Dr. Waterson at the University Avenue Church of

Christ in Knoxville preached an equally dogmatic sermon called "From Magog to *Baba*," in
which he declared that the appearance of the
blasphemous woman Jessie in their own vicinity
was abundant proof that the end of the world
was not far off, and that, in the final contest soon
to be waged, the Son of God would emerge vic-
torious and cast the horrid woman and all her
seditious paintings into the lake of everlasting
fire prepared for the devil and his angels.

Rev. Gary Sterling, publisher of *Christ Today*,
a major right-wing magazine, wrote a strident
editorial announcing that God had revealed to
him the true identity of the mystery artist Jessie,
whose paintings were doing so much to upset
Christians and confuse the heathen in East
Tennessee. She was really the great whore of
the book of Revelation, the resplendent harlot
whom God would throw down from the battle-
ments of heaven "the way Jezebel was hurled
down from the walls in the book of Kings,
so that wild dogs came and licked her blood.
People say they don't know her last name," he
wrote. "It is Bel. Jeze-bel."

Jessie herself was blissfully unaware of much
of the controversy surrounding her name, choos-
ing to go on with her painting and praying and
walking in the forest, with Columbo at her side.
A number of writers, reporters, and television
crews arrived in Cartersville every week to look
for her, and she sometimes interrupted her work
to visit with them. She had never thought very

highly of celebrities who treated others condescendingly; she did not intend to become a different person now that fame had been visited upon her. But she was often out tramping in the mountains when people sought her; assuming she might be away on some public relations tour or other, most of them were not very persistent about meeting her. They merely joined the crowds at Rymer's Chapel, took a few pictures of Father McKeown and the people coming out of the church—Father McKeown was still adamantly opposed to any photography in the sanctuary—and went away with half a story instead of the full one.

When she was interviewed, Jessie was simple and forthright in her responses. Whatever power her paintings had was from *Baba*. *Baba* was the name she had called God since she was a child. She believed in *Baba*'s power to heal the sick and the mentally disturbed. She focused on women in religion because that was where *Baba* was presently leading her to concentrate. At another time, in another place, *Baba* might lead her to do something else. She was sorry about the people who misunderstood her, because she never wished to confuse or hurt anyone. But she could not bow to the pressures of others and paint anything except what *Baba* directed. She did not know what her future paintings would be. *Baba* gave them to her only as she prepared to paint them. No, she had no plans for an exhibit or a book of her paintings.

The truth was that several publishers had contacted Harold about book projects, and Harold had mentioned the idea to Jessie. But Jessie had downplayed the suggestion, thinking it presumptuous to enter such negotiations when she had produced so few paintings. "Maybe next year," she said. "We'll see."

Visitors who saw the Rosa Parks painting, which Jessie had decided to call *Rosa's Gift*, described it as one of her most moving paintings to date. The faces peering in the bus window were priceless, they declared, and locals identified various ones as belonging to folks they knew, including a couple of deacons in the Baptist church. But it was Rosa's face, and the proud way she sat in the bus, determined and transfixed, that won the hearts of viewers. They could see in her eyes the entire future of her race, as if its guarantee depended on her and her alone.

Predictably—for two reporters had correctly foreseen the course of events—the exhibition of the completed portrait in the Moorefield Galleries produced even more controversy than already surrounded Jessie. "It's bad enough she has to paint all those awful feminist things," said one critic; "now she has gone and injected race into it."

Ed Preston, Tennessee Grand Wizard of the Klan, denounced Jessie as "a Jew-lovin', nigger-kissin' un-American" who was probably "one of them dirty lesbian atheists." Arnold Rainwater, head of a white supremacy group that trained at various secret locations in the mountains, called her "a symbol of the degenerate softness of the American left." And a number of preachers, politicians, and right-wing columnists questioned the morality of anybody who moved in from the North, as they knew Jessie had, and proceeded to criticize Southern ways and rewrite Southern history without a proper understanding of either.

The Coalition of Black Students and the Southeastern Association of African-Americans, however, praised Jessie for her sympathetic treatment of ethnic concerns, and the Interfaith Council of Knox County nominated her for their annual award as the person who in a given year is most successful in promoting spiritual and racial harmony. The chief of the Cherokee Indian nation in nearby Cherokee, North Carolina, hailed her as a model of interracial concern and suggested the names of four Native American women she might consider painting in the future.

And when the Rev. Dr. Reginald P. Waterson attacked Jessie in a sermon entitled "The Curse of Ham and the Eternal Separation of the Races," three of his own elders led a protest demonstration outside the University Avenue Church of Christ, calling for his immediate resignation as pastor of that congregation. "We came through that awful stuff twenty years ago," one of them told a reporter. "He must have been asleep."

D. M. Birkenstall read about all the controversy in the papers and made the decision one morning after breakfast to call her insurance agent in order to ask for a special rider on her homeowner's policy to cover the Jessie paintings she owned. She thought of setting the value at fifty thousand dollars each, but by the time she actually made the call she had raised it to one hundred thousand.

She realized when she hung up that the agent had probably not understood her allusion. "There aren't enough horses in the world," she said. "You never know when someone will do something foolish."

15

For the time being, Jessie was turning down the invitations she received to lecture. She realized that some of them would probably give her excellent forums for speaking about the things that mattered so much to her, such as *Baba*'s place in personal and public life, the recovery of a sense of morality, and the richness of the colorful, interesting world she lived in. But she felt, after praying about the various opportunities as they came, that this was a time for staying close to home and working on her paintings. It was the paintings, after all, that *Baba* was now using so powerfully to arrest people's attention and provoke their thinking about significant issues.

Perhaps later, when she needed a hiatus from this very creative period, she could more seriously consider traveling and speaking a bit.

But there was one exception to this self-imposed moratorium on speeches and public appearances. That was a visit to Jasmine's Christian group at the university. After the reports of interviews with Jessie appeared in the newspapers and on television, Jasmine's friends began pressing her to invite Jessie to one of their weekly meetings. In their naiveté, they had no idea of the kinds of invitations she received daily, and therefore anticipated no difficulty at all in securing her for one of their small, informal gatherings.

Perhaps this was what appealed most to Jessie about meeting with the group, although certainly it was her friendship with Jasmine that led her to accept her handwritten invitation when it came.

She spent most of the day in the woods with *Baba*, preparing her spirit for what she must say to the women at their meeting. Then she and Columbo walked into Gatlinburg and rode into Knoxville with Rowena, who had minded the studio that day so Harold could stay home and paint. It had been arranged that she would have dinner with Jasmine. After the session at the university, Harold would pick up her and Columbo and take them home with him and Rowena for the night.

The evening was cold and drizzly, but there

was a large crowd of young women present in the lounge of the dorm where they met. Jasmine introduced Jessie in her quiet, sincere way as the friend who had taught her about God and led her to an interest in the Christian faith. Then Jasmine took her place at the end of a sofa where Jessie had been sitting. Jessie stood in a clearing surrounded by several women sitting on the floor. Columbo remained by the sofa with Jasmine.

"I want to tell you about God from my per-spective," she began. "There are actually as many perspectives as there are people in the world, for each of us is equipped to know God in her own personal way."

Then she talked about her early years with *Baba*, and how wonderful they had been. *Baba* had always been her most intimate companion. She regarded with sorrow the many people who shut *Baba* out because of their busyness or blind-ness or wickedness. *Baba* did not hate them, she said; but they were missing the greatest happi-ness of their lives.

"How does one find *Baba* after years of ignor-ing or not even knowing *Baba*?" someone asked.

"Oh, it is very easy," said Jessie. "You merely have to realize that *Baba* has already found you. Then you open your heart and begin to visit with *Baba*. Everything will grow from that sim-ple beginning."

"What is the best church to belong to?" asked another.

"Probably a church where people love one another and seek to live humbly and meaningfully in the world. You can tell if *Baba* makes a difference in their lives."

"Why do you say 'probably'?" a voice asked.

"Because there may be a time when *Baba* leads you to belong to a church that is not worshipping *Baba*—where there is petty conflict and meanness and selfishness—so that you can model *Baba's* love and perhaps lead others into the way of *Baba's* spirit."

Someone asked if Jessie was working on a new painting. Yes, she replied, she was trying to make a portrait that would be an appropriate tribute to Mother Teresa, the saintly nun who worked with the poorest of the poor in India.

How did she choose the subjects of her paintings? She prayed and sought the guidance of *Baba*. So they were not entirely her work. *Baba* also had a large hand in them.

How did she feel about the controversy surrounding her works, especially *Rosa's Gift*? She was very sorry about the conflict, she said, but that was the nature of the world she lived in. The parables of Jesus, she reminded them, often alluded to the difficulties of ministry. He spoke of weeds growing in the wheat, of seed falling on stony ground where it couldn't take root, of wicked men killing the messengers and even the son of the owner of the vineyard.

"Is it true there have been miraculous healings of people looking at your picture of the Virgin

Mary?" asked a studious-looking woman with bangs and glasses.

"I have heard that," said Jessie. "But you must understand the nature of healing. Healing goes on all the time in our world. We only tend to notice it when something appears to expedite or hurry it beyond its usual pace. But if we live thoughtfully each day in *Baba's* spirit, we will be aware of the healing taking place inside us and all around us, and we will give thanks for the wonderful grace with which everything occurs."

"Is forgiveness a part of healing?" asked another girl.

"Oh yes. It is one of the ways we can all participate in the healing process. As we forgive the wrongs and mistakes of others, we allow our own hurts to heal. We make it possible for *Baba* to hasten the work of healing both in ourselves and in others."

Someone asked if God forgives us for taking drugs and getting our lives all screwed up.

Jessie looked gently and lovingly into her eyes. Everyone in the room could feel the tenderness radiating from her.

"Of course," she said. "There has never been a moment when *Baba* has not forgiven you. There is nothing you can possibly do to step outside the boundaries of *Baba's* love and forgiveness. The problem is in our own hearts. When we are made to feel guilty and awkward because of something we have done, that becomes a barrier to realizing *Baba's* forgiveness."

"But doesn't *Baba* hate sin?" asked a different student.

"Oh yes, the way a baker hates lumps in the dough or a potter hates impurities in the clay. Parents always hate the things that become problematic in their children's lives. But they still love their children and want the very best for them."

The questions and responses went on in this vein until a brown-haired, ordinary-looking woman near the back spoke up in a somewhat bitter tone.

"I have a question," she said, "that you would probably rather not answer. I know you and Jasmine are friends, and—well, Jasmine made it plain to us when she came here a month ago that she is a Buddhist, not a Christian. What I want to know is, if you are a Christian, how can you really have anything in common with her? The Bible teaches that there is only one way to salvation, and that is through Jesus Christ, so she cannot possibly be saved." She flicked her hair back out of her face with a quick, backward motion of her hand. "What do you say to that?"

Jessie smiled toward Jasmine and said that if it were not for her, she would not be there that evening.

"Jasmine is a beautiful person," she said. "You can all tell that. And she is very open to grace and love in her life. I don't know anything more Christlike than that. Don't you imagine that many of our doctrinal differences in this world are semantic in nature? I mean, we grow up in different situations and learn to call things by different names; then we let those names become barriers that separate us. Suppose when we die that we know everything directly and intuitively, without words and philosophical constructs. Then wouldn't we feel ashamed that in life we let ideas and doctrines stand between us and God's other children in the world?"

The woman was not satisfied. She said, "My pastor says that anyone who doesn't call upon the name of Jesus will spend eternity in hell."

Jessie stood there looking thoughtful for a moment. Then she asked, "What is hell, my dear? Is it really a place of fire and torment, or is that merely a metaphor for separation from God?"

She paused for the question to sink in, then continued. "If hell is really the absence of God, then for many people it begins here, not when they die. And when they die it is only intensified. I mean, maybe they realize then what they have been missing in not being close to God. That would be an awful punishment, wouldn't it?

"If Jesus were absolutely, undeniably the only way to know God, your pastor would certainly be right. But surely there have always been good Jews who knew God. After all, Jesus himself was one of them. And I have known some wonderful Muslim and Hindu and Buddhist people who clearly loved God and wanted to do God's will in their lives. I would feel awfully presumptuous in saying that they will not share an afterlife with the rest of us."

"But it's in the Bible, isn't it? Don't you believe the Bible?"

"Oh, honey, of course I believe the Bible. But the issue you are raising is, how do I believe the Bible? The Bible is very special, and it deserves a place of great reverence in our lives. But it is not a book of laws and ordinances and irrefutable facts. That is not its genius at all. Its real genius is its spirit. It is what it points to that matters. And what it points to is God and God's love in our lives.

"Maybe I can use an analogy. When you get a letter from home, you don't carry it around and underline parts of it and try to regulate everything in your life by it, do you?"

The woman hesitated and nodded no.

"Nor should we try to make the Bible more than it is, a letter from the past to our time about how God was acting then. It is the Bible's witness that is important, not its individual words and sentences. It points us to God, and we should look to God, not get lost in its myriads of details."

Jessie waited a minute to see if the young woman would respond. Everyone else waited too. But either she was satisfied with Jessie's answer or she was too confused in her thoughts to go on, so she remained silent.

After a few more questions and answers,

Jessie smiled and thanked them for sharing their time with her. Jasmine stood, said a sweet word of thanks to Jessie, and dismissed the meeting. A number of the women lingered to visit with Jessie, some wanting to ask questions they had not wished to raise more publicly, and others merely wishing to remain in her presence as long as possible.

When they finally said good-bye, several said they were coming to the Women of the Tomb service and would see her then.

16

Rowena and Harold were talking with Jessie in front of their crackling fire. At last Rowena said she would leave the rest of the evening to the young folks—she had to get her beauty rest. Columbo raised his head in acknowledgment as she arose and left the room, then lowered it onto his paws again.

"Jess," said Harold, "I really owe you a lot. It's wonderful to be able to afford to paint full time at last. I was beginning to think I never would."

"You deserve to. Your work is so special, so beautiful and lifelike. You help me to see the marvel of *Baba*'s world."

The firelight illuminated his smooth face, setting his dimples into shadowy prominence.

"I can't imagine anybody's being able to help you see anything," he said. "You have the most perfect, most wonderful vision I've ever known."

"Oh no. If I see anything, it's because I'm open to seeing, and that means I am helped by all sorts of people. You especially help me."

For a moment they simply looked at each other. Then Jessie glanced at the fire. She took a last drink of cocoa from the cup she had been holding and set it on the end table.

"Jess, we need to talk about us."

She looked back to him in the firelight, admiring his rugged frame and handsome features.

"We have been putting it off," she said.

"I know. We didn't want to complicate things. And we've both been so busy. Our output the last few weeks has been staggering."

They were both quiet, not quite knowing which door to take into the discussion. It was Harold who broke the silence.

"You know how I feel about you, Jess. You're the most special person I ever met."

Jessie reached for his hand and continued staring into the fire.

"I know how you feel," she said. "I feel the same about you. You're good and kind and thoughtful. And you have a wonderful gift for seeing things. I mean, really seeing them."

Harold wanted to put his arm around her and draw her close, but he hesitated, not wishing to shortcut the discussion. As if picking up on his thoughts, she scooted over and nestled down in his arms, still looking into the fire.

"I know you have a lot on your mind right

now," he said. "I don't have any right to push you." She was quiet. "Maybe later in the spring, when we've sort of caught up with things and this big Easter gathering is past, we can see our way more clearly."

She was grateful for his sensitivity. She did love him. She knew she did. But she wasn't entirely certain yet what *Baba* wanted, where the present train of events was leading. She had been through intense times before. But somehow this one was different. Something seemed to be building up. She wasn't sure, but she thought she could feel it.

He kissed the back of her head.

She stroked his hand in front of her.

"I really worry about some of the ugliness going on," he said. "I've never seen anything quite like it."

"There are some powerful, grinding conflicts in people's lives right now. My paintings just seem to have touched those."

"It's unbelievable how passionate people can become over issues they don't even understand or want to understand. I mean, your pictures are so beautiful and so good. Why would anyone get so upset by them? That's what I can't understand."

"I know. Sometimes I wish I could take them all back. You know how they run a film backward and make everything return to the state where it began. I find myself imagining how it would be if I could do that with my paintings —

just run everything back to the moment when I hadn't done them and stop there and go forward again without them."

"Oh Jess, that would be awful. Think how much poorer the world would be. I can't imagine life now without them."

"I don't really mean it, I suppose. But the thought does occur. I don't like being the center of attention. And I hate even worse stirring up resentment and anger."

"But the resentment and anger would be there, whether you stirred them up or not."

"That's true. But maybe at least they would lie dormant."

"And then spring up on somebody else."

"You're right, of course."

Harold got up to put another log on the fire. Columbo followed him with his eyes.

"I suppose that's always the dilemma of the prophet," he said, resettling and letting her snuggle into his arm again. "Whether to speak—or in your case, paint—and disturb the status quo, which may not be at all good, or to remain silent and let things rock along as they are."

"Yes. Only if you listen to *Baba* it isn't always your choice."

Harold nodded, brushing her hair with his jaw. "That's right. So it's a kind of catch-22. You're in trouble if you do it and trouble if you don't."

She waited, knowing he would explain further.

"If you listen to *Baba* you stir everything up, and if you don't you lose your intimacy with *Baba*. You lose either way."

"Or win either way, depending on how you look at it."

"I do wish you'd stay here with us, Jess. You could have that back bedroom upstairs. It gets a lot of morning light and would make a great place to paint. In fact, I've sometimes thought of installing my own studio there, and haven't done it because I'm in the habit of using the downstairs room."

She gazed silently into the flames, which were burning steadily again.

"It really bothers me for you to be out there alone in that location—even with *Baba* and Columbo. If anything happened out there, any ugliness or anything, nobody would even know about it."

"I'm sorry," she said. "I don't want you to worry. But I love to paint there. And I need the park. If I couldn't roam through those woods and hills, I don't know if I could paint at all. It's been a perfect place for me. And Columbo loves it too."

"I don't suppose you'd consider keeping a gun around the place?"

She shook her head no, this time brushing his face with her hair.

They sat a long time, staring and saying nothing. The fire sent an occasional ember popping onto the hearth. Columbo rolled over on his side and stretched his neck and hind legs. Presently they could hear a steady snoring noise coming from him.

"I guess it's time to hit the hay," Harold said finally.

Jessie nodded.

"Want me to call you in the morning?"

"I think I'll awaken in plenty of time. I'd better let Columbo out before I go up."

They stood and held each other a minute in the light and warmth of the fading embers. Columbo rolled over instantly, alerted by their motion, and gathered himself for the trip outside.

"I love you," Harold said, gently kissing her.

"And I love you," she said.

17

Of all the paintings Jessie had made, she liked the one of Mother Teresa best. When she began, she conceived of it with the saintly nun's face in the foreground and with portrayals of the Calcutta poor in the background, all looking at her. But now, as she worked on it, she was led to picture a pair of long, slender hands in the immediate foreground offering the holy chalice to Mother Teresa. Mother Teresa's face thus became a study in reverence and humility as she received the sacrament that would empower her, even beyond her eightieth year, to spend twelve to fifteen hours a day caring for lepers, cripples, and the abjectly poor.

Jessie thought she would name the painting simply *Mother Teresa Receiving the Blessed Sacrament.*

Perhaps the painting meant so much to Jessie because she knew how much she herself depended on *Baba*'s strength for the increasing demands of her own schedule. Everything had seemed so simple when she first moved into the converted schoolhouse and began to paint. Almost no one at that time knew she existed. Now her fame brought an almost steady stream of visitors to her door and a large volume of mail, which she felt compelled to read and answer. She found it necessary to be at her easel as soon as the light was good in order to get in two or three hours' work before people began to arrive; she often sat up until eleven or twelve at night, responding to cards and letters from friends, admirers, and just plain seekers.

Still, she thanked *Baba* for the gift of her art and the satisfaction she always felt when a painting was going well, and for each person who had taken the time and trouble to communicate with her. She was also grateful that the art provided the wherewithal to answer so many people's needs for a little monetary help.

Did the legislators in the nation's capitol have any idea, she wondered, how many of their citizens lived at the brink of perpetual worry and distress over unpaid bills, repossessed cars and furniture, disconnected utilities, unfilled prescriptions, and empty pantries? Surely a land so beautifully configured and bountifully endowed by *Baba* could devise better ways of caring for its perennially poor and hurting members.

She had visited a number of churches since her arrival in East Tennessee and been puzzled about why so few seemed to make any provision for the poor in their own congregations, much less in their larger communities and the world beyond. Invariably, in the congregations she had seen, there would be well dressed, affluent members who arrived in expensive automobiles sitting only a few feet from poorly dressed people who had arrived either on foot or in old jalopies that looked to be only a cough and a sputter from vehicular mortality. Yet there was seldom any evidence of the wealthier members making an effort to meet the needs of the poorer ones.

How carefully, she was forced to reflect, had they really considered the teachings of Jesus and the stories of the Gospels? Surely Jesus had been quite radical on this point. Wealth that is not used to alleviate the burdens of one's neighbors becomes a danger to one's own soul.

When she completed *Mother Teresa* and set it aside to dry, she began sketching a new picture, this time returning to a biblical setting for her theme. It was a painting of the woman described in the fourth chapter of the Gospel of John, and of her fruitful witness to Christ after her encounter with him that fateful day at

Jacob's well.

It would be called *A Woman Evangelizing Her Town* and would show the woman, keen-eyed and attractive, sitting in the midst of dozens of her townspeople, apparently answering their questions and holding them spellbound with the power of her insights. As she sketched in faces of the townspeople, Jessie recalled the interesting visages of people she had seen in various churches and along the streets of Cartersville and Gatlinburg. She also roughed in the features of three of the young women from the university, placing them together as if they were friends bound by confiding their secrets to one another.

She was finishing the last of these sketches when there came a knock at the door. It was D. M. Birkenstall and Delma Hirshfield-Jones, bearing a gift basket of wine, cheese, bread, and strawberries, and adorned at the top by a large red bow.

"We don't mean to intrude, my dear," said Dr. Birkenstall, "but Delma needed to contact you about the Women of the Tomb service. So I suggested we drop out and see if we could catch you. Is this a good time? We don't want to interrupt a masterpiece in the making."

Jessie was happy to see them and invited them in. When she said she would put some coffee on, they followed her into the kitchen, and were obviously delighted to see the new canvas on the easel and study the sketches for her next painting.

Then Dr. Birkenstall spotted the Mother Teresa painting at the end of the cabinets, and both women were momentarily transported by the sight. Delma said it was the finest portrait of Mother Teresa she had ever seen. Dr. Birkenstall was fascinated by the concept of it, with Mother Teresa receiving the sacrament in order to minister to the masses.

"I've always been a sacramentalist," she said. "The world as God's body, and all that."

"Oh, I do wish we could have this one at the Easter service too," said Delma. "Do you suppose there is any way we could?"

Jessie said she was sure they could work something out with Harold Moorefield, but he would have to be the one to say.

"I've seen how that young man looks at you," said Dr. Birkenstall. "Is there anything going on there?"

Jessie blushed and smiled.

"Shame on you, D. M.," said Delma. "That's none of your business. She always was a nosy one, Jessie. You'll have to forgive her."

"No nosier than you," rejoined Dr. Birkenstall. "You're just more polite than I am, that's all."

Delma laughed and said there might be some truth in that. What she needed to see Jessie about, she said, were some details about the service. The meeting would begin at seven a.m. and should conclude by eight-thirty; that way, people traveling from nearby towns could be back in their own churches in time for morning liturgies. Jessie should begin speaking about seven-forty-five and take approximately thirty minutes. There would be choral music both before and after she spoke. They would be happy to arrange transportation for her or she could arrange it herself, depending on her wishes.

Jessie said she would get there on her own.

There was one more thing, said Delma. She had been speaking with David Aldridge, president of the Gatlinburg Ministerial Association, about arranging for Jessie to meet with them sometime before Easter in order to disarm any of the ministers who had formed erroneous opinions of her or were opposed to having their members involved in the Women of the Tomb gathering. David had called a few days ago to say that the association's regular meeting date fell on Maundy Thursday. They had taken a vote at the last meeting about moving to a different day, but the majority of the ministers, members of churches that paid little attention to the liturgical calendar, had wanted to meet at the appointed time. David had also spoken with the program chairman, who had warmly received the idea of Jessie's meeting with them on that day.

Would she be available and willing to do this?

"I know it's an imposition, and I should have checked with you before going this far," said

Delma. "But I think it would be very helpful to the success of our Easter meeting, and, frankly, I would like to see it defuse some of the negative feelings a few of the ministers have gotten from somewhere."

Jessie looked around in time to see Dr. Birkenstall quickly removing her finger from her lips, as if she had been trying to shush Delma.

"Oh, I realize there is a lot of opposition to my paintings, and maybe to me myself," she said. She told them about the threats to the Moorefield Galleries and some of the things Harold and Chip had told her about the animosity she had provoked.

Delma shook her head. "I don't understand some people," she said. "Here we have in our midst the most remarkable person many of us have ever known, and they behave like—like horse's asses," she concluded, remembering Dr. Birkenstall's word the last time the three of them had been together.

"I'll meet with the ministers," said Jessie.

"Oh, thank you, dear," said Delma. "I think it will mean so much to the success of our meeting and to our future cooperation from the local churches. I'm sorry churches don't just naturally get behind anything good like this, but I suppose they're like the rest of the world; they have to be courted and cajoled and enticed to do the right thing.

"It's going to be such a great event! We already have word of forty-six busloads that are coming, some from as far away as Kingsport and Asheville. And station WATV in Knoxville has agreed to carry the whole program live, without any breaks for commercials. It's going to be a simply super affair."

"No thanks to some of the Christian bookstores," said Dr. Birkenstall.

Jessie looked from Dr. Birkenstall to Delma.

"Oh, honey," said Delma, "you know how some of these conservative Christians are. They don't think women have a place on God's earth except as housewives, TV hostesses, and singers. They just didn't want to give out our fliers, that's all. But they weren't all that way. Some were real sweet, and they've been dropping a flier in every package going out of their stores."

Before leaving, the two women studied the Mother Teresa portrait again. Dr. Birkenstall thought she recognized a couple of the faces in the background.

"That's what's so wonderful about your paintings, my dear," she said. "Or one of the things. They use the local, the real, the tangible, to create a sense of the presence beyond us all. They give us the feeling for incarnation."

Delma produced a small camera from her purse and asked if Jessie would permit her to make a snapshot of the sketches that would lie behind the next painting. "I could always remember that I was in on it at the beginning," she said with a slight giggle.

"If I know you," said Dr. Birkenstall, "then

you'll have to buy the painting so you can show everybody the 'before' and the 'after.'"

When the women had left, Jessie rinsed out the coffee pot, looked at the canvas on the easel, and said, "Come on, Columbo, let's go for a walk."

They climbed and climbed on one of the high mountain trails, until they rested at last on a ledge where they could see for miles and miles. It was a clear day, but a blue haze lay comfortably over the hills as far as the eye could see.

"Oh, *Baba*," said Jessie. "I need your strength for all of this. It isn't the sort of life I want. It's not who I am. But what you want is what matters. Help me to be faithful to that."

Columbo cocked his head backward at the sound of a squirrel darting through dry leaves and up a nearby oak tree. Then he too looked across the sky at the distant hills.

18

Jessie had finished most of *A Woman Evangelizing Her Town* but she wasn't satisfied with her sketch of the woman's face. As she often did when things were not flowing easily, she cleaned her brushes and went for a walk. It was time to pick up a few supplies in Cartersville. She and Columbo headed in that direction.

In some ways, she enjoyed being known by

the people of the little town; most of them now went out of their way to speak and be friendly. She bought a few groceries at the general store, stopped by the post office to mail some letters, and made a final stop at the feed store to purchase dog food for Columbo and sunflower seeds for the bird feeder. Denton Manning, the manager of the feed store, had promised to deliver the dog food if she bought a hundred pounds' worth at a time; Columbo had nearly finished the last hundred-pound bag.

When the woman and her dog turned into their driveway at home, they saw Chip Delaney's Rover parked at the house. Chip and a woman were walking around the yard, looking at some crocuses and jonquils in the first stages of blooming.

The woman was Chip's wife Margot, a pretty, strong-featured brunette in her mid-thirties. Her hair was curly and pulled up in a bun at the back. She was dressed in an old pair of jeans and a sweatshirt with a thigh-length car coat over them. Jessie liked her instantly.

"We thought if we came early enough, we could talk you into joining us for dinner," said Chip. "Margot's fixing country ham and gravy, and she made a Death-by-Chocolate cake this morning."

"Sounds wonderful," said Jessie.

"But I want to see your house first," said Margot. "Chip says it's a dollhouse."

Inside, Margot agreed with Chip's assessment. She was also fascinated by *Mother Teresa Receiving the Blessed Sacrament* and the emerging *A Woman Evangelizing Her Town.*

"I can't get over what you are doing for women's self-consciousness," she said. "I've seen your other paintings. I wish we could own one, but it's beyond our means right now. Maybe when Chip sells a motel or a restaurant. But not at the moment."

There was laughter in her voice as she talked. Whatever negative experiences they had had in the church, Jessie reflected, had not made her unhappy or bitter.

They were putting their coats on to leave when there was a knock at the door. It was Mike Pieratti and Dana Crouch, who had had the same idea as the Delaneys and wanted to take her to dinner.

"Hey, no sweat!" said Chip in his easy manner. "We have enough for all of us, don't we, Margot?"

"And anybody else we find along the way."

Mike looked at Dana. She smiled approval. He shrugged and said, "Sure."

"Settled and done," said Chip. "You can either follow us or leave your truck here, and we'll bring you back when we bring Jessie home."

They discussed it and decided to follow.

Chip and Margot's house was a chalet sitting high over Gatlinburg. As they wound this way and that on the narrow, crooked roads leading up to it, Jessie looked down at the early lights coming on all over town. They gave the appearance of a fairyland far below. The view from the sliding glass doors on the main floor of the chalet was even more enchanting. Jessie thanked *Baba* for making such a breathtaking world.

In the course of the dinner, Mike and Dana said they had come to see Jessie to make an announcement. They had decided not to wait till late spring to get married, but to do it two weeks hence, on St. Patrick's Day.

Jessie was delighted, and so were Chip and Margot.

"This calls for something special," said Chip. "Don't we have a bottle of champagne in the fridge, Margot?"

"You mean that one we meant to drink New Year's Eve and didn't because we both had the flu? I'm sure it's in there if you haven't touched it."

Glasses were produced, and they all laughed and clinked them together as Chip offered a toast.

"To life, to health, to happiness with the people we love."

"Hear! Hear!" said Mike, as he slipped his arm around Dana and kissed her on the cheek.

Then Mike proposed a toast. "To Jessie and our new friends."

When they had drunk that toast, Dana looked very serious for a moment. She stared briefly at Jessie with genuine affection. "To *Baba*," she said.

"To *Baba*," enjoined Chip and Mike.

Margot looked puzzled but drank the toast with them. Afterward, Chip explained to her who *Baba* was.

"I'll drink to that," she said.

The evening was full of merriment and planning. When Chip heard that Mike and Dana had not selected a minister to perform the ceremony, he volunteered. "I may not have a church," he said, "but I think my knot-tying is still valid."

"Oh, that's wonderful," said Dana. "And, Jessie, I hope you don't mind, but I've asked Jasmine to be my maid of honor. She was the one who first brought Mike and me together."

"I think that's wonderful," said Jessie. "I may even cry before the wedding."

When Mike and Dana talked about their plans to relocate to Atlanta so she could enter seminary in the fall, Margot's eyes lit up. "You're planning to go into the ministry?"

Margot admitted she had been feeling a similar inclination.

"I know it's crazy," she said. "We have one unemployed minister in the family, and I don't know why God would want another. But I've been feeling this way for six or eight months now, and the feeling just gets stronger and stronger."

She turned to Jessie. "You haven't helped, you know. All those paintings of great women in religion. I can't help thinking there's a revolution going on, and I don't want to miss it."

For the next two hours, she and Dana could talk of little else. They rehearsed their long-standing respect for the ministry, their earliest sense of anything resembling a calling, their fears about making it known lest they be met with ridicule, their certainty of the impracticality of the step Dana was taking, and yet their great excitement about the whole matter.

Finally Mike spoke up. "Jessie," he said, "you've been very quiet. It's clear you have had a strong influence on both these gals. What do you think about Dana's plans?"

Jessie was reaching down over Columbo, stroking his ears and neck. She sat upright again and looked at Mike.

"What do I think? I think each one of us has to do whatever *Baba* leads him or her to do. And sometimes we don't know that very far in advance. We're given one step at a time. That's the meaning of obedience. We take the one step that seems clear. Then another will be made clear. Isn't that how it has been with you, Chip?"

Chip was pouring an extra round of coffee. He put the pot back on the burner.

"Yes. At least, that's how it was. Right now there isn't a clear place in front of me. I seem to have been sidelined and have to wait to get back in the game."

"But isn't your present work also part of *Baba*'s plan? Everything is holy if it is what *Baba* wants—even working in a realty office."

"I suppose that's true. Somehow it just doesn't feel as important to me."

"Chip misses preaching," said Margot.

"And a few other things," he added. "But I suppose you're right, Jessie. It isn't whether we are doing what we prefer to do that matters. It's whether we're open to God—to *Baba*. And I think I am. I think I'm open to what Margot needs to do, and in a sense, that's a mission for both of us right now."

Margot leaned over and gave him a tender kiss on the cheek. Everyone sensed that it was a moment of significant emotion for them, as if they had reached a decision together without having been aware they were even trying to make it.

"Maybe we'll go to seminary together in the fall," she said to Dana.

"Wouldn't that be something!" said Dana.

"You know," said Jessie, "we may live at a modern turning point in the life of the church and the rule of God. Maybe something as important as the Constantinian era or the Reformation. Most of the old mainstream churches are diminishing. Congregations are dwindling, revenues are shrinking, programs are dying. Many churches that once flourished under male pastors can no longer afford full-time ministers; most male pastors cannot function on half a salary. Because of this, some of those same churches are now being forced to employ female pastors. When the practice becomes really widespread, the whole tone and theology of the church will be altered. More feminine perceptions of the spiritual life will be exalted, and everything will change."

"My brother-in-law is a priest," said Mike, "and he says there will be female priests by the end of the century. That's only a few years away."

"If they'll let us be married," laughed Margot, "maybe Dana and I will become priests."

"I don't think I would mind having a female pastor," said Chip. "Most of the women I was in seminary with outshone the men."

"I bet they were better at pastoral care," said Margot.

"Would you believe preaching and everything else?" asked Chip.

"It isn't really a matter of who's better at anything," said Jessie. "It's a matter of wholeness. Male and female are two halves of the same whole. God gave us to each other to complement one another, to supply one another's lack. And if the church is finally getting around to recognizing this, we should all be happy about it."

"Agreed," said Dana. "I'm happy about it."

"Me too, Reverend," said Mike, placing a big hairy hand over hers.

The following morning, Jessie completed her sketch of the woman evangelizing her town. She looked almost exactly like Margot Delaney.

19

The old-timers in the mountains had a saying that the number of snows in the winter would equal the number of fogs the previous summer. It was the consensus of most of those who counted that there had been sixteen fogs in the last summer, and thus far there had been only eight snows. But the two snows that fell in mid-March helped to redress the balance. Neither was very deep, but together they contributed to the snowpack at the higher elevations that would keep the mountains cool until summer and increase the volume of water cascading down the rocky streambeds until well into the month of August.

Columbo liked to go hiking with Jessie when there was fresh snow on the ground. It seemed to sharpen his sense of smell, and he loved to bound through the trees, following the spores of rabbits, squirrels, and other furry creatures. Once he caught a big, fat opossum and toyed with it for several minutes while the wily animal lay as still as a rag. Columbo obviously intended it no harm, and, when he could not nudge the recalcitrant faker into playing with him, retreated with an air of sad resignation.

The morning after the second snow, Jessie had just completed her painting of the burial of Jesus. Tradition held that two wealthy men, Joseph and Nicodemus, members of the Jewish ruling class, had obtained the body of the dead man and prepared it for burial. But Jessie knew that several of the women followers of Jesus were never far from his side, and that they had to have been present with Joseph and Nicodemus to perform the ablutions and perfume the body before entombment. How else did they know precisely where to go before daybreak on the day of Resurrection?

The painting, called *Faithful to the End,* showed one of the women cradling the head of Jesus in her lap and weeping as she bathed the face. Another, perhaps Mary Magdalene, who had once bathed his feet in perfume and wiped them with her hair, had one of his feet in her lap as she knelt plaintively, her long hair falling over her face and touching his leg. The two men were in the foreground, their backs to the viewer as they too cooperated in the ritual cleansing. A third woman, possibly Jesus's mother, was opposite them, her beautiful but sorrowful face bowed, yet plainly visible, as she touched her forehead in what Jessie suggested was the first-ever signing of the cross.

Those who knew them might have seen a resemblance to Dana in one of the women and to Jessie's Connecticut friend Phyllis in another. And as for the mother figure in the center, Jessie knew it had been created in the image of Rowena Moorefield as a younger woman, much like the photograph she had seen on the table by her bed the night she slept at Harold and Rowena's house.

This particular painting seemed to take a heavy toll on Jessie's energies. She felt a profound sorrow as she was painting it, a sorrow whose locus and perimeters were not exactly fixed. It seemed to be a sorrow for many things—for the jealousy and hatred in the world that lead to crucifixions, for mothers who hurt for their children, for idealists who get crushed by their enemies, for men and women who must deal in the realities of politics and economics, for women whose hearts are broken by sickness and death and injustice, for times when the whole world seems to be in the throes of war and confusion, for peoples too backward to provide for their own health and nourishment in eras of drought and scarcity. Occasionally Jessie felt tears sliding down her cheeks and would have to stop and wipe her face before continuing to paint.

Normally when she finished a painting she would experience a great release, as if a burden had been lifted and she was free to breathe and stretch again. This time it was different. The burden continued to rest on her, to be oppressive. She slept poorly the following night, and felt restless, as if the entire experience were a premonition of something dark and evil.

She was glad, therefore, to wake up to bright sunshine the morning after the snowfall, and to have the mountains to walk in. As soon as she and Columbo had eaten and she had spent a few minutes at her correspondence, she donned her boots and coat and the two of them struck out into the hills, greeting the shining blanket of flakes with eager spirits.

They climbed steadily for an hour or more, stopping at last to sit by a tumbling stream and admire the patterns of ice and snow at the edges and in the pools where the water was not moving. Rhododendron bushes were bent into arches by the snow on them, and it was difficult to imagine that in a few weeks' time they would blaze forth with beauty and color. The cloudless sky overhead was deepest azure, and the whole world seemed to breathe an air of purity and renewal.

Jessie loosened her scarf and coat and sprawled back on a large flat boulder, her face and neck open to the healing rays of the sun. She felt lazy and happy to be there, as if *Baba* were tending to all her needs, both physical and mental.

Columbo wandered off, putting his big paws down in the snow as carelessly as if it were cotton, sniffing at this trail and that in a desultory fashion, without any obvious intention of finding anything.

Half an hour went by, and Jessie was feeling wonderfully restored. She found herself thinking of her next painting. There were two medieval women on her mind, Catherine of Siena and Teresa of Avila. They were both mystics, very devout and dedicated to Christ, and the Roman Catholic Church had honored them in 1970 by naming them the first women Doctors of the Church. Catherine had linked the life of devotion and the life of service, and had once contracted the plague while treating plague-stricken patients. She had also spent much of her energy trying to reunify the Catholic Church and rebuild the nation of Italy. Teresa had turned her deep mystical experiences toward monastic reform, and had established numerous Carmelite convents and monasteries. Both women had run into considerable opposition to their activities from male prelates who taught that women should occupy only subservient places in the church.

What if she pictured the two women together, with a host of suspicious, evil-looking men watching them from the background? They lived a century apart, Catherine in fourteenth-century Italy and Teresa in fifteenth-century Spain, but their influence on their times and subsequent centuries was enormous.

Her reveries were suddenly interrupted by the sound of Columbo's throaty barking. Instantly alert, she sat up to listen for the direction of the sound. Dropping off the rock, she raced through the trees, down a steep incline, up the other side, and around a hill. From there she could tell that the barking was just on the other side of another hill.

When she reached the other side, she found a dell, a hollowed space about sixty feet wide cupped between two ridges. Columbo was poised at the perimeter of the space, his attention fully directed at the center. There, reared up on its back legs so that it looked to be seven or eight feet tall, was a great black bear.

"Whoa!" said Jessie when she saw the bear. "So this is what all the commotion is about. Is this the friend who gave you the shellacking before, old fellow? You seem to recognize her."

Columbo seemed reassured by Jessie's presence, but he did not advance on the bear.

"Now, now," said Jessie, patting his head and stroking his neck. "That's enough. You've sounded your warning."

Columbo stopped barking and sat hesitantly in the snow. Once, he seemed ready to leap up and begin the hullaballoo again. Then he relaxed all over and lay down, his forelegs straight in the snow before him, his head erect. He ducked his head toward his paws two or three times, made a slight whining noise, and then was quiet.

The bear too relaxed, dropping to all four paws, walking around in a circle for a minute, then collapsing backwards onto her hind quarters and merely sitting there, looking at Jessie and Columbo.

"Good bear," said Jessie, approaching the huge animal. "You want to be friends, don't you?"

She slowly walked up to the bear with her hand extended, speaking calmly and soothingly as she approached. The bear continued to loll on her backside, rolling her head slightly from left to right.

"Good girl," said Jessie, "good girl."

Then she was standing beside the bear and stroking the fur of her head. The bear made a deep, gurgling noise in her throat that passed for a sigh of contentment.

"See, Columbo," Jessie said, "she's a good bear. She doesn't want to hurt you again."

Columbo lowered his head to his paws, raised it, lowered it again, shuffled a moment in the snow, and finally rose and approached stealthily in their direction.

When he was four or five feet away, he whimpered and lay down again in the snow.

Jessie went on rubbing the bear a minute longer. Then the bear, as if she had only remembered an appointment she had to keep, turned suddenly away, pivoting on her backside, and started off into the woods.

Jessie watched as Columbo lay still, then, when the bear had disappeared in a grove of cedar trees, cautiously arose and began to sniff in the great tracks left in the snow.

Columbo had obviously had enough excitement for one day. As Jessie began the descent home, he trailed meekly a few feet behind her, no longer bounding through the snow to ferret out squirrels and woodchucks. Once, they startled a shrew that had left its lair in search of food it had probably cached a few yards away. It leapt in little arcs across the path in front of them, emitting a shrill, panicky noise as it dove in and out of the snow. Columbo didn't even display an interest in it, but passed by as indifferently as if it were some trick he had fallen for a dozen times before.

"Oh *Baba*, *Baba*," Jessie was praying. "If only your time would fully come, and we could all get along in peace and gentleness for the rest of the ages, the way you want us to. I long for the day when the lion will lie down with the lamb and the bear will eat straw with the ox, when Indian and Chinese and Balkan and Mexican will agree, when male and female, young and old, heterosexual and homosexual, liberal and conservative, fast and slow, blind and sighted, gifted and non-gifted, rich and poor will all come together in affection and joy, happy to share life on the planet and worship you together forever and ever. If only our eyes were on you, and not on ourselves, we would see only our likenesses and not our differences, we would honor one another for the image of you that we see in one another, instead of fighting and hurting and killing one another because we hate and fear anything not like ourselves. Oh, do hurry, *Baba*. Hurry, hurry, hurry."

20

It was a challenge for Jessie to combine the portraits of Catherine of Siena and Teresa of Avila in the same picture. Both were saintly women of great devotion to Christ. How could she show that without making one more attractive than the other? And how could she relate them to each another so that the picture was more than a mere double portrait? She thought of Mary and Elizabeth meeting before the births of their sons. Perhaps that was how Catherine and Teresa would greet one another, with a sense of transcendent joy because they were caught up in God's approaching rule.

Her models for the women's faces were two beautiful, mature women she had seen at Rymer's Chapel. Apparently they served together on the Chancel Guild, for when she first noticed them, they were arranging flowers in a large vase before the pulpit. They laughed and chatted as they tried different flowers and ferns, sometimes leaving them and sometimes removing them, until they had made a masterpiece of the kind one often identifies with cathedrals in Great Britain.

Jessie had thought of giving them white hair and making them somewhat elderly. But when she went to the library to do some research, she learned that Catherine was only thirty-three when she died, and Teresa sixty-seven. So she made Catherine dark-headed and gave Teresa some gray hair. They might even have been mother and daughter.

The important thing in both portraits was the translucence of the skin and the animation of the eyes. She wanted to give them the kind of saintly pallor that would come from spending a lot of time in an inner room in prayer, and yet make the eyes dance with the vivacity of lively faith.

The highly spiritual quality of the women formed a ready contrast with the nefarious appearance of the men staring at them from the background. The men's costumes marked them for fourteenth- and fifteenth-century prelates, including some bishops, monsignors, and cardinals. But their faces, dark and glowering, actually came from some of those Jessie had seen in local stores and churches.

She called the painting *Two Women of Spirit*. It was not one of her favorites, she had to admit. Artists do prefer some of their works to others. Yet she believed it would serve some purpose in the corpus of her work, and knew that *Baba* had given her the inspiration for it as for the others in her repertory that she enjoyed more.

Perhaps, she thought, it would lead to other double paintings of a historical nature in which she would bring together women who lived in different times and places, yet represented similar emphases or developments in the life of faith. Her mind went to Florence Nightingale and Clara Barton, women whose understanding of *Baba*'s tender care led them to the field of nursing. Did anyone today sufficiently appreciate, she wondered, the profound differences these two women had made in the care of the sick, the physically impaired, and the mentally ill throughout the world?

Her inventive mind leapt to another possibility, a triptych featuring Anne Frank, Corrie ten Boom, and Sabina Wurmbrand, three of the most notable women who suffered under the demonic Nazi regime in World War Two and whose heroic lives of faith and courage had since inspired millions of people. There were problems with such a canvas, of course. Anne Frank had died as a young girl, while Corrie and Sabina not only lived long and useful lives but also wrote and spoke with dramatic effect all over the world. How would she handle this? Perhaps she could depict Anne in an ethereal setting and show Corrie and Sabina moving toward her, hands extended in greeting, and call it *Corrie ten Boom and Sabina Wurmbrand Meet Anne Frank.*

Jessie was grateful to *Baba* for the gift of her imagination and the way it danced and pirouetted through memories, facts, and possibilities. She regarded the ability to combine hitherto discrete and unrelated materials into new and sometimes dazzling unities as one of the rarest forms of *Baba*'s grace. Only human beings, she believed, ever developed this talent to an amazing degree, and it related therefore, more than almost any other sign of intelligence or agility, to angels and purely spiritual beings.

By the time she had completed the Corrie painting, the snow had melted from everywhere except the northern sides of the mountains, where the sun didn't reach during the short days of winter, and the ravines and gullies, where it had drifted to a depth of up to two or three feet. Most Tennessee snows did not last very long because of the temperatures, which usually climbed into the thirties and forties, and sometimes the fifties, within a few days of a storm. And now that spring had virtually begun in the southern United States, no new snow and ice would lie on the ground more than two or three days.

As she and Columbo tramped through the forest, Jessie began to see crocuses, wild buttercups, and trillium blooming in the meadows and sunnier locations. From the thickening pods on the tulip trees, redbuds, and dogwoods, it was obvious that they were preparing to blossom in the near future. Jessie felt a wild surge of expectancy and excitement. She had heard about the magic of springtime in the Smokies. Now she would have a chance to see it.

She was filled with this mood of wonder and delight when she carried the Corrie painting into Gatlinburg to deliver it to Harold and Rowena, for the hillsides along the mountain roadway were beginning to bloom with wildflowers and the sugar maples were budding in preparation for their spring foliage.

Now that she was well-known in the area, she usually had invitations to ride with people who stopped their cars and trucks, but she often preferred to walk and enjoy the scenery. Columbo liked walking better too, for he explored every inch of territory along the way, plunging youthfully up and down steep banks, through rollicking creeks, and in and out of the edges of forest land that crept up to the road between farms and houses.

It seemed unlikely to Jessie that anything could spoil such a beautiful day; the temperature had risen into the forties, the sky was picture-blue with a few fluffy, cumulus clouds floating overhead; every few hundred feet she heard a mockingbird trilling its varied menu of tunes. But some presentiment, some sense of foreboding, crossed her mind like a shadow when she was two or three blocks from the gallery. At first she was disinclined to pay attention to it, thinking it was a momentary mood swing. By the time she turned a corner and saw the gallery, though, she was mentally prepared for the sight that greeted her.

The entire front of the studio, constructed of batten-board Western cedar, was charred and burned. There were large sheets of plywood where the plate glass windows had been; there were even signs of charring on the sidewalk in front.

As the partially destroyed but obviously repaired front doors were standing open, she looked inside. Harold was there, talking with two other men. He looked up as she stepped through the doorway, her painting still under her arm.

"Harold, what happened?"

"Oh, Jess..."

The two men said they would get back to him later and excused themselves. "What happened?" she asked again.

She could see that the gallery was empty. The walls were bare except for the hooks where paintings had hung. There was still an odor of smoke and charred wood, but, with the exception of some burned areas near the front of the room, there appeared to be little structural damage.

"Fire."

"Rowena! Is she all right?"

"Oh yes. She's fine. We weren't here when it happened. Somebody started it in the early morning, about one-thirty last night. Threw a can of gasoline against the doors there. Lucky for us, the night watchman for this area came along a split second after they'd done it. He saw two men running down the alley there. They had a truck and roared away. He raised the fire department; they came with extinguishers and got it under control in a hurry.

"Somebody called me. By the time I got over here, they'd carried out all the paintings and stored them over in Jim Larson's place across the way."

Jessie's eyes filled with tears.

"Oh, Harold, I'm so sorry. I know it was because of me."

"Hush," he said, pulling her against him. "We don't know why it was. It was senseless. Mean and senseless."

"I know," she said. "I know it was because of me."

"No, no, no." He rubbed her head and rocked gently with her in his arms.

Columbo, who had sat obediently outside the door, made a slight whining noise.

"Oh, Columbo boy," said Harold, patting his leg. "Come on in. It's okay."

The great dog trotted inside and lay down next to where they stood.

A firebombing was big news in a little town like Gatlinburg. Harold told Jessie that two television crews from Knoxville had already been by that morning. They photographed the building and interviewed him and the chief of police, who had been much in evidence until shortly before noon, giving directions to two or three detectives working on the case and to the men who came to board up the front of the gallery. One of the crews, with a more enterprising reporter than the other, had asked Harold about Jessie and the possible relationship of the bombing to controversies over her paintings. Harold had been obviously reluctant to pursue that line of thinking, but the persistent reporter had nevertheless led his photographers over to Jim Larson's souvenir shop and asked him about Jessie's paintings. Mr. Larson was very cooperative, thinking Harold had sent them over, and let them videotape the paintings in his storeroom, including one of the famous *Women in*

Religion works, which happened to be in the front of one of the stacks.

That evening Jessie and the firebombing were lead stories for both television news programs, and every thirty minutes a ten-second ad promised exclusive coverage of "the latest in the Jessie controversy" on the ten-o'clock news.

The following morning, people all over the United States heard about the fire on ABC, CBS, NBC, and CNN, and saw clips of Harold and the gutted front wall of the Moorefield Galleries where "the famous Jessie paintings" hung. The owner of two of Jessie's works, a Dr. D. M. Birkenstall, said CNN, had insured each of them for a hundred thousand dollars. Police were investigating the arson, but as yet had no significant clues. The night watchman who had witnessed the early seconds of the conflagration had not seen the faces of the arsonists. It was speculated that the incident was somehow related to the general controversy surrounding Jessie and her paintings, which depicted women in leadership roles in the development of the Judeo-Christian faith.

"That does it!" exclaimed Roxie when she and Joan were watching the news as they drank their morning coffee. "That girl needs us, Joanie."

"You're right," said Joan, indignation welling up like a heatwave in her heart. "She sure does."

21

Jessie did not feel like painting for three or four days after the fire. Her spirit was troubled by the harm she worried that she had brought to Harold and Rowena. They were such good, innocent people. Why did they have to be hurt by whatever forces were arrayed against her? Why were any innocent people ever hurt by the evil around them—by wars, by drunken drivers, by drug-crazed madmen, by the machinations of the greedy and the power hungry?

Probably she could not have painted if she wanted to, because there was a constant stream of visitors to her door. There were reporters and camera crews from all over; salespeople wanting to sell her insurance, alarm systems, and physical protection; people who were simply curious and wanted to meet her; religious people with interpretations of why she and her friends were marked for punishment; friends and well-wishers seeking to console and support her.

She was patient with all of them, even the salespeople and religious fanatics, but after a day of it she was exhausted in spirit and knew she had to get away from it. Early the next morning, when fog still hung upon the mountains and dripped from the eaves of the house and from the broader foliage of trees and bushes, she slipped out the back door with her sleeping bag and a knapsack of supplies, Columbo at her side, and headed into the mountains.

At first she gave herself the luxury of not trying to pray, of merely walking and climbing and stretching, of feeling the good pull of her muscles and tendons as she strove against the mountains, rising higher and higher. It was healing, for the time being, to live only in the realm of the physical, to give the body its rein and let it go, oblivious of mind and spirit. She was physically in good condition, so that she was able to walk for an hour or more without getting tired. But then she began to feel the shortness of breath, the slight weakness in the limbs, the growing exhaustion that comes to even the most experienced climbers, and she continued on, fighting against the enveloping inertia, happy to be wearing herself down.

At last she dropped her bedroll and knapsack and collapsed on an outcrop of granite. The sun had long since dispersed the fog and she could feel the perspiration under her jacket. Loosening it in the front, she sprawled back, propped on her arms, and turned her face upward to the light and heat.

Then, as Columbo explored the area around her, sniffing for spores and stopping to watch a noisy bee flying drunkenly from blossom to blossom, she began to pray.

She was prepared for anything that happened to her, she told *Baba*, but why must her friends be hurt? It made her feel awful, that she was the instrument of their pain and discomfort. Wouldn't *Baba* please, please cast a shield around them and see that no harm came to any of them?

For an hour or more, she prayed for her many friends, calling up images of them individually or in pairs or in family groupings, and holding them before *Baba* as she asked for particular blessings in their lives. She thought of Carol and Julia, who were in New York visiting Carol's mother and would soon be coming to see her; she recalled Ray and Rachel, and thanked *Baba* for the way they had given Carol a home and helped to transform her life.

She remembered the man named Sam she had met on the bus to Charlottesville, going to visit his daughter Billie. She had had a letter from Sam after he had seen the television segment about her first paintings and had written in care of General Delivery in Gatlinburg. By that time, the post office clerks knew her well enough to direct the letter to Moorefield Galleries, where Harold and Rowena often received mail for her.

Sam told her how it had been just as she said on the bus. When he got to the hospital, Billie was already feeling good and pestering the nurses to give her some solid food. The doctors were all astonished at her recovery. They never had figured out what was wrong with her, Sam said, and they were equally puzzled by the sudden remission. He was mighty grateful, he said, for Jessie's prayers and confidence. He was convinced that was the reason his dear little girl had gotten better so fast.

Jessie prayed for Sam and Billie and Billie's husband Howard.

Then she interceded for dozens of people she had met only through their letters and prayer requests in recent weeks—some with debilitating diseases like arthritis and cancer and multiple sclerosis, some with financial problems, some with great disappointments in life, some in difficult family situations. It did not matter that she had never seen them in person or even heard their voices on the telephone. She felt a true oneness with them in *Baba*, and was confident that *Baba* would help and encourage them.

By the end of the first day in the mountains, she was feeling relaxed and happy, and that night as she ate some bread and drank a carton of juice she had brought along, she was lifting prayers of gratitude to *Baba* for the wondrous complexity of life and human emotions. Columbo stood beside her, devouring a tin of dry dogfood she had put out for him; she stroked his beautiful coat, thinking how grateful she was for him as well.

For two more days, she and Columbo strode through the forests, stopping to drink at pure mountain streams, admiring new growth and promises of growth on plants that had stood dormant through the winter, and breathing deeply in the cool, fresh air. Jessie talked or made clucking noises to curious squirrels and rabbits and birds; Columbo chased an occasional animal back to its lair as if it were a duty he was expected to perform.

By the time they traced their way back down the mountainsides, Jessie had clarified in her mind what her next painting would be. She had initially thought of making one about Deborah, the prophetess in the Old Testament book of Judges, or Jael, the celebrated Jewish housewife who took the life of Sisera, commander of the Canaanite armies, with a hammer and a tent stake. But as she prayed and meditated, it became clear to her that *Baba* had another remarkable woman for her to treat now, the controversial Anne Hutchinson, who was banished from the Massachusetts Bay Colony in 1638 and massacred by Indians five years later. She didn't remember many details from Ms. Hutchinson's life, but she would do the necessary research in the Gatlinburg library before starting the painting. For now, she could merely train her unconscious mind on the subject and let it be doing its own kind of homework.

It was nearly dark when the two of them approached the clearing behind the schoolhouse. When they did, Jessie noticed smoke coming from the chimney. Then, as they entered the backyard, she saw that the lights were on. Someone was in the house. She stopped abruptly. Columbo, sensing her alarm, barked.

Jessie's eyes darted quickly to the side yard where the driveway terminated. She could hardly believe what she saw. There in the near darkness sat the familiar form of an old blue Volvo.

At precisely that moment the back door burst open and a voice called out, "Jessie!"

"Joan!"

The two of them rushed squealing into each other's arms as Columbo stood looking on.

"What in the world are you doing here?" asked Jessie.

"We're all here. Rox and Phyllis are inside."

"I can't believe it!"

"We thought we'd surprise you."

"You did that, all right. But how did you get in?"

"You know how handy Roxie is with a credit card."

"Oh golly, it's so good to see you."

They hugged and kissed again.

"Hmmm," Jessie sniffed the air as they stepped inside. "Somebody's cooking."

"Darn right," said the tall blonde at the stove. "Our hostess wasn't home, so somebody had to do it."

"Oh, Roxie!" said Jessie, walking into another embrace.

"Me too," said a voice from the doorway.

"And Phyllis," she said, disengaging from Roxie's arms to walk into Phyllis's. "Oh, you girls! I can't believe it. I'm so happy to see you."

"These steaks are about ready," said Roxie. "Phyl, did you get that wine open?"

"It's on the table."

"Then let's eat. We can talk over food."

"I think Jessie needs to," said Phyllis. "She feels thin as a rail to me, even with that coat on."

"No fair," said Jessie. "I haven't eaten all day."

Soon they were all eating, drinking, laughing, talking at the same time. Jessie answered questions about how she'd found such a wonderful house, about how she'd gotten into the painting deal, about Columbo and Harold and Rowena and all her new friends. Then, as things reached a more serious level, Roxie admitted that they had come south after hearing about the fire at the gallery. "We figured you needed some world-class protection," she said, "so here we are."

"But what about your jobs?!" Jessie asked. "I thought Joan had used all her vacation time for the next seventy-two years."

Joan looked down, guiltily.

"You didn't quit? Not your job at the commissary?!"

More looking down.

"Joan!"

"I got a new boss. I couldn't stand her. It's bad enough to work for a man you don't like — case in point, the last two years — but when they replace him with a woman you can't stand... Besides, Jess, it was time for me to get an outdoor job. I was getting a definite pallor in that place."

"What about Phyllis? You didn't quit your job too?"

Phyllis gave her head a little flip to the side, like a shrug. "It wasn't a very good job. I'd been promising myself to look for something better."

"I've still got my oar in at the bank, if that's any consolation to you," said Roxie. "Though I don't know why I bother. The last three promotions have gone to other employees with half my qualifications."

Phyllis looked quietly at Jessie. "Boy, you've really hit the big time, haven't you, hon? Imagine! A hundred thousand bucks a picture."

"And if I know Jess," said Joan, "she's giving the things away for free."

"What're they up to?" asked Roxie. "Trying to scare you off, or to hurt this Harold whatziz-name you're involved with?"

"I honestly don't know, Rox. I wish I could assign a particular reason to it, but I can't. It seems to be bigger than that—like there's something sinister in the air that keeps a lot of people stirred up, and some of them just let it get out of hand and do something like this." She shook her head. "Poor Harold. They nearly ruined his gallery. He's lost at least a week of sales, and had all the extra trouble to boot."

"Some men can't stand women," observed Phyllis.

"Or stand them getting any credit for anything," said Joan.

"But our Jess is so innocent," said Phyllis.

"Darn right," said Roxie, "and that's probably

one reason she's always getting in trouble. You know the old saying, 'Fools rush in.'" She tipped the wine bottle over her glass and let the last three drops run out. "But never fear, Jess. The troops are here. You'll sleep safely tonight."

"Speaking of which," said Phyllis, stifling a yawn.

"We left after work last night and drove straight through," said Joan, "except for a coupla hours at a roadside stop in Virginia."

The girls assured Jessie they didn't want to be a burden to her or interfere with her work. They had brought their sleeping bags and would spend the one night with her, but would go out the next day and find a place of their own. No, they wouldn't hear of staying there, but they would be close by, where they could keep an eye on her and lend support whenever she needed it.

Columbo was restless at first, having so many people in the house. But by the time the lights were out and all of them were stretched out on sleeping bags before the dying fire in the living room—Jessie refused to use the bed if they all slept on the floor—he had taken up with Joan and went to sleep peacefully with his head on her arm.

Jessie lay a long time watching the faint light and shadows in the room and listening to the occasional popping of an ember. She was happy to be reunited with her friends, for she loved them dearly. But she also felt a responsibility for their safety; she was concerned lest they had entered a matrix of danger by coming to her. She prayed earnestly that *Baba* would hold them too within the shield she had asked for Harold and Rowena.

22

Mike and Dana's wedding was the biggest affair Mike's restaurant had ever seen, bigger even than a victory celebration after a University of Tennessee football game. Many of Mike's regular customers were there, plus all of Dana's friends, many of Jasmine's friends from the university, Jessie and her friends who had recently arrived from the North, and of course Chip, the officiating minister, and his wife Margot, whose friendship with Dana had blossomed in the short time that had elapsed since they met. It was Margot, in fact, who accompanied Dana to select a wedding dress and who personally took her silk shoes to be dyed to match the dress.

Mike, Dana, Jasmine, and two other employees had worked for three days making lasagna, baking cakes, and getting everything ready for the big party. Mike had hired a combo; they arrived at three o'clock to set up their mikes and speakers and adjust their sound levels. By four o'clock, when the party was to begin, Mike had sweated through his tux shirt and was still hanging big green clovers around the room and frantically giving directions to the extra waiters he had employed.

By the time Jessie and her friends arrived in the old blue Volvo, the party was in full swing, with the band playing, the beer flowing, waiters coming out of the kitchen on the run with pizza and lasagna. People crowded into booths and around tables or were standing in the available floor space, while here and there a brave couple was attempting to dance.

"Glad I didn't wear my best shoes," said Roxie. "This looks like a real toe-scuffer."

A few minutes later, Mike appeared in a doorway, gave a signal to the bandleader, and the band played a fanfare as he and Dana came through the crowd hand-in-hand, followed by Jasmine in a soft pink, ankle-length dress, then a diminutive dark-haired girl carrying a tiny basket of flowers, and finally Chip Delaney, dressed in a dark suit and carrying a small black book.

"Oh look!" said Jessie. "That's Michelle, Mike's granddaughter. That must be her mother over there, the pretty one Michelle just smiled at."

The talking and clapping ceased when Chip lifted his hand, and he began the simple service, concluding with the traditional words of union and a prayer for the newly married couple. Mike was so nervous that he choked while saying his vow and almost didn't gain control again. But he found his voice the minute it was over and said, "We're glad you could all come. This is the happiest moment of my life. Now eat, drink, and be merry, because tomorrow you go back to paying for everything just like usual!"

There was a round of applause as the band began playing again. Mike gave Dana another kiss, this one longer and more serious than the one he had given her during the service. He and Dana circulated through the room during the next hour, introducing Michelle, whom Mike carried on his arm, and occasionally his daughter Janice and her husband Donovan, if they were within reach, to all their guests.

When they came to Jessie and her friends, Michelle and Jessie took such an immediate liking to each other that Michelle spent the remainder of the evening at Jessie's side.

"Who's the good-looking guy over by the counter?" Phyllis asked Mike.

"Who?" asked Mike, looking in that direction. "Him? That's my brother Steve. He's a taxi driver in Cincinnati. Drove down for the big event."

"Married?"

"Nah. Not any more. His wife Jeannine took him to the cleaners two years ago. Just like my first wife did me."

"Excuse me," said Phyllis, edging her way in the general direction of the bar. "See you all later."

Like all brides, Dana was radiant in her off-white, ankle-length taffeta dress. Jessie gave her a big hug and told her how happy she was for her. "Jess, hon," she said, "if it weren't for you, I doubt if I would have had the courage to do this."

"Nonsense," said Jessie. "*Baba* intended you for each other all along."

"Amen to that," said Mike. "I'll drink to that, soon as I get another glass of beer. Excuse me, everybody. Can I bring anyone else a glass?"

Roxie said yes, she could use another.

Mike came back in a minute with his face clouded by disappointment.

"What's wrong, honey?" asked Dana.

"That damn yo-yo who was supposed to bring the extra kegs of beer—pardon my French, ladies—completely forgot to do it. We're already outa beer, and the party isn't half over."

"Can't you call the distributor and have some more sent over?" asked Dana.

"No way. Not at this hour. Wait'll I see that slug. I'll nail him to the back of his own truck!"

"Oh, Mike," said Jessie, "don't let that spoil your whole wedding. I'm sure there's something we can do. Where do you keep the kegs, back there in the kitchen?"

"No, in the storeroom behind it."

"Come on, Michelle," said Jessie, leading her by the hand. Let's go see what Granddaddy's problem is, shall we?"

"Are those the empty beer kegs?" she asked a waiter who rushed into the storeroom for more napkins. "They seem to have something in them."

"Maybe somebody put water in them," he

said. "We're out of beer."

"It smells like beer to me," she said. "Would you bring me a glass?"

Presently the waiter returned with the glass, obviously in a tremendous hurry and annoyed at having to run a fool's errand.

"How do you work this?" Jessie asked, touching the spigot.

"Simple, lady. You just turn it with your glass under here. Hey! You're right! That is beer. Mike said we was all out. Hey, Mike!" He began shouting for Mike before he was even well into the kitchen.

"I can't believe it," said Mike when he had come to the storeroom to see for himself. "These others are full of beer too. And it's not that weak stuff they usually send. It's lager, better'n I paid for. Hey, get these out front! Drink up, everybody! This party's not over by a long shot!"

It seemed to Jessie that the more beer that flowed, the louder the party grew. She was ordinarily inclined to a quiet, meditative way of life. Nothing suited her more than being alone in her studio painting, with only the sounds of Columbo's padding over to take a drink from his water bowl, the popping of the fire in the next room, and the piping and trilling of birds outside her door. But she also loved parties like this one, especially if people were genuinely enjoying themselves, as the guests at Mike and Dana's wedding were.

Phyllis, she noticed, had spent most of the evening with Mike's brother Steve. She had seen them dancing several times, the last time cheek-to-cheek. Things are moving along swiftly, she thought.

About eight o'clock, Mike had the drummer do a roll to get everyone's attention.

"Okay, listen up. It's time for Dana and me to blow this joint. That means it's also time for you-know-what. So line up, all you bachelor types, while I deprive my wife of her garter."

There was some tugging and shoving and cajoling around the room, and soon half a dozen unmarried men, ranging in age from a university student about twenty years old to an elderly, bald-headed man whose equally elderly lady friend insisted he be in the lineup, had gathered at one side of the room. Dana stood on a table, and Mike gingerly removed her garter to a chorus of catcalls and whistles from the crowd and an impromptu burlesque tune from the band. With his back to the men, Mike held a hand over his eyes and hurled the garter over his shoulder. It flew unerringly into the hands of Steve Pieratti, who held it aloft like a hard-won trophy.

Descending from the table, Dana called for all the unmarried women to line up, including Michelle. Then, saying *one-two-three,* she tossed her bridal bouquet in their direction. It struck the ceiling in flight and cascaded down into Jasmine's waiting hands. She blushed and stammered that she did not even have a steady boyfriend, but several male voices called out that they would be glad to take care of that.

While Margot was helping Dana change into a more comfortable traveling dress—her wedding dress had a large bow in the back—Mike said to Jessie, "I've been thinking about that beer. There's no way those kegs had beer in them when I looked at them. I lifted every one and tested it before stacking them against the wall."

"Maybe the delivery man came after all," she said, "after you looked and before Michelle and I went back there."

"No chance. That guy never works after four o'clock. And besides, I have the only key to the padlock on that door."

Jessie merely raised her eyebrows and shrugged her shoulders. Mike regarded her knowingly.

"Will miracles never cease?" he said.

Joan and Jasmine passed by them, handing out paper flowers filled with rice to throw at the newlyweds as they left the restaurant.

"Dana told me where you're going on your honeymoon," said Jasmine. "She's thrilled to death."

"Ah, yeah, she's never been to Savannah. Neither have I, come to think of it."

"I know it will be beautiful, and you'll have a wonderful time together."

"Yeah, thanks."

Just then Dana reentered the room, and the band struck up "Sentimental Journey." There was a flurry of hugging and kissing and leave-taking. Then the guests formed a double line outside the restaurant and hurled rice all over the couple as they emerged and climbed into the white limousine Mike had rented to take them to a local hotel for the evening.

"Good-bye, everyone. And thank you," yelled Dana as the limousine pulled away from the curb.

"Bless them, *Baba*," Jessie said under her breath. "They deserve it."

23

It had taken three days of Chip's full-time attention, but Roxie, Joan, and Phyllis had final-ly found an attractive condominium they could sublet for a few months with an option to buy if they later decided to do so. Located on Airport Road in Gatlinburg, a hilly street that never really led to a real airport, the condo backed up to one of the rocky creeks for which the town was famous. It had a screened-in porch that was actually cantilevered over the stream.

Joan said she could sit out there for hours at a time, and just might start penning the account of Jessie's life she had always wanted to write.

The condo belonged to an elderly couple from Georgia who moved into it as a retirement home several months earlier. Unfortunately, the husband had a heart attack and a stroke from which he never fully recovered, and was now permanently confined to a nursing home in Knoxville. His wife, a quick-witted, round-faced little woman with neat, curly hair, said she was exhausted from running back and forth to Knoxville every day and had decided to take a small apartment there. She was happy to have three young women living in the place and knew they would take excellent care of it.

"Three men," she said, her eyes sparkling, "would be another story. But three women — one of them is bound to be a good housekeeper!"

Jessie enjoyed having her friends in Gatlinburg. It gave her a place to visit whenever she walked into town, and they were near enough to run out to see her every day or two. For the three girls living in the condo, it was like being on an extended vacation in a resort, and they clearly relished it.

Roxie and Joan soon found themselves gravitating toward Harold's gallery, which the insurance company had up and running again in a few days. Rowena was so busy from the extra publicity that she needed their help. Phyllis was spending a lot of time with Steve, who kept saying he had to get back to Cincinnati, but as it was his own taxi, who was to say when?

Jessie had a card from Dana in Savannah featuring a horse-drawn carriage on one of the shady squares of the city. Dana had written *US* on the photograph and drawn an arrow to the window of the carriage. They were having a wonderful time, she said, and Mike was everything she ever wanted in a husband, although she would never have guessed it before meeting him. She also said it didn't make sense to her, but Mike said to tell her he owed her a beer.

Roxie and Joan were overcome with emotion at seeing their faces in the *Martha and Mary* painting. They were also fascinated by the reports they heard of mysterious healings at Rymer's Chapel; they stopped several times to sit in the sanctuary and study the painting *Mary's Secret* or merely to chat with Father McKeown, whom they found likable and amusing. Joan made notes on several of the healing incidents Father McKeown told them about, thinking they would be helpful if she ever did write a book about Jessie.

Reports of the healings continued to create a stir in both official and unofficial quarters. The Vatican had sent a special envoy, a Monsignor Pattacini, on a discovery mission; several charismatic and Pentecostal groups had sent delegates as well. *Time, Newsweek,* and *People* magazine had all despatched reporters to interview Father McKeown and Jessie; *Time* and *Newsweek* featured Jessie and her paintings in their art sections. *Time*'s article appeared a week later than *Newsweek*'s, the time lapse enabling the magazine to include a paragraph about the firebomb at the gallery and speculation as to the kind of people who might wish to intimidate or silence a major artist. One of the reporters working on the piece suggested that it was reminiscent of what happened to many of the most notable artists in Hitler's Germany.

Jessie, meanwhile, went ahead with her research on Anne Hutchinson, the famous Congregationalist figure banished from the Massachusetts Bay Colony in 1638. She found only a couple of encyclopedia articles in the Gatlinburg library. Then she arranged with Harold and Rowena to visit them for two or three days in order to use the library at the University of Tennessee. There she found several books about Ms. Hutchinson, most of them written about 1930 or before, accepting at face value the accusations made against the intelligent, outspoken woman by Governor John Winthrop and several clergymen she had offended.

Much that Jessie read she already knew — that Ms. Hutchinson was born in a small town in England and admired the Puritan movement because of its independence of thought and its courage in relocating for religious freedom; that she emigrated with her husband William and several of her fourteen children to New England in 1634, when she was already forty-three years of age; that on the voyage over she gained a reputation as a woman of wit and learning, as well as of a ready tongue; that she often took exception to the sermons of the Massachusetts parsons, especially on the subject of original sin, which they espoused and she did not; that she organized discussion groups in her home that became more popular than the Sunday services at church; that the governor and the clergy, in their exasperation, finally dealt with her in the only way they knew how, by bringing her to trial and accusing her of heresy; that they found her guilty after she had bandied wits with them and exposed them for the prejudiced creatures they were, and expelled her from the colony; that she and her family removed to Rhode Island, then Long Island, and finally to Pelham Bay, where, a few years later, they were all massacred by Indians.

What she did learn that fascinated her immensely was that Ms. Hutchinson's father, a clergyman named Francis Marbury, had been an extremely independent thinker before her, spending time in jail on at least three occasions for his heretical opinions, and that it was he who taught his daughter to read, write, and entertain her own thoughts, however contrary they might be to accepted public opinion. She also discovered that, even as a girl, young Anne Hutchinson began acting as a midwife to her prolific mother, and that as an adult she continued to perform that important service for the women of the Massachusetts Bay Colony. It was her experiences as a midwife ushering wee ones into the world and as a mother of fourteen children of her own that convinced her of the utter foolishness of the Calvinist doctrine of original sin, which imputed eternal damnation to infants in their cradles, and led her to speak out against what she considered to be the vile and ignorant mouthings of slavishly imitative clergymen.

There was one more interesting thing. English Puritanism produced numerous woman preachers, many of whom claimed to have prophetic powers. King James I and his young successor Charles I, who both failed dismally as monarchs and knew that they lived under the shadow of the enormously popular Elizabeth I, strongly opposed outspokenness in women and encouraged the idea that women with public voices were likely to be witches. Anne Hutchinson thus grew up in an age when there was open debate about the place and authority of female ministers, and probably felt that she was being a responsible servant of Christ by following the Puritans to America, where she was assured that women were appreciated for their creative gifts.

On the passage over the Atlantic, Ms. Hutchinson found herself confined on a small ship, the *Griffin,* with a particularly noxious clergyman named Zechariah Symmes, an arrogant young university man who droned on for hours and hours in tedious, erudite sermons that generally denigrated womanhood and emphasized that all the woes of humanity had descended through our common mother Eve. Finally unable to bear Symmes's dogmatic pronouncements any longer, she declared that she would answer them once they arrived in Boston and that for the interim she planned to avoid him altogether and counseled all the other women to do likewise. Thus she sowed in the very voyage to America the seeds of destruction that would rise to do her in in the male-dominated theocracy of the New World.

The trial itself was tilted heavily against Ms. Hutchinson, as most of the ministers who gave testimony had felt the sting of her tongue. And when it was admitted into evidence that she often had prophetic visions, such as the one she received aboard the *Griffin* revealing to her that the ship was three weeks from land, Governor Winthrop concluded that she might be a witch. It did not seem to matter that her vision was correct, and that the *Griffin* did indeed dock in precisely three weeks. The only thing that counted was that she was an intelligent, strong-willed woman who refused to subjugate herself to clergymen with whom she had honest disagreements.

Jessie's mind whirled with images and ways of presenting this heroic Christian woman who may well have been the first American martyr for her faith. She thought of picturing Anne and her family at the moment of Anne's entering confinement for the winter before her banishment took effect. Anne and her husband William were very close and had often supported each other in times of stress or hardship. Jessie could show this in their tender regard for each other as they said good-bye to one another prior to William's leaving to make a new home for them in another place.

Then she thought of showing Anne on the witness stand, her arm half-raised in gesturing, humor on her face, making a witty point against Rev. Symmes and Governor Winthrop, who sat as her judge. When this picture came to her, she knew immediately whose face she would give Anne Hutchinson. It would be that of a younger D. M. Birkenstall, fire dancing in her eyes and wit exploding from her tongue as it had that day when she encountered Dr. Jack Garbie.

Again, it occurred to her to portray Ms. Hutchinson in a close-up view of her face, her eyes closed in the act of receiving a divine revelation, while behind her were ranged the accusing visages of the Boston governor and ministers.

She talked aloud with *Baba* about the possibilities as she walked back to Harold and Rowena's house from the university. "Oh, *Baba*," she said, "I am so excited about this painting! Maybe it is what is happening to me right now that makes me feel this way, but I sense an overwhelming identification with this woman. She was such a good woman. She loved her husband and her children. She was so good to the other women of Boston. She was so devoted to you. And she believed so strongly in truth and freedom and honesty. She was so modern. Her problem was the one so many of my friends are struggling with today. If only I can get this picture right, perhaps I can help to justify her sacrifice and make it easier for the thousands of women still trying to find places of service for you now."

That evening, as she helped Rowena and Harold with the dishes, she talked about what she had learned at the library.

"She sounds like a feminist ahead of her times," said Rowena.

"In a way, she was," said Jessie. "But she wasn't the only one. Apparently the reign of Elizabeth produced the incentive for many women to enter the ministry."

"And then it all got set back when King John or James or whatever his name was came to the throne."

"I think she'll make a great subject, Jess," said Harold.

Suddenly Jessie stopped, the dish and dish-towel motionless in her hands.

"What is it, Jess? Are you all right?"

"I just realized how selfish I'm being," she said, ""the trouble I can cause you with this painting."

"Bosh!" said Rowena. "It's time those preachers and nincompoops began facing up to the truth about women. God didn't make us smarter'n men so we could hide ourselves under a bushel all our lives!"

"Jess," said Harold, "if the time ever comes when you tailor your painting to the cut of their cloth, I'm going to give you a good spanking. They can burn me out a dozen times—they can burn me at the stake—and I'll still fight for your right to paint what you want to. Besides, I like this Anne Hutchinson woman too. She reminds me of you."

Jessie didn't start the Anne Hutchinson painting when she went home the next day. She still wasn't sure how *Baba* wanted her to do it. But she did begin sketching out a canvas for which she had received the idea one day while she was in the library looking for books on American women in religion. It was a triptych featuring three Americans who had founded religious movements—Ellen White, the theologian of the Seventh-Day Adventist Church; Mary Baker Eddy, who wrote *Science and Health with the Key to the Scriptures* and initiated the Christian Science movement; and Aimee Semple McPherson, the flamboyant Los Angeles evangelist who started the Four Square Gospel Church.

Two days later, she knew how she must arrange the Anne Hutchinson painting. She would have Anne making a point in the courtroom—or the church where the trial was held—and she would show Rev. Symmes on the stand and Governor Winthrop behind the table that served as a judge's bench. Standing beside her, proud and amused, with a hand on her shoulder, but painted like a wraith, as if he were present as a ghost, would be her father, Francis Marbury, who knew better than ever the worth of what he had taught his daughter.

24

Spring arrived early in the Smokies that year, and the wild dogwood trees, which usually reached their peak in mid-April when the Gatlinburg Chamber of Commerce scheduled their annual Dogwood Festival, began to show in full by the first of the month. The town fathers worried that word might get around and diminish the crowds that always packed the hotels and restaurants during the festival. The merchants, however, didn't show much anxiety, as Easter week fell late and coincided with the festival days, more or less guaranteeing a big crowd.

Roxie and Joan had been pleading with Jessie to show them "her" mountains, as they called them. One bright, clear day, she and Columbo appeared at their condo before breakfast, ready to lead an expedition. Steve Pieratti had finally gone back to Cincinnati, promising to return after the holidays, so Phyllis wanted to go with them too.

After some coffee and donuts, which Jessie had stopped and bought on her way through town, they put some drinks and sandwiches into their knapsacks, climbed into the Volvo, and headed up into the mountains for a scenic hike.

The path, which was fairly wide and well

traveled for the first mile or so, led down from the highway, across two or three streams, and then up into the woods. From time to time, it lay beside creeks where huge granite boulders forced the cold water to rush this way and that, sometimes bursting into spray and other times coursing through gorges and over ledges, forming thunderous little waterfalls.

Great clumps of mountain laurel and rhododendron grew near the water, where the roots could always find abundant moisture, and sent their heavy, wide-leafed arms out over the streams in search of sunlight. Behind them grew the giant fir and hardwood trees, many of which were hundreds of years old, their thick foliage now sheltering the forest floor, which was soft and spongy from decades of rotting pine needles.

Among these stately old trees, especially in places where the sun could still break through at angles during the day, grew the redbud and dogwood trees, occasionally symmetrical in shape but more often twisted and irregular from years of reaching this way and that toward the available light. The redbuds had blossomed earlier, with tiny rose-colored blooms clustered along spearlike branches; now, in place of the blooms, the branches were covered with small, waxy, heart-shaped leaves. The dogwood trees, however, were just coming into full bloom, their large, cross-shaped blossoms often appearing as great bursts of white amidst green fir trees. It was a rare treat to see a pink dogwood in the mountains, as they were mostly hybrids planted along the roadways or in people's yards. But over the years, the droppings of birds had transplanted a number of them in the forest; happening upon one was like suddenly coming upon a miracle of nature.

Joan and Phyllis continually oohed and aahed as they climbed the steep trail, stopping often to look back the way they had come or to survey the patchwork quilt of distant mountains seen through the broken leafcover of their own. Roxie said little, but Jessie knew her well enough to know that she was drinking it all in and feeding on it at levels not readily expressible.

Somewhere up the trail, after crossing back and forth over the same stream a number of times, they came upon a level place in the mountains, a kind of dell, where there was a clearing in the woods. Across this clearing, watered by a dozen tiny springs that made the ground soft and oozy to the foot, lay a veritable blanket of wildflowers. There were violets of several hues, trillium, black-eyed Susans, daisies, jack-in-the-pulpits, snow-on-the-mountain, aconytes, and other varieties unknown to the women.

Joan squealed with delight when she saw it.

"Oh God," said Phyllis, "it's so beautiful I can't believe it!"

They all sat down on a large poplar log that had apparently crashed, perhaps under the winter snows or during an early spring storm, and stared at the meadow in silent wonder, all four in a row, as if they were sitting on a pew and watching Low Mass being served in a dream.

About eleven o'clock, they were already hungry from the exertion of the climb and brought out the drinks and sandwiches on a large flat boulder by a rushing creek.

"I can't believe this place," said Phyllis again. It was getting to be her standard utterance. "I thought New England was gorgeous in the fall, but this is even more beautiful!"

"I think there are some times and some places where *Baba* simply likes to show off," said Jessie.

After eating they continued to climb for another hour or two. The path at times dwindled to a narrow way where it was necessary to brush aside the new growth of leaves and branches. But the scenery remained lush and exciting, with as many dogwoods dotting the forest as before. The streams were narrower and often steeper, with the result that the water leapt and thundered even more spectacularly than before. And there were still occasional little dells where flowers grew, surprising gifts forever hidden from those who did not aspire to heights or endure the hard toil of reaching them.

At last the women arrived at the peak of the mountain, which was still shrouded in woods, and followed the path along a narrow ridge leading to an outcropping of rocks and an open view across the entire range of the Smokies.

None of them said a word as they lowered their packs to the ground and stood gaping across the bluish haze at distant vistas.

Jessie noticed that Roxie, who had complained two or three times of being out of breath and suggested that they turn back, was simply shaking her head from side to side in wonder and disbelief. It was Roxie, in fact, who finally broke the silence.

"Well, since we've come this far, there's no rush to get back. I say let's stay a little while and catch a nap or something."

"Good idea," said Phyllis. "I'm a little out of shape, and I hear it's as hard going down as it is coming up."

So they took their packs and scattered, Roxie heading back into the trees where there was a soft bed of needles, each settling down for a rest with her own thoughts and ruminations.

Jessie sat leaning against a gnarled old fir tree, her face in the shadows, and gave thanks to *Baba* for the wonderful day, for her dear friends, for the beauty of the mountains as they were seeing them, and for Columbo, who lay contentedly by her feet, as glad for the surcease in climbing as the girls themselves.

She thought of the strange turns her life had taken, and expressed gratitude for each of the paintings *Baba* had given her. She was especially glad about the one yet to come, the portrait of Anne Hutchinson, and what she hoped it might mean in encouragement to thousands of people, especially women who felt a calling from *Baba* that they had difficulty in expressing because of patriarchalism in their religion.

She remembered Rachel and Ray, and Julia and Carol who would soon be arriving at the airport in Knoxville to spend a week with her. Her friends would love the girls, she knew, and they would all have such good times together. Maybe the dogwoods would still be in bloom, and they could all make this same hike together.

A hawk descended from somewhere in a narrowing spiral and landed on a dead tree branch on a little knoll a dozen yards away. Columbo, aware of the circling shadow, pricked his ears and raised his head to see the landing, then lowered it again.

Joan, who had taken repose against a tree a few feet from Jessie, was watching her face in love and admiration. For a moment, the sun in its westward travels dipped behind a cloud, which cast a slight shadow over the spot where Jessie sat. Then, reaching the edge of the cloud, the sun shone fully in her face, causing her to close her eyes and tilt her chin up until the rays transformed the planes of her cheeks into pools of light.

Joan's mouth dropped partly open, and she started, unable to breathe for a few seconds. It was as if heaven itself were anointing her dear friend Jessie, whose being, she had always believed, was the purest and most angelic the world had ever known.

The hawk sailed into the air again, breaking the spell of the moment. But Joan knew she would never forget what she had witnessed.

Presently Roxie came out of her resting place among the trees and stood, hands on hips, surveying the wideness of peaks and valleys.

"God," she said, "this really is the most fantastic place. Don't you think we could just stay up here, Jess, and never go down?"

Jessie smiled, thinking of all that lay below—Harold, Rowena, Chip, Margot, her studio, Rymer's Chapel, Father McKeown, all those people coming in and out of his sanctuary, D. M. Birkenstall, Delma Hirshfield-Jones, the convention center, the crowds of vacationers, the Women of the Tomb service.

"It would be nice, she said. "But think of everything we'd miss."

25

On the Saturday before Holy Week, Roxie and Joan both worked with Rowena in the galleries. That freed Harold to drive Jessie and Columbo to the Knoxville airport to meet Carol and Julia. Gatlinburg was filled to overflowing, with traffic bumper-to-bumper, and crowds of sightseers from all over the country converging on the Moorefield Galleries to see the Jessie paintings they had heard and read so much about.

Most people were very polite and respectful

and wrote comments like "Wonderful!" and "Wish I could own one" in the guest book by the door. A few had obviously come to scoff, and they were inclined to say, a little too loudly, "I can't see what all the fuss was about," and to write comments such as "Pure rubbish," "Dirty lesbian propaganda," "Shame on you." Roxie had a difficult time controlling her temper when she overheard the comments of the latter kind, and once Joan was sure she heard her mumble something under her breath.

Harold's works were enjoying a wonderful day by association. As none of Jessie's paintings were available for sale, many people purchased his oils and watercolors of local scenes and still lifes, all done with the incredible sensitivity that had first attracted Jessie to them.

"I can't believe how fast my things are going," Harold said on the way to the airport. "At this rate the place will be empty by the middle of next week. I'd better burn the midnight oil and get some new canvases up fast." He reached over and took her hand in his. "This wouldn't have happened at all if it hadn't been for you, Jess."

"Don't believe it."

"Jess, have you ever thought anymore about us?"

She squeezed his hand.

"Of course I have. But the future is still a little cloudy to me. I think things are building to some kind of climax. Let's give it a few more days, till after the holidays. Then maybe my mind will clear a bit."

"Okay. But I'd still feel better if you were staying with us."

She smiled at him and squeezed his hand.

"Thanks," she said. "I love you."

Carol and Julia were so long getting off the plane that Harold wondered aloud if something had happened and they hadn't come. But then they burst through the doorway, bumping against the frame with their carry-ons and packages as they came, laughing and excited as only two young women on vacation could be.

Jessie gave them big, long hugs and lots of kisses, and introduced them to Harold and Columbo. Both girls suddenly looked shy and awkward as they stared at the dimpled, handsome face above them. Then they dropped to their knees and smothered Columbo with affection, which he received in kindly toleration.

"Here," said Julia, happily thrusting a shopping bag at Jessie. "Mom sent you some of her challa bread. She knew you liked it."

The girls talked endlessly and energetically all the way to the base of the mountains, exclaiming at the beauty of the land and the trees, especially the brilliant dogwoods. When Harold turned the Rover off U.S. 411 and headed South into the blue hills, they suddenly fell awestruck at the spectacle of the mountains. At last Carol said, "Gee, Jess, this is the coolest sight I've ever seen. I couldn't understand why you wanted to come down here to the country and all, but now I understand. It's beautiful."

That evening Jessie had a welcoming party for the girls at her place. Roxie barbecued hamburgers, Joan made potato salad, Phyllis prepared the table. Harold and Rowena brought Cokes and beer when they came; Chip and Margot Delaney brought brownies and homemade ice cream. Mike and Dana had returned from Savannah earlier in the week; Dana drove Jasmine out, leaving Mike to come later, after the dinner rush at the restaurant. Mike said to tell Jessie he wouldn't give up his two best waitresses for just anybody, but he owed her one.

Julia and Carol were completely smitten by Jessie's house and its proximity to the forest. "You can go walking in the woods whenever you want to," said Carol. "That's neat!"

Jessie had draped a cloth over her Anne Hutchinson painting, which she had decided to call *The Vindication of Anne Hutchinson*, but her guests felt so much at home that they didn't hesitate to lift it and stare at what she had done. Anne Hutchinson's figure was essentially complete, as was Francis Marbury's ghost. And, in the actual sketching, Jessie had felt the inspiration to add a spectral figure of Christ as well, standing on the other side of Anne from her father.

"Oh God," said Carol, "it's absolutely fantastic."

"It's incredible," said Roxie.

"Your best, without a doubt," said Rowena.

"Oh Jessie," said Margot, "I can't describe what I feel when I look at it. It gives me such a sense of direction and empowerment."

Harold stood regarding it a long time, saying nothing. "Jess," he later admitted to her, "when I look at that, I know why you can't be completely free for us right now. You're serving something bigger than both of us. All I can say is, God bless you. I love you, and God bless you."

She put her arms around his waist and held him tight.

"Thank you for that."

The next morning, Sunday, dawned bright and clear. Jessie let the girls sleep—she had given them her bed and slept on the sofa in the living room—and she worked for a while on her painting.

When they arose and came to the kitchen, both squealed with delight, looking out and seeing three deer feeding off the ground under the bird feeder, where Jessie had gotten in the habit of throwing extra food for them and the squirrels.

"This place is so neat!" said Julia. "My dad would love it!"

Later, they all walked into Gatlinburg, Columbo trotting beside them. The girls were amazed at people's friendliness; many of the residents, recognizing Jessie, honked and waved as they passed.

The same air of cordiality greeted them everywhere they went in town. The streets were crowded with people who had come for the festival, and they were all in a happy mood. Almost everyone they saw was eating. Some were sitting in sidewalk restaurants or waiting to get into the Pancake Pantry, McDonald's, Burger King, and dozens of other restaurants along the main street. All those who were not in a restaurant or waiting to get into one seemed to be eating ice cream cones, donuts, caramel apples, candy, corndogs, or popcorn as they walked along, amiably jostling one another on the sidewalk.

Jessie led them to the large window where a man inside was making taffy on an unusual machine that stretched it back and forth on mechanical arms, fed it in long strips through a slicing machine, and eventually wrapped and sealed each piece before dropping it in a tub at the end of the assembly line. Then she took them to another window where two women were pouring out panfuls of fudge to cool.

They watched a young man spraying artistic scenes and messages on T-shirts and stopped in front of a booth where a man was using a routing tool to carve wooden signs bearing people's names and welcome messages for their homes.

Julia spotted the Space Needle, a tower reaching hundreds of feet into the sky, and had to ride up its elevator to a walled ledge that made her dizzy from the height. While they were up there, Carol spied the ski lift that carried people from the main street up to the mountains above the town; they rode that next.

From high in the air over the hillside, the neighboring mountains with their soft blankets of greenery appeared to be polka-dotted by thousands of white dogwood trees.

"Oh, look at the town!" said Julia, who had gotten over her sense of vertigo. "Everything seems so small. The cars look like toys. And see how busy it all is. You wouldn't believe it is Sunday afternoon!"

Some people recognized Jessie on the streets and stopped her to ask if she wasn't the artist who had been in *Time* and *Newsweek* recently. Several of them asked for her autograph; a few of the women told her how much what she was doing meant to them, that she had raised their confidence and self-esteem more than anything else in years.

Three or four persons also approached them, saying they had experienced miraculous healings at Rymer's Chapel while praying before *Mary's Secret.* A heavy-set man with a luxurious growth of reddish beard held up his right hand. "Look at this," he said, wiggling his fingers. "I'm a woodcarver. I had a stroke that left my right arm and hand completely paralyzed. Not a damn bit of feeling in them." He flexed the arm and wiggled the fingers vigorously. "March twenty-sixth. Three-forty-seven P.M. That's when it happened. In front of your picture."

He grabbed Jessie and kissed her. There

were tears in his eyes.

"Thank you," he said, his voice choking with emotion. "Thank you."

"Gee, you're so famous," said Carol as they walked on. "It's like you were a movie star or something, the way all these people come up to you."

"It doesn't take much to win some people's admiration, I'm afraid," said Jessie with a laugh. "We live in a celebrity-conscious world."

When they went to the gallery to visit Rowena, Roxie, and Joan, Jessie's presence started a near-riot. Some people said they had driven more than six hundred miles to see her paintings, and had no idea they would get to see her as well. She signed autographs on gallery guides and studio cards until the entire supply was exhausted. People thrust napkins, packages, and other articles at her for a signature. Finally Rowena said, "Folks, give the girl a rest! We don't want to injure those precious hands she uses to paint with." She had to interpose herself bodily between Jessie and the crowd of people pressing upon her.

Afterward, Jessie, Julie, Carol, and Columbo walked down River Road, which followed a wide, rocky creek, with big motels on the other side of it and the mountains rising precipitously behind them. They stopped from time to time to lean on the railing and watch the ducks swimming in the creek below them.

"Jessie," Carol said on one of these stops,

"why are people like that?"

"Like what, dear?"

"I mean, those awful things some of them wrote in the guest book at Harold's gallery. Why do they do that?"

Jessie put her arms around both girls as they continued to look at the ducks.

"Honey, I don't really know. There is both bad and good in the world, and in people too, I'm afraid. It must be awful for the people who have bad feelings and behave spitefully to others."

"But if *Baba* is so powerful, why does *Baba* let things happen that way? Can't *Baba* make everything okay?"

Jessie thought for a moment. She wanted to answer the question as well as she possibly could.

"I believe, dear," she said, "that *Baba* is working on it. But the world is like a piece of art—a statue or a painting or a musical composition, let's say. Sometimes they don't come right instantly or without difficulty. The artist uses all of his or her skill, but there seems to be an independent will in the material that resists the final beauty the artist is seeking. So the artist has to be patient. If she isn't—well, things will never turn out the way they ought to."

Carol slipped her arm around Jessie's waist.

"You know everything," she said.

"No, not really. I'm just older than you. I've lived more and seen more. And I'll tell you something," Jessie said, kissing both girls on the sides of their foreheads, first Carol and then Julia, "it's a wonderful world in spite of all the problems in it. We are privileged to live in it, regardless of how much we may hurt or suffer while we're here."

"Do you hurt and suffer?" asked Julia.

"Oh yes, dear, a lot. You can't see people in pain or ignorance or bad situations without hurting for them. But you pray for them and go on. You do what you can to help *Baba*, and then you let it go and give thanks for everything."

"Even the pain and the suffering?"

"Absolutely. They're part of what makes us human, what makes the world so beautiful. They remind us that *Baba* is still working on this masterpiece of a universe."

"But wouldn't it be better to live in it when the masterpiece is finished and everything is as it should be?"

"Oh, that will be wonderful, of course, and we all live looking forward to it. But sometimes I think it is a greater privilege to live now, when things aren't as finished as they will be. There is a lot of passion, a lot of energy, in masterpieces early on, when they're just under way. That's the way it is with our world now, and I'm glad to be a part of it."

It was beginning to grow dark and cool around them.

"I'm hungry," Jessie said. "Anybody else hungry?"

"I am," said Carol.

"Me too," said Julia.

"Long John Silver's is just down the street from here," said Jessie. "Let's go have some fish."

26

Roxie and Joan had promised to take the girls hiking on Monday, but Monday was rainy. Jessie let them sleep late again. She built a fire in the living room to take the chill off the house, made herself some hot chocolate, and looked at her painting of Anne Hutchinson.

Then instinctively, as she sometimes did, she set aside the canvas she was working on for another, and put her triptych of Ellen White, Mary Baker Eddy, and Aimee Semple McPherson back on the easel. She had been thinking about it at odd moments and wondering if she ought not to add a fourth figure behind and above the others, that of the woman who was instrumental in the Azusa Street meeting in Los Angeles and the beginnings of modern Pentecostalism. She couldn't recall the woman's name, but she remembered the part she played.

"Funny," she thought, sketching in a rudimentary figure where the extra woman would be added, "two of the modern movements came out of Los Angeles. I'd like to go there for a while sometime. It must be a fantastic city."

The rain didn't let up that day or the next, but

by Tuesday the girls were getting cabin fever. Jessie suggested they walk over to Rymer's Chapel, which was not far away. She said she wanted them to meet her friend Father McKeown, but she also wanted Carol to see *Mary's Secret* and watch her reaction to it.

They made Columbo wait for them in the tiny narthex. The rain had brought out his canine odor and they didn't want to offend anyone else who might be in the church. Despite the rain, there were several persons in the sanctuary, some seated around the room and a couple praying at the altar before the painting. Father McKeown apparently was not there.

Jessie genuflected and made the sign of the cross. Carol and Julia made awkward little efforts at imitating her, and followed her down to one of the front pews, where they all sat.

The girls recognized Carol's face in the painting at the same time, and turned excitedly to one another to point it out.

"Oh, wow!" said Carol. Almost as if forgetting where she was, she rose, walked to the chancel, and stood behind the people praying there. She shook her head slowly and incredulously from side to side, studying the picture as she did.

The candlelight on the altar seemed to highlight the beautiful face of Mary, so that the love and adoration of the children around her appeared natural and wonderful, even inevitable. In the background, it was the red poppies that stood out most. The entire painting seemed to be alive with spiritual presence.

The girls could understand why people sometimes felt healing there. As they gazed on the remarkable picture, they did not see how anything could possibly be wrong in their own lives.

"Oh, Jessie," Carol said when they reached the narthex again, still whispering as if they were inside, "I don't know what to say. Why did you put me in that painting? How could you honor me by using my face for her? She's so beautiful I want to cry."

And she did. Putting her hands over her face, she sobbed.

Jessie encircled her with her arms and gently rocked her.

"I am so unworthy," Carol said between sobs.

"That's what Mary said," replied Jessie. "In fact, that's what we all say. It takes so much to be worthy of *Baba*'s favor. But *Baba* never stops at that. *Baba* bestows the worth. *Baba* makes us worthy."

"And to think"—sob—"to think that people have been healed looking at my—at her—picture!"

She sobbed all the harder.

"You couldn't have reacted more beautifully," Jessie said when the crying had finally subsided. "It makes me see even more clearly why *Baba* wanted your face on Mary. *Baba* knew."

Carol was unusually quiet the rest of the afternoon and at supper, which consisted of wieners roasted in the fireplace, sugar-baked beans, and some of Joan's potato salad left over from Saturday night.

Finally, as the food began to make her more talkative, Carol said, apropos of nothing that had been remarked by Jessie or Julia, "I think I'll go home when we get back to Alexandria. My mama needs me now, and I think I can help her. Before, I probably couldn't. Now I think I can."

"You haven't mentioned your last trip home," said Jessie. "Was it okay?"

Carol was quiet. She looked at Julia, then spoke. "No, not really. But that's all right. I can handle it."

She rose, went over and poked the firewood, sending a shower of sparks up the flue, and added another log—she had accepted the role of unofficial firetender—and sat down before speaking again.

"It's time I started paying my way in the world," she said. "Jessie, I want to be like you. I want my life to count for something. I don't want to be a drughead or stupid anymore. I don't feel the way I used to feel about things. You've taught me a lot—about love, about caring, about belonging—about mattering. I want to matter in other people's lives. I want to help them."

Jessie's eyes filled with tears and she couldn't speak. She just leaned over on the sofa and gave Carol a big hug and rubbed her head gently.

Julia reached over too, and held on to the two of them.

Columbo opened his eyes to look at them, then closed them again.

Wednesday dawned bright and beautiful, and the world around the schoolhouse seemed particularly luminous, as almost always happens after a rain in the mountains. The sound of the creek a few hundred feet away, often audible at night when everything was still, was augmented by thousands of gallons of extra water pouring through it. Jessie left the back door open while they ate breakfast.

"Agenda time," she said after they had eaten the last piece of freshly baked sweet roll. "I propose that we all go outside in our grubbies and do some yard work I've been postponing. Then this afternoon I'll take you up the mountain behind the house. Or we can walk into Cartersville. I'll introduce you to some of the home folks."

"Why can't we do all three?" asked Julia.

"We can," declared Jessie. "Agenda set."

They found some old yard tools in the small shed at the edge of the woods. Carol set about pruning the bushes while Julia cleared the grass from the flagstones in the front yard. Jessie took a pick and shovel and dug around an old plum tree in the side yard that hadn't survived the winter. It was difficult to budge, but after all three of them had taken turns hacking at the roots with the adze end of a pick, Jessie finally managed to pull it over and out of the hole. Then she got a wheelbarrow, went up into the woods, and brought a load of dirt to fill the cavity.

"I never could stand a plant that wasn't doing its thing," she said, smiling at the recollection of another tree in another place.

They joined together in attacking the weeds in the fencerow on the left side of the house, and then decided that was about all they could do; there was no lawn mower in the shed; Jessie would have to buy or borrow one another time.

Their trip up the mountain was limited by both the time they had allotted to it before going into town and the climbing stamina of the girls. Jessie told them they were both soft from riding everywhere they went and not participating in any vigorous sports.

"I'm a soccer player," said Julia, "but that's on a level playing field."

The girls were charmed by the little town of Cartersville, but had trouble believing that people actually chose to live in communities too small to support libraries or sports clubs or movie houses or even their own high school.

"But where do the kids go to high school?" asked Carol.

"They ride the bus to an area high school in Gatlinburg."

"But doesn't that ruin their group spirit? I mean, for teams and things like that."

"I don't know," said Jessie, feeling some

amusement at Carol's passion about something that had not occurred to her. "Maybe it does."

Both girls were delighted to meet Sarah, the dishwasher at the restaurant, whom they recognized from having seen *Rosa's Gift* in the magazines.

"I'm surprised you're still working here," said Carol.

Sarah looked at her quizzically.

"I mean, now that you're famous and all."

"Famous don't pay the bills, child."

They all laughed together.

That evening as they roasted marshmallows in the fire, they talked about the advantages and disadvantages of small-town life.

"I can't get over the little post office," said Julia. "The woman in there seems to know everybody around here. When I go to the post office at home, I don't know anybody and nobody knows me."

"I guess a big city's good if you want to remain anonymous," said Carol. "I mean, if you've done wrong or anything, and you don't want people to know who you are."

"I wouldn't know what to do out of a city," said Julia.

Jessie listened to their discussion and thought about her life here by the woods. Had living here changed her in any way, she wondered? Did she ever want to return to the big city? She didn't have to answer the questions now. Somehow they didn't seem to matter very greatly. She was happy here, doing what she knew *Baba* wanted her to do. She felt comfortable with most of the people — especially Harold and Rowena. Who knew what the future held?

What was the old saying, "Sufficient unto the day is the evil thereof"? Why didn't it say "the good," she thought? Let the good be sufficient for the day they were living in.

27

On Maundy Thursday, Roxie picked up Jessie, Carol, and Julia at nine-thirty and drove them to the restaurant where the Gatlinburg Ministerial Association would be meeting. They arrived in plenty of time for Jessie to be introduced to the presiding minister before ten-thirty. Joan and Phyllis merely walked down from their condo, which was not far away.

There were only four or five ministers present when they arrived; they had gathered near a table with old-fashioned white china mugs and a large metal coffee urn.

A youngish man in a light-blue polyester sports jacket and navy tie that matched his navy trousers left the group and walked toward the girls. "Hi, I'm Russell Dwyer, minister of the Twin Oaks Christian Church. You must be Jessie. I'll be introducing you today."

The president of the association, he explained, had a funeral to perform and would not be there.

Jessie introduced her friends. The other ministers remained near the coffee table.

By ten-thirty, the room was filled. Some of the men went out and brought in extra chairs for those still standing. Roxie, who sat near the back of the room, counted fifty-six men and four women in the crowd, plus Jessie and her friends. One of the women was Margot Delaney, who had come with Chip, and another was Trish McCann, the editor of *This Month in Gatlinburg.* Roxie assumed that the other two were ministers or staff members of local churches.

The meeting began with the singing of a hymn, followed by a prayer given by an Episcopal priest. An elderly minister wearing a boldly checked sport coat accompanied the hymn on the piano. The Episcopalian and two Roman Catholic priests were the only ones wearing clerical collars. The hymn and prayer were followed by about ten minutes of announcements of various kinds, vice president Rev. Billy Hargett reading from slips of paper he had been handed, and others being offered from the floor. Most of them concerned special Good Friday and Easter services or spring revival meetings scheduled in the churches. Most of the latter were in Baptist or United Methodist churches, though one was in a Nazarene church, two were in Churches of Christ, and one was in an Assemblies of God church.

When Rev. Hargett had ascertained that all the announcements had been made, he announced that Rev. Russell O'Dwyer of the Twin Oaks Church of Christ would introduce the speaker. Rev. Dwyer stepped over to the speaker's desk with the microphone and corrected the information.

Someone called out, "That's pretty good for Billy Hargett. He still thinks David defeated Goliath at the battle of Jericho!"

Laughter and catcalls.

"It is my privilege today," said Rev. Dwyer, "to be able to introduce to you a woman who no longer needs an introduction in these parts. Although she has lived among us less than six months now—is that right, Jessie?—she has already made a name for herself that reaches beyond these hills."

He proceeded to speak of the various magazine articles and television programs that had focused on Jessie's work, and to read from the *Newsweek* article he held in his hand. Although he did not specifically refer to the painting *Mary's Secret*, he did allude to "various and sundry rumors" about "the unusual powers" of some of her paintings, and remarked that while he himself had not seen any of her works, he was sure that they must be "pretty good" to have drawn such wide attention.

When Jessie began to speak, the sound did not project well; the microphone had not been adjusted for a person of her height. Rev. Hargett walked over and unceremoniously corrected it as she waited, producing two or three loud, squawking noises in the process. "Way to go, Billy!" someone called. Jessie had no notes. She merely began to speak very simply and clearly about how richly and beautifully *Baba* had made the world, and how grateful and loving and peaceful we should be as a result. The problem is, she said, we sometimes fail to see this because we fasten upon prejudices, pains, personal injuries, and the like, and become blinded to the utter graciousness of *Baba*.

She used the word "God," not *Baba*, for she did not wish to confuse them with her own personal terminology.

But when she had completed her remarks, Rev. Dwyer said it was their custom to have a few minutes of questions and answers. The first question, raised by a raven-haired minister in his late fifties or early sixties, was about her terminology. His voice was deep and resonant, as if rising from a dark well; he spoke with an air of authority.

"It is reported that you have your own name for God, that you call Him '*Baba*'." He pronounced it slowly and with strong emphasis, baaah-baaah. "Is that true, and if so, by what authority do you do so?"

Jessie admitted that that was the name by which she knew God best, and explained about its transexuality and sense of intimacy.

"But the God of our fathers has always been masculine," said the minister with a pleased tone, as if he had heard the admission he was seeking and was moving in for the kill. "In the Old Testament He was Yahweh, a male deity who revealed Himself through a man, Moses. In the New Testament, Jesus said to call Him Abba, which means Father or Daddy. The model prayer that Jesus gave to his disciples to pray begins 'Our Father, who art in heaven.' God has always been masculine. God will always be masculine. Who are you to challenge the central assertion of the Judeo-Christian faith since its very beginning?"

Jessie blinked, unsure whether there was any point in trying to respond to the truculent spirit she recognized in the question. But then she thought of the others in the room, and especially of Carol and Julia.

"It was always my understanding," she said, "that the central assertion of Judeo-Christian faith is that God is one, not that God is masculine, and that God's oneness means that we are all united in God, whether rich or poor, male or female, white or colored. Shakespeare, one of the greatest poets of all times, asked, 'What's in a name?' It isn't what we call God that matters as much as how we conceive of God and our relationship to the divine."

The minister wanted to continue, but Rev. Dwyer interposed and said others had questions too.

A buxom young man whose stomach hung prominently over his belt, stretching the broad expanse of his shirt so that it shone in the light, addressed Jessie in an incongruously high-pitched voice, slightly less aggressive and authoritative than his predecessor's.

"These paintings you have done—this series, I guess you call it—about women in religion. How do you explain the fact that the Apostle Paul says, 'Let your women keep silence in the churches'? You seem to think women ought to preach and do the work of evangelists and everything else a man does. Isn't that nonscriptural, and aren't you defying the very Word of God you pretend to honor by elevating women above the position God intended for them to occupy?"

Jessie smiled at the man, considering his background and ignorance about many things.

"Yes," she said, "Paul did say that, in one of his letters to the Corinthians. But have you ever considered why he said it? Have you ever worshipped in a remote Middle-Eastern church even today? The men sit on one side of the aisle and the women on the other. The women have a very short interest-span. When someone is up speaking or praying, they very quickly fall to whispering and gossiping among themselves. This continues until one of the men slaps the bench he is sitting on and says, 'Will you women please be quiet so we can hear what is being said?!'

"Paul was not making a rule to forbid women to speak in church. Heavens! Most of the churches he dealt with were in the homes of women. He himself wrote to the people of Galatia and said there is no longer any such thing as male or female in Christ, but all are one, as God is one. Paul was only addressing a troublesome situation in a local church, which had to do with women who talked too freely. It would be foolish of us—has been foolish—to turn such a statement into a law for all times and places."

"Don't you believe the Holy Scriptures?" someone called out.

"Oh yes," said Jessie. "I believe the scriptures. But I also believe it takes as much help from the Spirit of God to read and understand them as it did to write them, and unfortunately ideas sometimes get enshrined in our traditions that were not intended at all by the scriptures themselves."

Someone said in a near-shout, "Ask her where she stands on abortion!"

Jessie looked in the man's direction and waited. When it seemed that no one was going to pick up on the matter, someone else asked, "Where do you stand on abortion? Is it right for a woman to abort a fetus that has already been given a soul by God Almighty at the moment of conception?"

Jessie had hoped the question wouldn't be asked, for she knew what was in their hearts. She herself was generally opposed to abortion, especially in the callous way it had come to be employed as a method of birth control. But she knew it wasn't a simple matter and that she must not perjure her true understanding. She spoke very quietly, praying that *Baba* would guide her words.

"I believe in the sacredness of all life. For that matter, of all non-life as well—trees, rocks, streams, oceans, the air around us. It is a matter of attitude. God has given us a wonderful world to live in, and we should live reverently and joyfully before all of it.

"That extends to fetuses as well. They are part of the beautiful process of sexuality and reproduction, which we should also take very seriously."

She paused almost imperceptibly, knowing that her next words were the ones the ministers would misunderstand. She wished she didn't have to speak them, that she could leave the matter where it was. But she had agonized over the divisiveness in the human community by the abortion issue and knew she had not said all she must. She prayed for the men to be open-minded and sensitive, for them to hear what she was about to say.

"But our reverence should also lead us to take seriously the rights and opinions and feelings of others. We cannot legislate respect for God or for human fetuses. There are times when individual women must decide whether it is right for them to follow through the entire process of giving birth or to abort the process. That is between them and God."

"What about murder?" asked the raven-haired minister who had started the questioning. "Is it all right for people to decide whether they can kill someone if they feel like it? God's law says, 'Thou shalt not kill.'"

"Murder is a social matter," said Jessie. "It affects other people who are already sentient beings. Abortion does not bear the same consequences for general society."

"You say it doesn't," countered the minister. "Who do you think you are, some kind of savior? Well, lady, I will answer for you, you are not. You have neither the authority of ordination nor the proper theological indoctrination to make the kind of speculative judgments you make, either in your speaking or in the paintings we have heard about. You are an upstart, that's what you are. You are an impertinent upstart in a world that seems to be full of upstarts today, and you will reap the reward that God in heaven, who is a male God, is preparing for all of them. Atheism, secular humanism, New Age, it's all the same. The devil is always going to and fro in the earth, seeking whom he may devour. But our God, the male God, who made women to be helpmates to men and to live in quiet submission to their husbands, the same God who condemns abortion and will send all these women who get abortions and the sleazy doctors who perform them to suffer for eternity in the fires of hell, is more cunning than the devil, and more powerful, and He will smite the devil, He will smite all of you, and you will beg for pardon, you will cry out from the flames and ask for a drop of cool water on your tongue, your blaspheming tongue, and God will say no, you would not repent and be humble when you had the chance, now you must suffer for all eternity!"

"Amen!" shouted someone. "Amen!" shouted another. And soon there was a chorus of amens and most of the men broke into loud applause.

Jessie merely stood behind the lectern looking very small and powerless.

Rev. Dwyer looked awkward and helpless. It was obvious that he felt some embarrassment for the way their speaker was being treated, but he did not know what to do about it. These were his colleagues, the ministers of the other churches in the area. Finally, he did the only thing he could think to do. He took Jessie by the elbow and led her out of the room.

The clapping grew even louder behind them as the swinging door opened, then swung shut again.

"Jess, I'm sorry," said Roxie later at the condo. "I didn't know what to do. I really felt angry at first, when they started in on you. I wanted to box that older minister's ears off. But they were all against you. I began to think, This is Jessie they're talking to. I've always believed in her, believed everything you said. It always seemed so reasonable. But they're the ministers of churches. They've been to seminary. They all seem to agree about what is right and what is wrong. My God, I thought, what if they are right? I mean, why should they all be wrong? Could they possibly all be wrong? And somehow, Jess, I didn't know what to think. I didn't know what I believed. I know now, now that we're out of there and I can think again. Oh, Jess, it was wrong of me—wrong of all of us—to sit there and say nothing and let you take that—that inexcusable crap—by yourself. Can you ever forgive us?"

Jessie looked at her from somewhere deep inside the tiredness of her being. "Oh, Roxie, I know you love me. There wasn't anything you could do. I'm not sure there was anything anybody could do. Of course I forgive you."

Chip and Margot came by to offer their apologies too.

"I can't believe Chip and I sat there and didn't get up and say anything in your behalf," she said. "We just sat there and let you get crucified like that. We're so sorry."

That evening the girls all gathered at Jessie's house for dinner. Most of them were still in shock at the experience of the morning. It was as if they had had their first real, definitive look into the maw of the world's evil and hatred and were unable to speak of what they had seen.

All except Carol, that is. Despite her youth, Carol seemed to have an almost mystical capacity for understanding the world and its ways. She also trusted Jessie implicitly, and saw in her a model of patience and endurance for living in the midst of difficulty and evil.

"They weren't all chauvinist pigs," she said. "I watched them. Some of them were ashamed of what happened. They probably wanted to speak out but were afraid to. I understand that. Some people are able to go into combat, and others aren't. It's that simple."

No one responded. She went on gnawing on a barbecued rib as nonchalantly as if she'd said, "I think it will rain tomorrow."

They were having ribs, baked potatoes, slaw, and homemade bread. Jessie had needed to bake the bread to settle her emotions. There was always something about working the dough that did that; she went straight to the kitchen and started rattling pans the minute she had gotten in the house. After that, she scrubbed out the bathroom, for that humbling act had a similar effect on her. Roxie, Joan, and Phyllis had stopped on their way out and bought two half-gallons of red wine, saying they thought everybody ought to get sloshed. Phyllis kept filling their glasses whenever they appeared to be even half-empty.

Jessie had a fresh loaf of bread in her hands—she liked to "hunk" off homemade bread rather than slice it, as it seemed to preserve the flavor better—when she decided to make a little speech.

"You are all my dear friends," she said. "You know how much I love you, and I know how much you love me. I want to apologize to you for what I put you through today. No, hear me out. If it hadn't been for me, you wouldn't have had to sit through that somewhat humiliating experience.

"But I want you to know that it didn't really humiliate me. Humility is something you have inside yourself. Nobody can impose it on you from without unless you will it. I felt humility instead for all of us—for the whole human race—because we never seem to learn. Scenes like that have a way of repeating themselves over and over, in every age. I wish it weren't true, but it is."

Remembering that she had the bread in her hands, she pulled off a piece and passed the rest to Joan.

"What I really want to say is that something seems to be happening in my life, and I don't know where it's all going to lead. I appear to have touched some nerves that I didn't expect to touch, and there are angry reactions."

Phyllis was up refilling their cups for the umpteenth time.

"I am concerned about how it may affect you all. I don't want any of you to be hurt on my account, and I'm beginning to see that you might."

"Stop right there," said Roxie. "I'm not sure what you're getting at, but I for one, or two, or three"—it was obvious that she had had a little too much wine—"I for one do not intend to stand idly by again and have you treated the way those bastards treated you today. Oops, sorry, Carol and Julia. Strike that last remark, but not the sentiment. Why do you think we drove all the way down here, Jessie? Not to attend a freaking dogwood festival, I can tell you. We came because we're your friends. We came because we love you. And whatever happens, we're going to be here. Right, girls?"

"Right!" said Joan.

"Right!" said Phyllis a split-second later; she was concentrating on where to set down the wine bottle, not realizing that Julia had set the bread in the space where it had been.

Jessie's eyes filled with tears.

"I love you all," she said, "so much."

Carol reached over from her left and gave her a squeeze. "We love you."

Joan hugged her from the other side. "Oh, Jess, you know we do."

In the euphoria of the evening, filled with wine and love, it was decided that on the following morning Joan and Phyllis would take Carol and Julia on the hike that had been rained out on Monday. Roxie said she was needed at the gallery. Jessie said she would stay home and try to finish *The Vindication of Anne Hutchinson*. The day's experience had yielded some new male faces to go in the painting.

It was further agreed that the girls should return to the condo with Roxie, Joan, and Phyllis so that the hikers could get an early start. This thrilled the girls, especially when it was decided that Columbo should go with them.

So after hugs and kisses all around, they piled into the old blue Volvo with Columbo spread across the laps of Carol and Julia, who were sitting beside Phyllis in the back seat. He looked a little apprehensive, but trusted the girls enough to give it a try.

Jessie waved them away with a kiss and returned to clean up the kitchen. The others had volunteered to help, but she said she needed to do it for therapy, so they cheerily abandoned all insistence.

Most of the kitchen cleaned up easily enough, but the pan she had done the ribs in was a hard case; she filled it with soapy water to let it stand in the sink until morning.

Invigorated by the quietness in the house, she uncovered *The Vindication of Anne Hutchinson* and studied it. No painting she had done yet, she was sure, had afforded her so much inner satisfaction. Almost without making a conscious decision, she picked up a pencil and began sketching in the faces of Governor Winthrop and Zechariah Symmes. It's funny, she thought. Before, she had imagined Symmes as a thin, angular man, somewhat like Ichabod Crane in Washington Irving's story. Now she found herself giving him a corpulent face and body, with his stomach hanging over the top of his black trousers.

She did not know what time she stopped working on the painting, but supposed it must be nearly midnight. Yet she was too excited to go to bed. She looked out through the kitchen window and saw that the backyard was bathed in moonlight.

Taking a flashlight and slipping into a little fleece-lined jacket, she stepped outside and started into the woods. It was much darker there than in the clearing; she switched on the light in order to see the path. How different it all looked at night, she thought. She had walked this path dozens of times, maybe more, and yet it had never appeared as it did now in the dark.

She climbed and climbed, exhilarated by the cool air, the sounds of frogs, crickets, and owls, and the strangeness of the woods. Eventually she reached a familiar outcropping of rocks where she sometimes basked in the sunlight. Now she sat on a boulder in the moonlight, looking out at the luminous haze that lay like a voluptuous gauze over the valleys and lower parts of the hills.

"Oh, *Baba*," she sighed, feeling the grandeur of the natural world. "Even the night is beautiful. What a wonderful job you have done with it all."

She prayed, remembering the events of the day and trying to be charitable to those who had sought to wound her spirit. Then she asked for *Baba*'s protection for all her friends, the little circle who had been with her that evening and the larger circle stretching out to Knoxville and Alexandria and New Haven.

She thought of Thomas and Matilda and their beautiful children, and prayed for them.

"I don't want any trouble, *Baba*," she prayed at last. "But neither do I want to shrink from any that it is your will for me to face. I must leave it all to you."

28

Sometime after daybreak, Jessie heard a vehicle drive up outside the house. She had already started painting, and was about to wipe the paint from the brush she was using when there was a sudden noise at the front of the house, as if the door had exploded off its hinges.

Within a second or two, four men in stocking masks had rushed upon her in the kitchen, expertly seizing her, placing a large piece of duct tape over her mouth, and binding her hands behind her with more tape.

One man was tall, another short, one fat, the fourth unusually thin.

The short man had a three-foot piece of chain in his hands. He went throughout the house, came back, and asked of no one in particular, certainly not of Jessie, who could not utter a word, where the damn dog was. Apparently he had been planning to catch Columbo by the throat and strangle him.

The tall man, obviously the leader, pulled off his mask, and the others followed suit. "Nobody else around," he said, "so no need for these."

He looked around, saw the coffee pot on the stove, walked over, opened cabinet doors until he found a cup, and poured himself some coffee.

"Got any sugar?" He was looking at Jessie.

She stared back without moving.

"No matter," he said. "I'll drink it without."

The fat one went to the cabinet, got a cup, and poured some coffee for himself.

The other two merely stood by Jessie, the short one nervously slapping the chain against his leg.

"Well, lookee here," said the tall one, standing in front of *The Vindication of Anne Hutchinson* as he drank his coffee. "The lady is an artiste." He gave it the French pronunciation, but with a derogatory slur.

"C'mon, Frank," said the short one. "Let's do it and get outa here. Somebody might come."

"Ain't nobody gonna come. Not this early in the morning."

He picked up the brush Jessie had dropped on the floor and looked around for the palette that was lying on the counter behind him. He daubed the brush heavily in the brightest red.

"This looks like it needs a little more color here," he said, painting a rough beard on the face of Ms. Hutchinson.

He rubbed the brush through the yellow, producing orange with dark streaks through it.

"And here too," he said, decorating Francis Marbury's ghostly figure. "Couldn't see him good. He was pale as a ghost the way you had him."

He drew the brush back and forth through the black, then smeared out the face of Jesus.

"He was a little pale too. Now I've made a nigger out of him."

The fat one laughed.

"You shoulda studied with me," the tall one said to Jessie. "I coulda taught you some things you didn't know."

Then he opened some drawers until he found a knife. He returned to the canvas, stuck the knife into the upper left-hand corner, and ripped it to the lower right-hand corner. Jabbing the knife into the upper right-hand corner, he then tore the canvas in the other direction.

"So much for art," he said. "Now let's try sex."

The short man half-carried, half-dragged Jessie into the living room.

"Up there," said the tall man.

The short man put her over his shoulder and carried her up the ladder. The thin man was carrying the duct tape. They roughly pulled the tape from around her arms, spread her out on the bed, and taped her wrists and ankles to the four corners. Then the tall one took the knife and sawed through her clothes.

The four men took turns raping her.

Once, because she was not cooperative, the short one hit her hard on the side of the face with his chain.

Then the tall one said to the thin one, "Bring the gas."

He returned presently with a five-gallon gasoline can in each hand. Taking one from him, the tall man removed the cap and liberally soaked Jessie and the bed. Then he ran a trail from the bed down the sides of the ladder to the floor below. Downstairs, he and the thin man poured gas everywhere. The tall one even took a moment to throw some on the canvas he had slashed. They ran a trail out the front door and poured the last of the can into a small puddle there.

"Okay, Shortie," said the tall man.

The short man reached in his pocket for a book of matches. They stood in the yard only a minute after he had thrown the match. By the time their van eased out of the driveway and down the road, the house was an inferno.

A truck driver noticed the fire ten minutes later. It took the engines from Gatlinburg thirty-five minutes to get there. By the time they did, there was no point in hooking up the hoses.

"Just hope there warn't nobody in there," said the deputy chief to some of the crowd of passers-by who had stopped to watch. Spitting a great chunk of chewing tobacco, he added, "Not a chance in hell if they was."

D. M. Birkenstall and Delma Hirshfield-Jones were the first of Jessie's friends to discover the fire. They had heard how disastrously the meeting with the ministerial association had gone and drove out with a potted plant to say how sorry they were. When they arrived, in the early afternoon, everyone had left. The ruins of the house were smoldering, emitting a sickly, charred odor.

They supposed that anyone in the house had gotten out safely, but felt more than ever that they had to find Jessie and speak with her.

"The gallery," said Dr. Birkenstall. Delma Hirshfield-Jones had obediently headed the car in that direction.

Rowena and Roxie were beside themselves at the news. As Roxie reported with alarm, Jessie had been home alone, painting. The others had gone hiking in the national park.

Rowena phoned Harold. Harold said to call the sheriff; he himself was on his way.

Rowena did as she was instructed, then locked up the gallery, explaining to visitors that it was an emergency. She and Roxie headed for the burned-out schoolhouse as fast as they could, with Dr. Birkenstall and Delma Hirshfield-Jones following at a slightly more sedate speed.

"Just pray she was up in the woods," said Roxie. "Just pray she wasn't in that house."

It was obvious within a few hours that Jessie had been in the house. The sheriff had called one of the fire trucks back; a man in an asbestos suit was sent into the rubble to look for evidence. After searching through the lower floor, he came out for a ladder, which he carried back in and leaned against the charred timbers of the wall to reach the balcony. There he found pieces of what he was sure were human bones. They were sealed in a large plastic bag and taken away to be delivered to the forensics lab in Knoxville.

Harold got the truth from the sheriff, who got it from the fireman, and carried it back to the others, who were standing helplessly under the shade of a large maple tree in the side yard.

Roxie screamed when she heard the news.

Delma Hirshfield-Jones fainted.

Harold sent the others back to town in case the hikers returned to the condo. He and Rowena would wait there for them in case they came to the house.

The truth was, he needed to walk around and around in the yard, trying to absorb what had happened.

29

It was nearly dark when the Volvo drove into the yard. Joan was the first to see that the house was gone. Shocked, they all poured out of the car. Columbo ran frantically around the edge of the ruins, sniffing for familiar odors and trying to understand what had transpired.

They could tell, when Harold and Rowena emerged from the shadows and walked toward them, that something terrible had happened to Jessie.

Joan screamed, "No, it can't be!" Then she and Phyllis fell into each other's arms and wept.

Carol and Julia stared into the ashes in stunned disbelief. When Rowena asked Carol if she was okay, she said she felt completely numb.

Columbo seemed to sense from the others that something had happened to Jessie. Once, he ran swiftly up the path they had so often taken into the woods and mountains. When he returned, he merely lay on the ground close to the others, occasionally raising his head to utter a slight whimper.

Eventually Harold and Rowena drove back to Knoxville, and the girls returned to the condo to be with Roxie. They found her with red and swollen eyes, pacing the condo, inside, then out onto the screened porch, then back again, a glass of beer in one hand and a cigarette in the other.

Joan didn't say anything about the cigarette. Roxie had stopped smoking two years ago, but there was a Stop-and-Go market next to the condo.

Phyllis went down the street for some hamburgers. None of them felt really hungry, but their climbing had consumed a lot of energy; they were surprised at how quickly they devoured the burgers and fries. Columbo was the only one who did not touch his food. Carol removed the bun, thinking he would eat the meat. But he didn't even appear interested in smelling it.

The two younger girls fell asleep with their clothes on about ten o'clock. Roxie, Phyllis, and Joan sat in the living room, staring vacantly at one another. Roxie lit a cigarette, snuffed it out a few minutes later, and lit another. She was up and down, up and down, pacing about like a big cat in a cage.

Sometimes she shook her head.

"I feel guilty as hell," she said once.

"Why, dear?" asked Joan.

"Because I should have been there. We shouldn't have left her alone. We came down here to protect her. We knew there was some kind of trouble, and we went on partying and living as if there weren't."

The others were silent. They too felt guilty. They were alive, and Jessie wasn't.

"Who would have done such a thing? I can't understand it. Some people hated her. We saw that yesterday. Or was it the day before yesterday? Whenever. But kill her, even burn down the house?"

She left the question hanging. There was no answer.

They talked about having some kind of memorial service. Maybe Chip Delaney would conduct it. It should be somewhere in the woods, they thought. Jesse would have liked that.

One by one, they all managed to fall asleep. Joan stayed in the easy chair and just seemed to drift off. Roxie and Phyllis fell across the bed. Roxie put on her gown, but Phyllis didn't bother to change. She simply plowed into the bed head-first and was asleep crosswise on it when

Roxie came. Roxie left her there and managed to ease down enough cover to slip under at the top by lying crosswise herself.

Sometime in the night Julia awakened all of them with a loud, eerie-sounding fit of sobbing. The three older women converged on her room, but Carol was already holding her, rocking her back and forth, and telling her it was all right. They stumbled back to their beds and fell alseep again.

The phone rang about nine-thirty. Joan answered it in the kitchen. None of the others was up yet. It was Harold, calling to see how they were. He was going over to the sheriff's office, he said, and would come by later in the day.

Of course there was no question about opening the gallery. He didn't care if they never opened it again. But he did have to meet D. M. Birkenstall and Delma Hirshfield-Jones there at two o'clock to give Dr. Birkenstall's paintings to her.

Ms. Hirshfield-Jones had called to say they had decided to go ahead with the Women of the Tomb service, as it would be impossible to notify everyone who planned to attend. Hard as going ahead might be, they felt that an Easter celebration was one event that should never be canceled for a death.

Dr. Birkenstall had once known a pastor who had a heart attack and died during the early service at his church; when the deacons met, they decided to proceed with the eleven o'clock liturgy, and turned it into one of the most moving services the church had ever had. Maybe the Women of the Tomb service would turn out that way, they hoped.

They were also going ahead with plans to have Jessie's paintings flanking the podium. Dr. Birkenstall intended to offer a few remarks about Jessie and the appropriateness of remembering her on that particular morning. They would like to invite Harold or any other of her friends to say a few words if they felt led to do so. Harold told her he didn't think he would be able to say anything, but he would pass the word on to the others.

Presently, the women were all up and sitting around the kitchen table, not quite knowing what to do with themselves and the day. The bright sunlight seemed invasive. Surely a dark, cloudy day would have been more appropriate for their aching spirits.

Phyllis noticed that Roxie wasn't smoking again.

"I promised myself only one pack," Roxie said. She took the crumpled package out of her sweater pocket and laid it on the table.

"What are we going to do?" Phyllis finally asked.

"I think we should go home," Roxie said. "The sooner, the better."

"We have to stay till next week," said Joan. "We can't leave before we have some kind of service for Jess."

"Whenever. But the sooner, the better. Next weekend, maybe. I can drive into Knoxville and arrange it with our landlady. She'll understand. We're three weeks ahead on the rent. She should be happy with that. We'll even pay another month if we have to."

"Oh God," said Phyllis. "Chip and Margot! I wonder if they know."

Margot was crying when Joan called. Harold had just phoned to talk to Chip about a memorial service. Chip was out with a client. She had tried to call through on his car phone, but he wasn't in the car. She couldn't believe it. Jessie dead. Anybody else, but not Jessie.

Joan told her what Harold had said about going ahead with the Women of the Tomb service. No, they didn't think there were any suspects yet. The sheriff's department was working on it, and Harold was going over to the sheriff's now. Yes, Margot knew that. Harold had told her that much.

Most of the major television networks were enjoying a lazy weekend, with many staffers on spring breaks, but CNN in Atlanta had despatched a helicopter unit as soon as a bulletin hit the wire service. At noon they had a segment showing photographs of Jessie and her paintings, plus footage of the charred remains of the house and part of an interview with the sheriff. The sheriff was obviously nervous and self-conscious. He kept adjusting the tilt of his

Stetson and correcting his own grammar. They didn't presently know who the killer or killers might be, he said. They understood the woman had some enemies. "Cain't be a celebrity like she was and not have some," he opined. They were working on the case.

If most of the visitors to Gatlinburg had heard the news by mid-afternoon, it was hard to tell. The streets were as crowded with cars and people as ever; the restaurants and shops were doing a record business; and morning hikers in their boots and nylon backpacks were beginning to filter back into town from their morning walks.

Roxie stared at a bunch of them crossing the street in front of the Volvo as she and the others waited at a stoplight before turning left and heading up into the National Park. She felt a distant impulse to slap the wheel and yell "Damn! Damn! Damn! Damn!" But it did not materialize through the intervening hollowness of her spirit.

They had not seen the CNN news broadcast, had not wanted the incessant noise of network emptiness mocking their own emptiness. And they had stood the sense of confinement in the condo as long as they could before leaving a note on the door for Harold and evacuating for the mountains. Maybe they could wear themselves down, become more senseless of their present, unbearable senselessness.

They found themselves lingering listlessly on

the bridges across the streams, focusing on their great loss. They trudged slowly up the rocky paths, with no real motivation to energize their steps. Even Columbo, who normally dashed about with the enthusiasm of a puppy, following mystic spores out of some primordial instinct, plodded along zestlessly and mechanically at their heels, as lost as if he had been deprived of all his senses.

Finally, at dusk, they turned the car toward town and stopped at Long John Silver's, where Carol suggested they go in memory of Jessie.

There they found their tongues and began to talk about Jessie, recalling how they had met her, things she had said, what she had done for each of them.

"She was the wisest person I ever knew," said Carol.

"And the best," added Joan.

"My dad said she used to know more than any of their professors in college," said Julia. "You know, not necessarily in terms of data and stuff like that. But she was so sensitive. She could always go right to the heart of a thing, while everybody else was still asleep or groping around trying to understand."

Roxie smiled a quizzical little smile, as if seeing something she had long forgotten.

"I remember once, not long after we met. I had this pig of a boss. He was always sending me for coffee or something, just to prove he had the power to do it. I told Jess I was going to belt him into next week if he did it again.

"She started asking questions about him. What was he like? Did he have a wife? How did they get along? What about his children? Did I think his life was fulfilled, and all that stuff. I finally said I would introduce them. A day or two later, I did. We ran into one another in the lunch room. 'Jessie, this is Mr. Whatzizname,' I said.

"By the time that lunch hour was over, she knew everything about him. And the darned funny thing was, he was different that afternoon. I swear to God he was.

"I thought it was only temporary, that he would be his old self the next day. But he wasn't. Somehow, in half an hour, forty-five minutes, she had gotten through to that geek and changed his whole way of looking at things."

"Jess could do that," said Joan.

"She was really there for me when my husband left," said Phyllis. "I sort of went to pieces. But she was so whole, so complete in the way she looked at life, it helped me to see everything in a new way. I think I came out stronger than when I went in, thanks to her."

Joan bit a long french fry in two. "How is it with you and Steve?" she asked.

Phyllis smiled shyly.

"He's coming in sometime tonight."

"You mean in the night?"

"He's a taxi driver. He's used to staying awake all night."

Carol said, "I don't envy you for having to tell him the news."

"He only met her the one night. It can't be as bad as telling Mike. I thought Mike had had a stroke. The phone went dead, and all I heard were some funny little gurgling noises."

"What were they?"

"I don't know. He never explained. He came back on in a minute and asked some questions. But I think he was just in deep shock."

"How did Dana take it?" asked Julia.

"I don't know. Mike was going to wait a while to tell her. He said he had to get under better control himself before doing it."

"Poor thing," said Joan. "She'll take it awful hard, I think. She thought the moon rose and set in our Jess."

"She was right," said Roxie. "It did."

"I almost forgot," said Carol. "Julia and I have to fly back tomorrow."

"What time?" asked Roxie.

"Not till four o'clock. We planned to be here for the service tomorrow."

"We'll take you."

"What about us?" said Joan. "Did you get in touch with our landlady?"

"Damn," said Roxie. "I completely forgot. I meant to go see her this afternoon, and I didn't even think to call."

"We can do it tomorrow after we take Carol and Julia to the airport."

Joan noticed that Julia was looking pensive

and asked what was on her mind.

"Oh, I was just thinking about Jessie and her *Baba*. I thought that was so neat, to have your own special name for God."

They were quiet a moment. Then Roxie said, "*Baba* didn't do her much good in the end."

"Oh, I disagree," said Joan. "We don't know what really happened, but I bet *Baba* was right there with her, whatever it was."

"And if I know Jessie," said Carol, "she probably even prayed for whoever did it. That's who she was."

"I never saw her get angry," said Phyllis, "except when something wasn't right. She could get real indignant then. But other times she could take more than a saint."

Roxie went back to the counter for another cup of coffee. She came back, set it down, and scooted into the booth beside Julia.

"I just hope, whatever happened," she said, "that she didn't suffer."

They were all quiet, and obviously thinking about it despite the attempt not to.

It was Carol who finally broke the silence.

"I think she could stand her own suffering. It was other people's she had a hard time with."

30

Easter Day dawned clear and cool. There was a faint mist in the valleys, but the weather reports forecasted an early burnoff and temperatures well above normal for the time of year.

Cars, trucks, campers, and buses were already pouring into the convention center parking lot when the girls walked down from their condo at six-thirty. Many of the buses had large banners with mottoes such as WOMEN OF THE TOMB, MARYVILLE CHURCH WOMEN UNITED, KNOXVILLE FIRST CHURCH, WOMEN FOR JESUS, and WOMEN TO THE MOUNTAINS. The women came forth from them in great streams, adjusting pantyhose, straightening dresses, and chattering with excitement as they formed a mighty confluence heading for the arena.

The girls had agreed to wait until after the service to eat, perhaps to go to brunch somewhere with Harold, Rowena, Chip, Margot, Jasmine, Mike, and Dana, if the others had no plans.

They had barely passed the parking entrance when a hearty voice called out "Roxie! Joan! Phyllis!"

Turning toward the parking area, they saw Thomas, Matilda, Leah, Matthew, and Mark coming toward them, great white smiles radiating from the parents' dark faces.

"Thomas! Matilda! What are you doing here?" exclaimed Roxie, who was closest and first to recognize them.

"We have come for the important service," said Thomas proudly.

By this time it had dawned on all the women.

277

They didn't know. They had come to hear Jessie. They had driven all the way from Connecticut for the special occasion, planning to surprise her. Each women considered whether it was her duty to speak first and tell them the news.

Matilda picked up on the pause, saw the awkwardness in their faces. "Is something wrong? Something is wrong, isn't it? What is it?"

"It's awful," said Joan. "Jessie is dead. She was killed Friday in a fire."

Thomas looked as if someone had just struck him in the stomach with a fifty-pound sledge hammer.

"In a fire? How?"

"We think she was murdered, to tell the truth," said Roxie. "Her body was found in the bedroom, even though the fire didn't start until between eight and nine in the morning. Jessie was always up and out long before then."

"But the police?"

"The police are looking into it. We haven't heard anything yet."

"Oh my," said Thomas, suddenly sitting right on the ground at their feet and holding his head in both hands. "Oh my."

The arena of the Convention Center was huge. The women, accompanied by Thomas, Matilda, and the children, walked nearly to the front, wanting to sit where they could see the paintings clearly during the service. The paintings were already in place on attractive gold-colored easels at the sides of a large wooden pulpit draped with a white cloth and topped by three microphones. Surrounding both easels and banked against the sides and front of the pulpit was a tasteful array of Easter lilies, whose perfume could be smelled halfway back in the room. Large, potted ficus trees adorned the sides and back of the stage, which was bathed in a soft blue light. High up behind the podium hung an enormous tapestry depicting the Gospel scene of the two women at the empty tomb meeting an angel. It was framed at the top and on the sides by a dark-blue valance and drapes, and under it hung a huge WOMEN OF THE TOMB banner, with the letters all in bright, shiny sequins.

A very large lady in a yellow and orange flowered dress was laboring at an impressive-looking electronic organ that had probably been brought in for the occasion.

D. M. Birkenstall sat on the edge of one of the chairs behind the podium, apparently concentrating on her notes, which lay in her lap on yellow foolscap. Delma Hirshfield-Jones came hurrying out from the wings of the stage and spoke into the microphones to ask the person in the control booth to give her a sound level.

"We're expecting the soloist to be here at any moment," she said. "Stay right there, and I'll get her up here the minute she walks in."

Thomas sat bent over in his chair, his head again in his hands. Matilda was gently rubbing his back. Matthew and Mark arched their necks to look around the vast room. They had never been inside such an enormous arena.

Joan looked over to the far right and saw Chip and Margot come in. They looked very sad and unhappy.

Almost at the same time, Mike, Dana, Steve, and Jasmine showed up on the other side of them. Phyllis and Steve embraced, and Roxie introduced them to Thomas and his family.

Then Harold and Rowena came in on the right and joined Chip and Margot.

The prelude began, and the heavy lady threw herself mightily into its drama, her huge shape shifting suddenly and unpredictably as she lunged at various sections of the console. She was accompanied now by an older gentleman on stage playing a grand piano; he ran his hands up and down the keyboard in pyrotechnical fashion while she sustained the longer notes.

A tall, blondish young man named Tim O'Keefe, whom the program identified as a regular performer at nearby Dollywood, stepped to the microphone to lead the hymns. Roxie thought he was insufferably upbeat and therefore callous under the circumstances. She looked straight at Jessie's paintings, first one, then the other, and back and forth, instead of joining in the singing. It felt strange to her to see her and Joan's faces again in the *Martha and Mary* painting, especially in that setting.

Delma Hirshfield-Jones gave a brief welcoming address on behalf of the spiritual-life committee of the Episcopal diocese and the other churches that had joined to sponsor the Women of the Tomb event, and said how saddened the entire community, and indeed the nation, was to have lost on Friday the eminent local artist Jessie, who was to have been their featured speaker. The audible gasps of surprise and sighs of commiseration all over the giant arena indicated that many had not already heard the sad news. Yes, said Ms. Hirshfield-Jones, it was true; they had all suffered a great loss, an irreparable loss, a loss that could not be measured as ordinary losses are measured. Later in the service, she said, they would hear a tribute to Jessie from Dr. D. M. Birkenstall, the noted author and owner of the two famous Jessie paintings on display before them that morning.

A two-hundred voice choir that had paraded onto the stage during the prelude and occupied a long set of three-tiered bleachers sang a medley of Easter hymns, followed by a brief scriptural drama about the resurrection read by five women clustered at the pulpit. One of them was too near the microphones; every time she pronounced a word beginning with the letter *p* it seemed to send a brief electrical disturbance through the amplifying system.

The choir next sang an anthem called "Blessed Are the Man and Woman," which the program said was based on Psalm 1 and was written by John and Anne Prather especially for the service. The solo parts were sung by country-music star JoAnn Paisley. Dressed in a choir robe like all the others, she was identifiable by her position a couple of feet in front of the choir and by her strong spotlight.

The music was lively and crisp, and Roxie found herself listening to the words:

> Bless-ed, bless-ed, bless-ed,
> Bless-ed are the man and woman
> Who listen not to the worldly voices
> Nor behave in a manner ungodly.
> Bless-ed, I say bless-ed,
> Are those whose God is the Lord.
> They shall be like trees,
> Trees, trees, trees, trees, trees, trees, trees,
> Planted by the living waters,
> And they shall be bless-ed,
> They shall be bless-ed,
> Bless-ed, bless-ed, bless-ed.

The choral voices became very soft and light during the repetition of the word "trees," and the piano in the background made accompanying noises like a waterfall or wind chimes tinkling in the breeze. JoAnn Paisley's voice was slightly nasal, but not in an unpleasant way; the manner in which it blended with the voices of the chorus in the background produced a haunting, lyrical effect.

Following this, Dr. Birkenstall rose and traversed the distance to the pulpit, unselfconsciously carrying her yellow foolscap in front of her and laying it on the pulpit. She paused before speaking.

"I consider it a very great personal honor," she began, and then had to pause again for static to clear from the amplifying system, for she had stood too close and produced a harsh, grating rumble that went on for several seconds. She began again: "I consider it a very great personal honor to have known the woman named Jessie, and to possess these paintings, which are the first in her acclaimed series entitled 'Women in Religion.'"

She went on to speak of the importance of the series for its focus on women's contributions to the history of Judeo-Christianity. She quoted from some of the national magazine articles about Jessie, citing particularly what some of the critics had remarked about her extraordinary combination of sensitivity and passion. Then she talked more personally about how Jessie had affected her—how sweet and simple and unassuming she was, and how she had helped to restore her faith in God.

"Like many of us, I'm afraid," she said, "I had become blasé about mystery and transcendence. The course of world affairs, the growth of technology and information, the sheer busyness of modern existence, had all combined to make me feel cynical, saturated, isolated, and self-protective. I had decided, perhaps without giving the matter much thought, that God had abandoned the world and we might as well make the best of it.

"But Jessie brought me back to God. Or maybe she brought God back to me. There was something about her eyes, and the way she saw everything, that made me look again and see what I had been missing. I owe more to her than I can say. I suspect we all do. And I would like to think that this service, which was planned with her in mind as the speaker, is a testimony to what she tried to teach us, and that it will live on in our minds and hearts for the rest of our lives as her service, for what she did for us."

Then Dr. Birkenstall asked if anyone else whose life was touched by Jessie would like to offer a comment. She looked in the direction of Roxie, Joan, and Phyllis, and seemed to be searching for Harold and Rowena as well, but did not see them as they were positioned behind several unusually large persons.

Suddenly Carol was standing and going forward to the podium. Dr. Birkenstall looked slightly doubtful for a moment, but recovered her composure and gracefully retreated in a manner that bespoke Carol's right to the microphones.

"Jessie changed my life completely," Carol said with a firm, confident voice. "We met by accident—or maybe it wasn't an accident—at a bus station in New York. I was running away from home. I didn't think there was anybody in the world who loved or cared for me. And then there she was, loving and caring for me."

She told about Ray and Rachel and Julia—pointing out Julia—and how they had accepted her and bestowed new worth on her life. But it was Jessie, she said, who...

At precisely that moment, Carol saw them coming down the center aisle from the back of the arena, and her mouth hung open in mid-sentence. Others looked too, and those who knew and recognized the figure experienced the same shock of astonishment.

It was Jessie, coming down the aisle, accompanied by Columbo, jouncing effortlessly beside her.

The recognition was like a wave that began at the rear of the auditorium, among those who saw her first—after Carol's sighting of course—and then simply rolled forward as if it would inundate the stage when it reached that point of its movement. No one said a word. It all happened as if in a dream. And there she was, mounting the steps, Columbo trotting beside her. With a barely audible squeal, Carol embraced her, then stepped back as Jessie proceeded to the microphones.

She stood there looking happy and radiant. There was a very definite mark on her face, as if she had been struck by a piece of chain. But her eyes sparkled and her smile was beatific.

What happened next would be a topic of discussion and debate for years to come among those who were present that morning. Some said Jessie began to speak. Others said she stood there as the entire crowd went wild with hugging, kissing, crying, and praising God.

Whatever the particulars, which depended on individual points of view and recollection, the consensus was solid that *Baba*'s spirit fell on the entire auditorium, moving people to tears, to confessions, and to exaltations the like of which they had never experienced. There were multiple healings, with people's arthritis and digestive problems and even cancers disappearing, with bones being straightened and slipped discs restored, and with at least one case of blindness being cured. Those present would remember the rest of their lives the feeling of love that pervaded the entire space of the arena, as if it were something thick and tangible, like a heavy, perfumed mist that enveloped them. Some said they could actually taste it, like a sweet confection. Others said they heard music, like angels' choirs and thousands of harps. Still others reported a sensation of light, as if the sun had suddenly come to stand in the arena, and of lightness in their own beings, as if they could float upwards at will and intermingle without encountering any resistance of the flesh. All agreed that it was the most singular experience of their lives, one that would transform their thinking about life, the world, and life beyond death for as long as any of them lived, and then pave the way for a joyous transportation into the world that was yet to be.

At some point in all this, whether at the beginning or in the middle or at the end there was some disagreement, Jessie spoke to them about the wholeness of *Baba*, and how everything looks different to the person who can transcend discrete and immediate phenomena to see them against the pattern to which they belong, the eternal unity of which they are parts.

Suffering is not the same to the person who sees the whole, she said. Neither is hatred, nor violence, nor even death.

In this life, she said, our vision is only partial. We are growing toward the light, traveling toward the day when we shall see everything, when all will be revealed. For now, we are given only parts of the picture. But there are enough, if we are thoughtful and patient and sensitive, to suggest the whole, the way bits and pieces of a familiar picture eventually lead us to recognize it in its entirety.

This is what religions are about—or ought to be about—all of them. Not just Judaism and Christianity, but Hinduism, Buddhism, Sufism, Mohammedanism, Native American faith, and every other religion. We should not hate or despise those whose vision of parts of the whole is different from our own, but embrace them, that we may combine the parts we all know and see more together than we could ever see alone.

What we begin to see when the entire picture starts becoming plain, she said, is that *Baba* is love. *Baba* is love overcoming hate and darkness and prejudice and everything that stands in the way of love. One day, *Baba* will have conquered everything and all the hate and darkness will be expelled, like gases forced to leave the whole and seek another place to be, even though there will be no other place, for *Baba* will be all in all.

For now, said Jessie, they must all live and walk in love, as much as possible. They must think love, practice love, pray for love, receive love, celebrate love, and even eat and sleep and breathe love, so that *Baba*'s plan of wholeness for everything may be implemented even more quickly, and reach its consummation as soon as possible.

This extraordinary occurrence came to an end—or perhaps reached its hiatus would be a better way of putting it—when Jessie and Columbo turned from the podium and, as lightly as they had come, proceeded down the steps, up the aisle, and right through the double doors at the back of the auditorium. She did not pause to embrace any of them—not Roxie or Joan or Phyllis or Thomas or Matilda or Harold or Rowena or Mike or Dana or Jasmine or Chip or Margot or any other—and yet they all felt her aura so closely and personally that they knew they had been embraced, that her presence had settled on each one of them in the room and blessed them beyond their deepest needs and fondest expectations.

—

For several days, there were numerous sightings of Jessie and Columbo reported in the vicinity. Two boys saw them in the woods above the burned-out schoolhouse. Several hikers or groups of hikers thought they had encountered them on various trails throughout the mountain region, one as far away as Cherokee, North Carolina, and another not far from Helen, Georgia. Father McKeown swore he had seen them twice outside Rymer's Chapel and once in the little sanctuary itself, where Jessie touched a poor, crippled old homeless man and restored him to vigor and wholeness. And three teenage girls got off the Obergatlinburg ski lift one day breathless with excitement over having spotted Jessie and Columbo in the carriage ahead of theirs.

"We watched them get off at the top and just disappear," they said.